ENDING GENTLY

A MEMOIR BY
FRANK GENTLY

ISBN: 978-0-9976259-0-5

Cover art collage by Frank Gently.
Cover art acknowledgements:
Belhoula Amir
Hajime Sorayama
Alberto Vargas

Dedicated to my family
and low-hanging fruit.

"The mass of men lead lives of quiet desperation . . . there is no play in them, for this comes after work."

- Henry David Thoreau

"If you go home with somebody and they don't have books, don't fuck them."

- John Waters

"I shall tell you these things not because you need to know them and certainly not because you have to. I shall tell you these things solely because I believe I am good company and I believe that when anyone decides to sit down with a book, they are deciding to sit down with the person who wrote it. I submit to you that the following pages were laid down purely from an attempt to make you feel at home and in good hands."

- Frank

ENDING GENTLY

Note:

The author would like the reader to observe this piece's original intent and that nothing as follows is to be taken seriously, that is, of course, unless the reader wishes it to be taken as such. However, according to Frank, "that will be all fine and dandy – but if it is taken literally, or damned if I say it, fundamentally," then the author will see to it that a "death warrant is served and lord willing, carried out."

- Executor of *Gently Gentry & Co.*

Prologue

This Whole Executor Business

As the record will no doubt show, I have no executor and nor do I want one. I seem to be handling the entire thing just fine on my own thank you very much. At least, I *think* I am. Why don't you do me a solid and have another gander at the above note just one more time. See, I wrote that – I'm the executor, Frank.

Frank Gently, delighted to have you on board.

Now back to the point.

The point being that the above note seems to be pretty executive stuff, don't you think? Some homegrown jargony riff-raff, some bureaucratic BS, some legitimate loony tunes language, yeah? See that's what I thought, too – fake it till ya make it. Do what everyone else does and blow it out your ass and hope it smells good. And I must say it's overwhelming, whatever the scent.

I'm sure this all sounds absurd to you, what with me handling my own affairs and all but if we're being completely,
wholly,   right-hand-on-the-book-of-tall-tales-honest,   this
whole executor business wasn't *supposed* to be on me. It
wasn't *supposed* to be on anyone. Hell, none of it was. It was
all *supposed* to stay in the hands of a man I didn't know,
didn't care to know, and for all I knew – was long dead
before I ever found out about his passing.

So much for supposition.

You see, it was there in the fading warmth of late October, well over four months ago now and my thirty second
birthday to be exact, that I was sitting in my cheap ass apartment of New York's burgeoning burp of an art town, Peekskill (or The Kill as you'll come to know it), when I received
word of the funeral arrangements. I remember it rather vivid-
ly. I was perched as I always was, leaning back on the arthritic
legs of my desk chair and staring out the large frosty window
of my third floor shoebox. Ha! *Frosty. That's a good one.*
This is to say that the panes of glass were painted with a
cheap, artsy-fartsy glaze in an attempt to make it seem as
though winter and its effects were a year round event. I don't
think hilarity was exactly what Doris was going for but she
surely nailed it on the head.

I always considered the glaze a poor decision on Doris'
part, but seeing how my Russian-Jewish landlady was now
nearing a solid eighty years of age with her eyes fuzzily following suit, I figured she had laid the faux-frost on thick just
to give her tenants a taste of what losing one's vision feels
like. A sort of forced empathy, if you will. It kind of worked,
and it kind of made you hate her. *A wash. A white-wash.* The
homemade serum was applied to every window on the old
rickety gingerbread house and was done so poorly, in fact,

that the effect resembled a blurred shower door – the exact opposite of what one might want when looking out the lone window of a living space. The only way to know what resided on the other side was to keep it permanently open and that was how it remained throughout my ten year stay in the attic of 112 Hudson. I didn't mind it so much though, being the rampant cigar smoker and ardent cold-weather-lover that I am, as well as living atop of two tenants who kept their thermostats boiling at a steamy eighty-five or higher – the heat was never an issue, only over-heating was. Keeping that window open became everything to me; the life source, the breath of fresh rejuvenating air that was needed when licking clean the hot-headed wounds of whiskey and wine; and the reason you turned to those two in the first place – work.

My beloved window to the world did The Kill justice. Its grand, liberating view of this historic town that sits roughly forty miles north of The Island was the only way to cope with the infinitesimals of depression. Its perspective, like all scenic landscapes, offered a world much bigger and brighter than anything my broke, floundering, unoriginal ass could cook up. You see, you get a rather special feeling and the only feeling worth mentioning from 112 Hudson when you open that window. Equal parts magic, charm, and reality, all of its sobering qualities eventually melt their way down into one barely expressible finish: weightlessness. For that uplifting view caught the rolling, graceful hill of Peekskill perfectly and lived on in my mind as a resilient buoy to life. One that was strong enough to keep this sinking soul afloat when drowning didn't sound like a bad way out.

But, ah! Through that window was another way out!

And beyond the slow, sloping streetlights and recessive rooftops, beyond the jarring chimneys and decaying remnants of pristine pre-war architecture, beyond all that; beyond the beauty of man lay the perfection of nature – for beyond all of it lays The Hudson. And snaking its way through Appalachia with one stoic downward exhale, strong and majestic with its roaring deep blue and powerful gray and sometimes menacing black . . . I often found myself wasting hours there at that window, chatting up the earthly therapist.

Centered below that window was my little wooden single-drawered desk and it wasn't much to look at. It was cheap and wobbly. Okay, it was a shitty desk. The annoying back and forth tilting was kept at bay by four measly matchbooks, two of each propped under its left legs. The drawer itself was unusable if anything weighing over two pounds was laid inside and squeaked an insidious whimper when opened and closed. Still, I loved that thing. It was old and pathetic but I had grown attached to it. It was my partner in crime, after all. My steady guide through literary bouts of insanity, my silent ranger through the thunderous storms of pounding fists and obscene tirades that were the side effects of bad writing. (Oh yeah. I guess I should tell you that. I'm a writer. It's okay, you can go now.)

The odd sense of pride I took in that POS desk and every other piece of junk in my room was all the more reason to denote them "treasures of character and relics deserving of stories," to anyone who visited. What can I say, I liked to kid myself. I think you know exactly what I'm getting at: my room, to the untrained eye, was chock full of the kind of authentic crapola and vintage hogwash that goes with any piece of furniture over twenty years old. It was delicately curated some might say. Others might ask about bed bugs. All sarcastic and ass-kicking comments were welcomed here. It was only the serious remarks I had problems with. A man once told me the desk was "actually a lovely piece and the room would've been a total loss without it." I laughed at first but seeing the confusion in the man's face from my humorous reaction led me to believe that his dick-sneeze of an utterance hadn't one iota of a joke in it! Can you imagine? I know, you can never be too sure with dry humor so I asked him. He shook his head no and happily said he wasn't kidding. I asked him if he spoke pig-latin too and he said he didn't. I then went on to inform him that I didn't either and that flattery might as well be bear-oil rubbed on a pair of pig's lips so he'd better hit the road or cut the shit. It was at that exact moment where he relieved himself of built up gas and said he'd rather cut cheese so I let him hang around.

Speaking of cutting through the poo, I shit you not when I say that the only thing lovely about the space I lived in was the opportunity to look outside of it. Be it in times of light, playful questioning or deep darkened distress, I would constantly twiddle thumbs and thoughts while looking out that window; restless, in a sort of hopeful creative stupor. And there, with my feet up, gnawing on a cigar, huffing and puffing about women, lamenting over last night's particular lady who left this morning without a goodbye, agonizing, always agonizing over what comes next, would I wait propped up by the sole belief that the river or the time-capsule town or the comedic garish frost might help procure some answers...and eventually, some words.

I was in this usual tortuous state when I heard a loud knock at the door. This was odd. As any apartment dweller will no doubt tell you, a knock on the door is as uncommon as someone complimenting you about your living space. *My! This is a lovely shoebox you have here.* Seriously, everyone, friends and family alike, used the buzzer. Hell, even Doris never took it upon herself to climb up to the top floor to let me know the hot water would be off. She'd just buzz and lazily leave a handwritten note in my mailbox with the most horrific smelling perfume seeping out from the corners of the envelope:

Mr. Gently,

I just finished your book, *The Unbearable White-ness of Being (Having A Small Penis and Owning Your Space)*. I found it on the dollar rack of Bruised Apple. I must say, I wasn't amused. However, I can see how young boys might like it. If you ask me (which you won't so I will go ahead and tell you anyway), if you are going to call this a Romance Novel, perhaps a re-working of the title would give it some much needed direction. Or, maybe this is one of those golden oppor-tunities to rethink the direction of your career in gen-eral.

Best of luck, Doris

PS. There won't be any hot water for a week. The sodomites on the second floor saw to it to run the hot water for the entire day Monday to "humidify the room," and have now broken the heater. "Humidify." Sure. They think I don't know what happens in bath-houses. Just revolting. If you expect or want any sever-ance for rent, I suggest you ask them.

The sodomites she was so kindly referring to are the de-lightful and unbearably handsome, gay couple who live below me – Sean and Jay. And it was these two, the prior a brown-haired jackal and the latter his silver-foxed counterpart, charming and cheeky men who were on the other side of the knock. I was hung over as hell and a tad spaced when I answered the door. Something barring masochism, perhaps the fact that I never, not once have answered a knock at my apartment door, kept me from realizing that I was in nothing but my briefs. It was a delicious scene for Sean and Jay who needed nothing else to set their fiery wits ablaze.

"Jesus. H. Frank. Your cock is out."

"What?" I said, embarrassingly, still in shock that it was these two at the door. I glanced downward to check. "No it's not." Looking down, I couldn't help but notice a certain protruding blob of the mid-section. My lager-logged belly was now nearing that scary world of no return where sucking it in makes no difference. I sucked it in anyway. *Here's to thirty-two.*

"I know." Sean said. "I just wanted to draw attention to the fact that you're homophobic and we love cock." He paused for a second and wiggled his nose at the escaping smoke. "Still fecklessly smoking cigars, eh, Twain?"

"God *you* two. Give it a rest, will ya? It's still morning."

I spun around and picked up a pair of jeans that were strewn across the floor from the previous night's debauchery. I brought them to my face — stale beer and embarrassment filled my nostrils — and threw them back down. Dust bunnies scampered about.

"Oh, *that's right*, you're only functional after noon," continued Sean. "I guess that explains the deafening moans at 4 AM. What was her name again, Jay? Juh…Judy?"

"No, no. Jewel? Or wait.." Jay said, squinting and scratching his head theatrically. "Well, whatever it was, she wanted the world to know it."

'*It's June you shmucks,*' I wanted to say. Truth be told, I wanted to say a helluva lot more than that, but I'd be dammed if I was going to add any fodder to this pair's bottomless trough of social savagery.

"Yeah, no. That's it, *Julie.*" Sean carried on, wry smile front and center. "I never heard-a-girl beg to have her name screamed like that. Some pair of vocal chords she's got on her. Jay and I agree, her performance was spectacular."

"Streep-esque." Jay chimed, elbowing Sean playfully in the ribs.

"Indeed." Sean rebounded, ball-tapping Jay lightly but all-too-solidly on his Schlonze.

"AH! YOU CUNT MUSCLE."

"Don't suppose we'll be seeing too much of her again? Do tell us, was she an aspiring actress or are you just *that* good?"

I blushed. I blushed like a schoolboy who had just been caught staring down the blouse of his fifth grade teacher. However proud one might be of getting laid the night before, the fact that strangers can know your living habits and know them so well, so intimately that one-night stands have now become foregone conclusions, well, when the mask is unveiled, no matter what lies underneath, the audience is always surprised. And more often than not in my case, reddened.

"Yes. I mean. No. I mean — what was it again that I can do for you two?"

"Two things," said Sean. "If Doris told you we broke the water heater, she's lying. We had our contractor friend look into it and he tells us that she's had the same water heater running this joint since she bought it. So, we're gonna try to get some money off the rent and want to know if you'd like to form a coalition?"

"Hm." I saw a golden in. "So you two weren't turning your place into an Adonis-ridden bath house then? Like, doing headstands and towel slaps and all-you-can-eat-butt-buffets? Ya know? Like wrestling and tickling each other, carrying on and singing show tunes and all that?" It was always tiring to keep up with these two. But if I was on, it was more than just joyful – it was brotherhood.

"Oh. *We were.*" Sean snapped. "But she's not getting a new water heater off of us just because we were shower-ing...with men. Lots and lots of men."

"And besides," continued Jay, bringing us back around to the point at hand. "The old bag is tighter than a freshman at BYU. It's gonna take all of us together to get anything out of her. That is, unless you're cool with living with shrinkage for seven days straight?"

"Guys. That hurts. This isn't shrinkage. This is genetics."

They laughed and I agreed to be a part of their anti-Doris campaign. Jay then took the brief pause in banter as a sign to finally hand me the envelope he had been holding the entire time. It was the second reason for their visit. They apologeti-cally mentioned how they had received it two days ago in the mail but had forgotten up until now to deliver it to me, hence the abrupt visit. I thanked them and bid them adieu. I mo-tioned to close the door but it was all Sean could do to restrain himself from the deplorable sight of my studio.

"Women actually step inside this place?" He quipped, peering his head around the closing door. "You must dine on the sushi all day. You know there's mercury in some o'that shit...do you even come up for air? Or are you one of those fish-mongers who has gills and can breathe down there like Costner in *Waterworld?*"

"Thank you!" I said, through the door. I had shut it mid-way through his delivery but it certainly hadn't stopped him from yelling the rest of his barrage through the shoddy wood paneling.

"You're welcome!" They roared in unison. Faint gleeful laughing could be made out as they descended the stairs back down to their place.

'Gay men have entirely too much energy,' I thought. I looked around, fuzzy eyed at the room. 'The place isn't *that* bad, is it?' I stepped over two or three or four piles of dirty clothes and moseyed on over to my desk. There were stacks of books and albums scattered about. Old dusty frames of friends and classic films and pop art claimed the wall space along the bottom of the floor as well as rare black and white photos of celebrities from the 40's and 50's, all of which I had grand schemes of hanging but then didn't. (Don't ask me why – leaning art on walls is a thing now, right? Yes, that's why I didn't hang anything, for aesthetic value.) The bed was suffering from a lack of tidiness too, as was the clutter of solo cups and empty beer bottles and paper pads and journals that decorated the floor and coffee table like some compulsive interior decorator's real life nightmare. I sat down and took a long deep breath and found myself far more shook up over the lack of tidiness in myself: the gut being the major thing, the long over-due beard and hair being the other. I played the bongos on my tummy while I pondered the perks of going for a run. I couldn't keep a beat for shit so I stopped – both the drumming and the dreaming of aerobic exercise.

I felt lousy about myself. I figured my lack of tidiness had something to do with the lady June leaving so early this morning without a goodbye. I tried to think of something I was good at. Nothing came to mind. I temporarily convinced myself that I had decent hygiene and that was something to behold. And what a thing to behold! White teeth and fresh breath . . . life is like a Tic-tac, my friends, small and meaningless and its enjoyment was over before it started.

How effing morbid.

I snapped out of it – Sean did have a point, after all. I needed to get my act together, especially with writing... *Writing!* I looked at the laptop screen. Word Processor was still open. Its contents neat and orderly and I realized my digital life was quite organized.

'Shove that up your loose rectum, Sean!'

*

I furrowed my brow in a lame attempt to force myself back into the work. It was a cheese-dicked state of contemplation. I was too hungover for anything good to happen and as I leaned forward I felt my pooch-of-a-gut push up against the envelope now sitting in my lap. I had completely forgotten about it. I picked it up, took a big long drag of my Toscano and scowled a Spaghetti Western grimace that would've made Eastwood proud. I put the cigar down and finally assessed what now rested in my hands: a large, beautifully hand crafted envelope that was obviously handled with great care up until its final delivery. The materials, the craftsmanship, the calligraphy, all of it resembling something you might've expected from a Freemason's invite circa 1939. There was even a wax seal on it stamped with a significantly stylized, typographic "G." When you added up all the ingredients and downed them whole, they forced even the most oblivious of men – one of them being yours truly – to turn their nose up to its scent. The smell was lofty and far away, at the same time palpable and purposeful – it was the smell of money. The envelope reeked of opulence and it turned my stomach. The fact that this piece of well-manicured station-ery was sitting in my hands and addressed to me had caught me more off guard than answering the door half naked to a pair of gay men.

This is most likely because I have always loathed money and it has always returned the feeling. Throughout my entire thirty-two years of existence on this big racquetball, anything that ever took on the symbol of wealth seemed to purposeful-ly evade me. It had now irritated me to the point of indiffer-ence and I actually thought about pitching the envelope directly in the trash because of it.

Call it childhood brainwashing, but I've always seen mon-ey as the salt poured on the wounds of the soul. Or at the very least, a lousy band-aid, a flimsy adhesive laid on top of a cut so deep that it won't ever heal without the proper dress-ings. I know this deep-rooted resentment comes from my mother. You want to know how I know? The band-aid metaphor is her metaphor. Yeap, my bona-fide, bat shit, whack-job of a mother came up with it. Her craziness is legendary, by the way. I suppose it all started with her un-adjusted schooling techniques – the radical rhetoric that spewed forth daily throughout my adolescence left me with little escape. Her political rantings were notorious around town and much more humiliating than any horror story my friends would offer in times of sympathy. At its most severe, her behavior can only most accurately be described as a threat to national security. I remember her shouting – I think I was four or five at the time – spit flying from teeth like rockets shot into space, fists gesticulating high like Teddy Roosevelt taking on a Bull Moose, shouting manically about "Reagan's fuck-ups." The best part is that this was all happening in a K-mart shopping line. She viciously decried the latest five-cent jump in the price of a ring-pop. "We can't afford ring-pops anymore, Frank. Thank the Pagan for that!" She called Reagan 'The Pagan.' I had no idea why at the time but now that I know a little more I'm sure it had something to do with spiting Gerry Falwell and the Christian State. Like I said, she was full-blown...but hey, what can I say? Some of it, despite my ardent attempts at dissention, stuck with me over the years and oddly enough, rang truer and truer as I got older.

But let's not confuse things; the woman is a complete and utter lunatic. An astronaut fallen from the space shuttle. Sure, a blind squirrel can find a nut a couple times a year, but let's be clear here, she is out there right now, floating in orbit and spinning violently out of control around the rest of us normies. She and I don't even speak the same language half the time, let alone talk in general, but when it came to the topic of money, most of our stars did align. As time passed, the whole band-aid metaphor began to make more and more sense. And hell, if I thought about it long and hard enough, that aforementioned gash always resulted from the trials and tribulations that came from wanting a stylish and expensive and unneeded Band-Aid in the first place! Money and its wounds on the world were to me, as Marx once referred to religion, "the opiate of man." It was his one true addiction. His placebo-pain-killer and corrupter alike.

Sorry. I don't mean to turn you off here with the whole rancid *"I presume to know how the world works,"* bunch of jack-assed-nonsense-bullshit. But I can for now, at least, tell you that I am not wealthy and am somehow slightly okay with it. Well if I'm being honest, I'm barely getting by, but the fact that I can be happy and find contentment elsewhere should, at least some part of it, be attributed to my mad mother. You see, I do not have a savings account and don't understand many of those who do. The more I hung around those who had wealth, especially throughout my adolescent years at NYU – schmoozing with affluent Upper West Siders born of lawyers, Tribeca punksters born of I-bankers, Soho model douchebags born of douchebag models – the more absurd it all became. Prosperous terms like 401K or Trust Fund quickly became preposterous. The whole scheme became so abstract and convoluted to me that it was soon relegated to where it rightfully belonged in my brain: somewhere up there next to Quantum Theory and Self-Flagellation . . . Except, I could always grasp Quantum Theory, or at least understand why it existed. But the one thing I'll never be able to grasp is Wall Street. Of course, both are intangible and to the logical brain, creativity gone awry – like hazing or torture or Iggy Azalea – but hey, at least Quantum Theory's aim is to be constant and true and seeks to answer a question about the ways of the world. Where as the money market seems to seek the exact opposite. In fact, I find that Wall Street was built purely to keep people guessing, keep people wanting; to exist as nothing else but gambling on its grandest and most ridiculously legal scale.

And the best part?

You guessed it, the house always wins.

After returning home from one of my many late nights in Manhattan during my sophomore year at NYU, something of a conscience found me. I recalled the careless flights of abounding wealth furnished by a deeply built, inherent lack of regard towards humanity...watching a stilettoed princess stomp on the hand of a homeless man, a boat-shoed coked-up prince throw a beer bottle into a storefront window while bragging, and I quote, "C'est petite bourgeoisie," to his twee-dle-dee and tweedle-dumb counterparts. The tossing of crumpled up Washington's at taxi-drivers' backs, the disdain for those who didn't know art, the hatred for those who didn't know labels, the belittling of those who were already little, the fortune of being able to delight in the gross enter-tainment of life less fortunate. And, well, as far as last straws go, witnessing the obnoxious little Fire-Red-wearing-fuck purposefully vomit on the bar top at Kettle of Fish, who, after intentionally pulling the trigger to spite the bartender cutting him off, then went on to grab a stack of bar napkins, launch them into the air — white-bats of disgrace flapping in the red and green and blue colored dinge of Christmas lights — and Fire Red yelling "Clean it up, *help*," to the Latino bar back before walking out the door, eyes redder than the fires of hell, his face glowing pure evil with a snide untouchable grin...

Yeah.

I was done.

Finito.

I turned my back on it all. The Scene, that is. I left NYU and saw to it to retreat back up the river and round out the rest of academia by commuting to Hunter College.

It was upsetting and difficult of course — leaving all that behind — but more often than not, the begrudging moans that accompanied staying in and moving back up river would soon manifest themselves solely as twitching and turning in my seat. At its most dramatic of occasions, I would throw my cigar out the window, cantankerous as all hell and mutter: "Are we that bored in life that we need risk to survive! Or

was Easy Street coined just to make us all slobber over prop-
erty?"

And yes, I do speak that way, but only to myself.
Things haven't gotten medical – at least, not yet.

Which reminds me of what got me going in the first
place: El Madre. The Mad Queen. The one who is genuinely
certifiable, I'm talking patented straightjacket material (okay,
she doesn't belong in an asylum. Hyperbole, as with most
mothers I imagine, comes all too easy with the woman) and
the reason I went off on this petty diatribe. She is the only
explanation for such a pathological reaction to an envelope.
I'd like to apologize for the idiotic ranting – bad form and all
that it is – but I can tell you however painful it was to read
all that it couldn't have been half as painful as it was to live
through it. Both of us are long estranged now, mom and me,
and haven't spoken or seen one another since my graduation
from Hunter. (She thought that educational institutions were
propagating the corrupt system and I thought she needed
more Xanax). Christ, that's almost a decade ago now. Water
long under the bridge and out to sea, but still, any reflections
on the dollar always brings me back to the parable she used
to preach throughout my youth:
    "There's two things that run the world, Frank. This,"
She'd hold up her hand and rub her two fore-fingers against
her thumb to form the universal sign for money, "and that."
She'd point, and more often than not if I were in arms-length
of her, tap me firmly on the head, to reinforce the power of
the mind.

It was always This or That.

Black or White.
Money or Art.
Crazy or Sane.
Yin or Yang.
The ever-plaguing two-sided coin of life.
Gawd, shut up, mom.
You think you know everything!

Despite her loose grip on reality, she was a well-educated woman, strong-minded almost to the point of weakness and aside from a few rare spitballs of genius, innately ineffectual to her offspring. She came from serious money and that alien world of boarding schools and west-island nannies and parents who gallivanted around the globe while their kids used family portraits to build bonds. *Gallivanting. Shit.* Apparently they invented the word for people like my grandparents. I wouldn't know. I never met them. My mother excommunicated herself from that entire world when she hit eighteen. I think about that now at the prime, overweight age of thirty-two — leaving everything I'd ever known behind at such a scary age with a newborn on the way...and to have the courage to up and run away from all the privileges and perks of title and wealth...just walk away from all of it to play gypsy and feign a bit of motherhood in the process, well, it was more than my small brain could handle.

I dosed off in unhappy nostalgia for another minute or two and then remembered what brought me to this random stroll down memory lane: this fucking envelope. The fact that such a little thing could curdle my stomach and bring back such an odd and dismal childhood, well, let's just say I cranked open the damned thing anyway. Out of spite, perhaps, but more so in hopes that a winning lottery ticket had finally found my door. I mean, let's be real here, despite all the above bullshit, I would only be kidding myself and don't intend to: *I want to be on Easy Street — whatever the hell that is — just as much as the next shmo.*

Inside the envelope was a handwritten letter. It read:

Franklin my boy,

If you are reading this letter it means I've finally kicked the bucket. What a crock. I always figured I would have had the time to explain myself to you and right what may have been wronged these past three decades. Unfortunately, it seems the finish line has caught up with me rather quickly and unexpectedly, and to my infinite despair; the checkered flag didn't see fit to allow that which I never built up the courage to mend.

In a meek attempt to ease the pain my absence may have caused you, I leave to you, my son, the entire Garcon De Garrison Estate and all that goes with it:

Regret, Sorrow and Hope for New Beginnings.

Your Father,
Edward F. Gently

PS. The family lawyer will be in touch with you soon, a Mr. Gerald Goldstein. He is a good man and will see to it that you are taken care of. You are the last of the Gentlys and I couldn't be happier than to leave now, knowing full well that the lineage lives on…in you.

"Lineage?"

I turned the letter over. I was ready for a gotchya-April-Fools-type moment. You know, something to the tune of Ashton Kutcher popping out of my closet with a camera crew and then I could happily punch him in the face. But nothing happened. No camera crew. No Kutcher. Just continued disbelief in a haze of cigar smoke, confusion and awkwardness cloaked in boxers and a beer gut.

I turned the letter back over and scanned its contents again. There was nothing to insinuate fraud. My buds were real pranksters so I could've seen them getting one over on me like this. I flipped it back over maybe two or three more times, felt the paper and rubbed it with my thumb and forefinger. It felt real.

We tend to look for anything and everything when in shock, anything to make sense of the agony of confusion, anything to maybe nullify the onslaught of new conspicuous information...I find that we do this most when all of the signs point toward the most obvious of answers – the truth.

"Father!?"

"What the fuck, Mom!"

Intermission

(The Author Takes a Moment — Four Months Worth)

Reopen on Gatsby's American Dream realized. A young man sits outside of a gargantuan, towering, multi-faceted gray and cream stoned chateau. It is garlanded with colossal chimneys and step-outs and the most obscene excuse for good taste. It is a monstrous mess of influences ranging from a French Renaissance exterior to a desperate attempt at Venetian splendor in its hand-cut floor-to-ceiling oak blinds to the Victorian tree-lined driveway to the much uncalled for Rodin sculptures that sprinkled the grassy knoll which still lays eerily unattended to. The whole design was laid out in such a manner, so desperate for attention — one that screamed please love me, approve of me — that you might've thought a man with an ego the size of a pea had drawn up its floor plan. A man loaded to the gills, of course. Walking through the spacious, hollow decorum inside was like someone playing jazz piano with feng shui except the improv chords were laced to dynamite fuses of fugly. Who ever created this tragedy was playing the wrong tune and by god it showed.

The young man's face looked dumb and aloof against the backdrop of the deafening manor. He was teetering on the edge of the empty outdoor pool, tossing tiny pebbles he'd gathered from the driveway into the cavity just to hear the soft clinking noise. The shallow echo of the pearly white stones matched the hollow blood coursing through his veins uncomfortably well. The noise reminded him that all of it was true; that everything that had transpired in the past four months was real and this was, indeed, *all his.* It was infuriating. The sound and the fury would soon fade as the early February snow thickened, covering the base of the pool and his anger with a fresh exotic white. He looked up to admire the painless precipitation and took rest in the large snowflakes that found his face. They landed softly, happily dedicating their demise to his flushed cheek's enjoyment. He peered back down from the blinding gray-white sky and swigged the rest of his flask. He spilled some whiskey on his beard, foolishly – he felt foolish. In all that he did, all that he was – a fool. But then there was The Hudson. Time stopped and he could feel it now, the river, lying before him more powerful and prominent than he ever could have imagined.

The rushing water was one hundred feet beneath the manor and only thirty off the shoreline. It was completely arresting and had real feeling, a consistency not felt from afar. A force unrealized from 112 Hudson, it was the sound: a low roaring hum, an ominous clatter that was somehow pleasant. Its rippling temperament matched the quaking of his bones and stillness took him. 'It wasn't real,' he thought. 'It can't be real.' It was so near and constant and forever that you wound up with a funny feeling in your gut if you looked at it for too long. 'No one is supposed to see it like this,' he reeled. 'So…perfectly.' He was baffled by how quickly he fell victim to it, and somewhere in the forefront of its enormity and the backdrop of its immensity, was the memory of his father's funeral.

Just then a foghorn sounded two hundred yards down the river. The sound was so close, so remindful of reality that its loud bellow sent a shiver down his spine. The jolt rebounded off his toes dangling in Danners and worked its way back up to his shoulders huskily hunched forward in a blue-knit wool sweater, eventually wiggling its way down his arms flowing outward through his fingertips. He dropped the remainder of the stones in his hands, bent forward, grabbed his knees and began to cry.

It was a reflecting pool with no water in it. And yet, there he was reflecting...all the water in his eyes.

*

As I eventually came to, I'd do well to let you in on a little secret: there was no sweat-drenched pillow at the end of this story. There was no dream, no nightmare. I was the one wiping away frosted tears from my eyes. I was the one who buried a father I never knew existed three and a half months ago. I was the one whose mother schemed to keep both me from him and him from me all on account of "principles and integrity." Can you even imagine doing such a thing? She had kept him from me all because he "wouldn't turn from the life they were handed" just as she did.

Hate was too small of a word for what burned in my heart. The burning was too hot and never lasted long but the tears...

The tears wouldn't stop.

I couldn't stand crying but I couldn't help it. I didn't even *feel* bad – it was all too surreal, all too early, but I just couldn't stop. No matter how hard I tried, they came and came…I'm serious when I tell you they didn't have feeling. I tried to break them down. Psychoanalyze. But I couldn't pinpoint what was causing this soap opera response. Was it Absence? Emptiness? Betrayal? The tears existed merely as salty droplets of disbelief. And as they made their way to the ridge of my mouth, their flavor reminiscent of an oyster that had gone south, nausea took hold. The more I cried, the more it all sank in, only starting the thought process over again and hitting the reset button on this cursed cycle of agony.

To recap, not only had my mother lied to me about my father since birth, going so far as to say that he was a traveling techie of The Clash whom she had spent a couple months frolicking with in the summer of '82 in Great Britain, but also coldly led me to believe that he had died in a fucking airplane crash the following year – the year I was born! All of which, obviously, turned out to be a complete fabrication.

My God!

Call me gullible but what witch, what cold-blooded creature could do such a thing? Let alone keep something like that a secret for three decades? It's inconceivable. The time? The effort! The ability to never let it slip that "your father isn't dead, he actually has a manor thirty minutes up The Hudson from you. That he isn't British, but from New York and has some money and god awful taste but he still might've loved you had he known you existed!" Oh just fuck everything. I wanted her dead now too.

'Who gets dealt a hand like this?' I asked the river.

'Only literary characters and people nobody ever cares to know in real life.' The river answered back.

Self-pity had never been my thing but I had now glimpsed its purpose.

I saw her (if you're wondering why I haven't written her name here or previously, it is because she is undeserving of the notoriety) at the funeral and let her know just how I felt after demanding an explanation. As she sobbed she let it all out – the hidden past; the inexplicable course of actions, the cunning fabrications and deceit, the hiding of me from my father's knowledge till the very twilight years of his life when she learned he was dying of cancer and guilt had over-whelmed her. All of it led to one permanent outcome: hatred. A visceral resentment of the fact that I share blood with this woman, this reptile, this ice-veined snake who ruins lives. And at the funeral I let her know it. I told her that she didn't belong down there in the hole with my father. I told her that they didn't dig holes deep enough for her. Nothing on earth was low enough for this. She screamed and wailed and said I didn't know everything but I had had enough and turned my back on her and walked away.

Forever.

✻

I threw another stone into the pool, this time with such force and anger that it felt borderline theatrical. It made a poofing noise and was easily swallowed up by the now two-inch thick, powdery plush. The soft reply to my enraged toss only reminded me how futile and unfulfilling my life had been up until now. I was getting cold. Snow was accumulat-ing on my hat and shoulders and I missed Peekskill. I missed my shoebox and my frosted view and my neighbors and my horrible landlady and my friends – I missed them most. They were mine...*this*...this house, if you can call it that, was everything but that.

Seeing my friends' faces flash in front of my eyes finally brings me back to this whole dammed executor business. If you recall, I am the executor, Frank – and despite the tears and the emotional roller coaster, the sentiment and the detriment, I still think I'm doing an okay job at it. This business is the reason you and I are meeting on black and white ground after all:

It only took a couple of days for the news that I inherited a "mansion" to spread around the small town of Peekskill. I've never loathed a buzzword more. Close friends who caught wind of my unfortunate fortune recommended that I write a memoir. You know, "something to help make sense of all this." I told them it was the last thing I wanted to do, but seeing how I didn't believe in, nor could afford any therapy and still couldn't make sense of anything anymore, they thought it would help with everything I was *feeling*. Christ. *Now I had feelings.* What's next? Maury?

Nope...

...just more tears.

I put the idea of a memoir out of mind for a while. It felt like such a cheap way out. And to me, the estimable and unaccomplished writer that I am – a memoir wasn't writing, it was reporting. Not to mention it making a complete mockery out of everything I just went through.

Friends are persuasive, though. Friends and alcohol, that is. I should've known better. The agreement to do this book came after a long bout of bourbon and banter with my good bud, Jack Thornhill. The man has always had a knack for cutting through the bull and laying it down straight:

"Ya gotta face facts, man." He said. "That is what wealthy, accomplished people do when they have reached the finish line of their lives. They write a memoir."

The prick.

The irony, of course, exists in one word and one word only.

Executor.

I am now one highly unaccomplished, newly dumbfounded and spitefully damaged, Executor.

Fooey.

For what it's worth I am the Executor of *my* estate, the Garcon de Garrison, in Garrison, New York — a town slightly less stuffy than Beverly Hills. If that doesn't give you a sense of the neighborly affluence around these parts, the fact that most of the 'cottages' in Garrison have their own helicopter pads and equestrian caretakers should. My father's estate was only twenty heart-breaking minutes up the river from Peekskill and twenty minutes too far. I know, it seems almost unfathomable that our paths had never crossed. But, eventually, I'd learn that the man avoided the lower classes with the same regard and fervor one used to apply when avoiding leprosy. It wasn't so much a keep-them-at-arms-length approach as it was a keep-them-out-of-sight-and-out-of-mind philosophy that ensured we'd never meet...

Anyway, it is with this unexpected title that I now find myself fatherless, motherless, listless and well housed.

What a fuck-all-of-a-trade.

In spite of it all, I have taken to writing a memoir for *Gently Gentry & Co.*, my father's failed publishing house, and have resolved to let the cards fall where they may, so they say.

The catch?

There is no catch.

But...there was a girl.

And where there is a girl, there is hope.

Chapter I

Beans and Franks and June

(Four Months And One Night Ago)

Yes. There was a girl. Her name was June but I didn't know that yet. I didn't know anything yet. And until Jack, in that assholish tone friends come to know so well, purposefully reminded me that tomorrow would be my birthday, I didn't even know that tonight would mark my last few hours as an under-accomplished, effluent thirty-one year old.

"You're like a good cheap wine without the hangover," Jack said, as he threw on his jacket and made his way for the door. "Constantly aging, never maturing."

I let him know just how much I appreciated the sarcasm by slapping him on the back and nudging him playfully out the door.

"Thanks bud, I'll see ya tomorrow."

"Alright then."

"Alright."

He tottered a bit and then scampered on down the three flights of stairs and out into the blustery streets of The Kill.

Knowing the man well over a decade now, I'm sure he was headed to the brewery to raise hell and dodge bad demons. His early evening visit had earned me a good writer's drunk and left me feeling warm and cheery. The buzz of a couple IPAs always tended to hit me neatly, squarely on the head. Its reassuring warmth always churned out a foolish confidence backed by an incurable wont to write something better – anything better than what I had previously written. So, I figured why not sit down and strike keys for a bit?

"It is time for the next book." I had said it aloud, drunkenly to myself and myself drunkenly nodded back in full agreement. I shook off the embarrassment one has when hearing oneself think aloud and lit a Toscano. As I sat down and looked out over The Kill, I felt confident that tonight might be the night I *actually* start the damn thing.

Maybe.

I stared at the blank white page for a minute or two and it glared right back at me. Its vague illusion of heaven was all I ever needed to keep the eye-burning, mind-numbing dregs of a staring contest at bay, but lately, purgatory seemed to be its only promise. It always won the head-to-head eyeballing by the way and its unnerving emptiness forced me to think about just how big of a lie my previous statement was: nobody "just sits down and strikes keys for a bit." Jesus, that's laughable. "Like it's some goddammed leisurely activity or something." I liked to joke to myself in an absurd Shakespearean voice when I was drunk:

'I say, joyous were the days when I wrote sonnets by the lake and lay with Lady Gwendolyn and unwrapped her bonnet. Ah Yes. To writing and unwrapping bonnets and cupping buxom breastesses in the evening hour! Here, here.'

And hell, if people do think that, if they really think it is some hobby or act where scribbling down one's thoughts equals solid gold, then they are kidding themselves. It is either that or they are producing trash of the highest order. *Fools Gold.* My recent attempts have been anything but successful, perhaps not compactor-quality, but as my lackluster review from Doris and others have verified – they ain't making the cut.

My latest comic tragedy, *The Unbearable Whiteness of Being (Having a Small Penis and Owning Your Space)* was my first attempt at a Romance Novel for men. A rather remarkable disaster; its hopeful tongue-in-cheek effect on the masses palate was impotent to say the least – a real rarity for tongues, I must say. (You don't often hear of a tongue having that problem, if you catch my drift.) And not so ironically enough, it wasn't the oral irony that hurt, it was just the flat-out-failure that left me broken. Its literal non-reception and the neutral effect it had on people, considering the severe amount of time and effort and words was overwhelming. Especially when you add in the fact that I had somehow managed to save up enough scratch to have the one hundred and fifty page, fictional self-help novel printed and bound three thousand times. Good God. Every bloody, blithering copy had found its way to a shelf well over five months ago now with the overall sales, to this day, totaling a whopping ninety-eight. That's right, ninety-eight copies sold. NINETY fucking-tuck-your-dick-back-up-inside-itself-EIGHT.

Break out the bubbly boys and then break the bottle over my head. Thanks.

I know what you're thinking; 'men don't read romance novels, let alone self-help-sex-fantasies so why on earth are you surprised?' Or may be you're thinking 'how come they still make Cadbury eggs?' *Who knows what you're thinking.* But I will say this: the amount of people reading romance novels for men these days is equivalent to those eating Cadbury eggs. Ninety-eight. 'So, why go on doing this, then? Why the hell continue to torture yourself?' You might ask. And the most truthful answer I can give you is I don't know. Why does anyone do anything that might be worthwhile? *Because they have to.* Why does anyone attempt anything that might not be loved by the masses? *Because they have to.* Why does anyone believe that Cadbury eggs are edible? *Because they have to.* Why does anyone seek to create something that might be considered valuable? Might entertain? Might intrigue? Might help? Might edify? Might right the wrongs of the past? *Because they effing have to. Got it?*

Now, rest assured I am not going so far as to say that penis jokes can procure actual civil rights, nor could the description of a robust, rubicund raspberry change the staunchly corrupted attitude of a fundamentalist, but hopefully, it can distract and entertain and make good people laugh while they do the legwork. *You with me here?* The end goal is to do something worthwhile. And drumming up something that feels worthy of someone's time is the most painful thing I have ever experienced in my life. Believe it or not, I have always laid most of the blame on time itself for this enduring pain. And before both of us roll our eyes at that abstract ass-clown of a comment and throw this thing deservedly out the window, just hear me out.

If time weren't so damned valuable, people would have the leisure to read trashy good-natured filth in the first place and I, along with a lot of other more meaningful and helpful artists, might actually earn themselves a damned audience.

Capeesh?

Great. *Thanks for your time.*

However horrible that pun, time still remains our most fleeting and incorrigible customer, the most stubborn and snobbish of patrons. The unchangeable, enduring reminder that the job of life is difficult and its difficulty is continuous. Yes, time is the one who comes in, buys one cup of coffee, stays for far too long while making jokes at your expense and then, unexpectedly, gets up, sprints out the door and never leaves a tip. That's time for you:

Oh indifferent youth, your twinkle eludes me.
Oh father time, your hands grow arthritic.
Oh mother vine, your wrinkles amuse me.
Oh senile truth, your brain is so slow and stammering it doesn't remember how to rhyme and has peed itself, once again, yellowing yet another poem's ending.

Excuse me, you'll have to pardon the poetry – the clock strikes midnight tonight in under an hour, and with it, the icy dagger of thirty-two. So you might be able to grasp how abstract malarkey like time and success might not be in my good graces at the moment. I guess the point I was trying to make was that if we are all subjects to time, we should all try to leave a tip in its stead; a bit of learned advice, some wisdom aquired along the way, what have you. Anything to help make life a little easier for everyone else making the passage, especially all of those innocent bystanders who've yet to snag boarding passes.

I suppose that is actually what I am doing as I sit here, wailing, pissing and moaning, desperately trying to create something that is worthwhile.

All because I have to.

I brought the pen down to the paper and still nothing.
Wait a second...what was it the poets' said?
"If you don't know where to start, start with a joke?"
I'm sure that's not what they said but here goes nothing:

What's the best slogan for a penis ever written?

Life's hard.

Best motto for a vagina ever written?

It's what's on the inside that counts.

'Not bad. Not bad. Not brilliant either...*decent.* Maybe
keep the tone and switch up the direction?' I thought. "One
more drink oughtta do it," I said aloud to myself again,
burping out confidence. For better or worse, liquid courage is
a hell of a thing. I got up, filled a rock glass with ice and
poured bourbon the only way I knew how – to the top. I
splashed on some ginger ale and sat back down, readied to
bleed and let the ink run.

Ah! Finally:

He saw her and she saw him as they were meant to be
seen, skin-lit by moonlight. The tinge of smoky bourbon still clinging to their lips set the sight of new skin
on fire. He felt vulnerable and confident and eager and
she reflected his gait. A slow metallic taste returned to
his tongue and sat there, bitterly awaiting the mechanical
motions to come. His heart pounded out of his ears as
he reached out and grasped her swollen sleeve-hole,
firmly – if only to let her know who was in charge.

He was.

He rotated his forefingers lightly around her button and then proceeded to methodically spread her apart. Slowly. Always slow. Always patient. Always precise...she whimpered. Warmth and water sprang forth, and just as the sun does to the budding flower, so did she open up to him. She shivered as his demeanor changed and with the confident movement of an aged-lover, he hooked his fingers inside her. He pumped a couple of times. Steadily at first and then moving faster and more solidly, rigidly inviting her toward him with only his fingers. The moaning that followed struck a tuning fork in his loins. The pulsing vibrations of her vocal chords triggered something deep inside of him, a real change. He was letting go of the human and submitting to the wild within. The animalistic, instinctual nature of it all. The Switch. Her entire body was moved by his changed person, his newly inspired vigor. Stiffness took on new meaning. He was solid now, unbreakable. A wizard's staff swung in the air readied to make magic. Spreading her legs apart, the twisting, gripping nature of her toes on his calf and the slight tilt of her head splashed sweet brown hair across his face and told him she was ready for all he had to offer. Before he knew it he was inside her.

Blank thoughts and obscurity.

He nibbled on her earlobe and braced her arms together violently, pulling her trunk onto his. He looked down and admired the scene of his unsheathed sword slowly penetrating her shorn-lipped glove. He took a stroll down her holy hallway and left himself for what seemed a permanent vacation. Time slowed and he was away from her, away from himself, away from everything...he was gone.

But there he still was, furious and forever and, of

course, over before it started. He had made a complete
fool of himself. 'Shotguns have more pump-action than
this,' he thought. 'Beer commercials last longer than that,'
she thought. As he flopped off to the side of her like an
over cooked noodle, the joy from the fleeting buzz of
climax had left him and the hangover of a poor performance was setting in. When he finally rolled over, regaining full consciousness and memories from childhood,
he noticed her areolas were the size of sand dollars.
'How the hell did I miss that,' he thought. It made no
difference. He liked them just the same. He played with
them a moment. Not sexual but toyish. He glanced over
at her, unsatisfied as she was and stopped the toying,
ashamed. But then he noticed how warm and beautiful
she remained, how he might be able to love someone
like her, and, to his astonishment, how well she had hid
her disbelief at his record-breaking performance. He
knew right there and then that it was his duty to rise to
the occasion once more. He would do so, reimagining
the plethora of details he had missed previously and
oddly enough, didn't require to enjoy the deed before
hand. He focused his perversion with a wizard's intensity and remembered the nuances of their friction perfectly: just how tropical she was downstairs, the mineral
saltiness of her brine that still lingered on his fingertips,
the minor movements of her torso as he pummeled her
pie, the way she would firmly press back on him when
he gyrated and how her jaw opened wider and wider as
he protruded forth like a conquistador on the path of
chaos and destruction – 'whose adventure ended in failure.' He thought. Wait, wait. Bad thoughts. Bad
thoughts. Another approach was sorely needed so he
switched to another angle, another way in – or shall I
say, *up.* He thought about the exact moment he entered
her. He imagined, and emphasis on imagined, that he

had filled every inch of her...and finally, with his ego-peaking from this fantastically phallic boost, his bamboo grew rapidly and strong enough to hold up his end of the bargain: 'We, as in the both of us, will enjoy this and enjoy it good.' And so they did.

I put down the pen and closed the laptop. I figured then that writing romance novels for men was what I was *supposed* to do — lackluster or not. The alcohol was fading now as was the potency of *Jean-Luc Wharm*, the best and most pussified pen name in the biz.

But a title? Dammit. There need be a title before His Lukewarmness, the Philosopher of Phallus Minimus, could rest...I scribbled something down so quickly and haphazard-ly it was almost illegible when I reread it on the notepad:

"My Red Hot Winter in June"
By Jean-Luc Wharm

Just then, a buzz at the door. I closed up shop and hazily made my way down to the entryway. It was Jack again, back and in rare, weird form. He had tears streaming down his face. He was crying and evidently distracted for he couldn't bring himself to look me in the eye.

"I slept with Carla," he said, muscling through tears.

"What?"

He sighed a long, desperate sigh. "I slept with her, Frank. I mean. I've been seeing her."

"Okay. Well which is it?"

"God man, I don't know, I'm drunk. Okay? I didn't have the balls to tell you earlier."

He pouted some more. The spectacle of a two hundred and fifty pound lumberjack sobbing, looking for forgiveness was far more than I needed this evening. It was something about the way we found ourselves talking about the topic and not just the topic itself that had a souring effect on me. Perhaps it was that we were already tilted, well on our way to hiccups and headaches and beyond, or maybe it was simply that it was happening twenty minutes before my birthday. Whatever it was, it stirred something red in me. I began to clench my teeth and boil with rage but quickly shook it off. It was the whiskey whispering hate into my ear and I knew better. *I was the one who broke up with Carla, anyway. Remember?*

"We're talking about Carla as in – my ex, Carla – right?"

"Yes," he could not bring himself to look me in the eye. "Listen if you want to hit me or something, just do it. I feel horrible. Just do me a favor – stay away from the face, all right? I have an audition tomorrow."

"God you're dramatic."

"I'm serious man, just hit me if it'll make you feel better."

"Listen, If I'd-a-wanted to hit you it would've happened already. And if it did it would've destroyed your beloved face, Jack. I mean, look at you. You look like a sad clown. All you need is some white powder and I'd be happy to hit you, you bearded Pagliacci."

Despite my even-keeled sarcasm, neither of us could move much due to the extreme awkwardness that sat there like a thick wall of ambiguity between us. So, naturally, we both continued to stand outside, shivering like idiots in some stupid state of friction with no end in sight. As we waited to find the right course of action, the tension built and our breath struck the cold air and steamed with the force of two castrated bulls expecting battle, like two steers staring down each other for the cow. Except I had already left the cow two years ago and I had a hankering that old Jack here didn't really want the cow either, he just wanted someone. . . someone who might want him too. You know, make him feel special and all that. Hell, what we all want. I glanced up at the sky and back at Jack and started to laugh a little at the ridiculousness of the situation. 'The fucking incestuous nature of a small town.' I thought. There was a sort of inescapable inbred absurdity to it all. We tend to weave webs more tangled than Charlotte's in places like The Kill, and fuck-all if we can't help it. The only chance we're given is to decide whether we call these intricately entangled, sticky personal histories a miserable mesh of the past or a happy coincidence for the future. More and more I have been finding myself choosing the latter and I must tell you, things have been going much better. I finally stopped chuckling and found what it was I wanted to say:

"I only have one question for you."

"Yeah?" He finally mustered the courage to look me in the eye.

"Were you sleeping with her or talking to her while I was with her?"

"No. Not at all." He re-centered himself, his boots finding new roots in cement. "I swear Frank, on our crazy mothers' lives, I swear it."

"Okay then. Stop crying and come inside. You look like a blubbering idiot out there."

Jack started to cry more after my nonchalant reaction finally sank in. He launched himself at me and the result was nothing short of bromance. A bear-man-hug in full effect, my feet were off the ground and the son of a bitch planted one on my cheek.

"I love you, man." He said.

"Ease up!" He was separating cartilage from my ribs. "Cah-rist! How drunk are you?"

"Drunk enough."

"Alright-alright." I said as I wiggled out of his grip, pushing the burly overbearing lush back on to the sidewalk. "Come on in. I reckon I got some Trace left over upstairs – enough for a night cap."

"Naw-naw. Let's go out! Hell, it's almost your birthday. Fuck it. Let's go get sideways at the brewery – my treat."

"Jack. I don't really feel like going to the same bar that I will have to work at on my actual birthday night."

"Well Christ had cankles, are you serious?"

"Yeah. I have to work there tomorrow, on my birthday."

"Well then. It's obvious you need to go out *tonight*. It's Friday you philandering fuck. C'mon, even you can't resist the scenery that crawls its way up from the city on weekends."

"Eh. I'm supposin' you're right."

I didn't feel like arguing with the man. Too many years spent working behind a bar has taught me one thing and one thing only: drunken arguments aren't arguments, they're one-sided vomit contests. And besides, it was Friday night at the brewery and Jack had a point.

I turned around to head inside and grab my jacket only to see Doris shaking her head at us through her frosty front window. I could see from the seething disapproval in her eyes that she thought Jack and I were an item. New found gay lovers who only happened to look otherwise. I smiled at her and offered a sultry, flamboyant hand-wave. She reared her nose up at me at which point I blew her a kiss. I couldn't help it – the woman needed to be shocked out of her old world mindset. I added a flair of estrogen and pageantry as I cat walked inside. She shot me another look of contempt and shut her curtain firmly. I shook my head and laughed for I was all the better for it – she wasn't necessarily easy on the eyes so to say, resembling something closer to a Boris these days.

When I came back down stairs, Jack asked me why I continued to live with such a miserable mope of a landlady for so long (part of me figured he was purposefully changing the subject) but I had plenty of excuses and was happy to give them. They all revolved around the rent and the almost nonexistent amount of money I paid to live there. He then joked that I obviously paid for it in other ways and I agreed with him but then abruptly told him that as long as her abuse wasn't bruising my wallet, I could put up with her backwards, petrified temperament a little while longer. The real question was how on earth could Sean and Jay stomach it for so long...I had a feeling their answer would be pretty close to mine.

The beginning of the walk down to the brewery proved to be an odd one for Jack and me. With things resolving so quickly and so drunkenly between us, I never really had time to fully digest everything. I knew deep down that some part of me was fine with Jack seeing Carla, but there were shallower layers of me that felt off, like an engine whose conveyor belt had now taken to that rancid screeching noise that only stops when the car is either fully in motion or completely in neutral. It was something like being functional while still being horrendously annoyed at the same time. When it came down to it – Jack and Carla seeing one another – I knew it wasn't wrong but it somehow still wasn't right either. I decided to let it roll off my back and smartly mellow for another time. Jack cracked wise about the new waitress at the Brewery being something of a c-word and we strolled merrily, jokingly down the Hudson St. hill to the brewery.

Enter the Peekskill Brewery, my place of income or stability or whatever (I haven't yet been able to call it my place of employment – I am a writer by trade, goddammit, and a laborer for survival). It has now resided in an old gutted furniture factory for little more than two years. Its four-storied façade of red brick and large modern windows tended to catch the early winter sunsets crisply and the warmer pastels kept the place aglow, heating the brick and churning the brew and spinning the dialogue, long after the sun had ducked behind the western Appalachian skyline. Its lone presence in this rather slow-to-rise town sits right on the water and is only a short two-minute walk off the Metro-North Hudson Line. Aside from the craft beer and artisanal fare, it was these last two qualities that continuously guaranteed a fair amount of females, desperate to escape the city and smell something other than the shallow musk of obnoxious urban men, to migrate in beautiful droves into its dressed-down gastro-pub. I must tell you that the migration is highly appreciated around these parts and weekends at the brewery, more often than not, produced the most enjoyable scenery this side of suburbia. It is a unique talent show of sorts; where ladies of leisure, women of woe and harlots of hope, all hell bent on a rather carefree night up the Hudson, get what they're looking for – locals and libations. Well, they probably don't care too much for the locals, but we liked to kid ourselves nonetheless.

I'm guessing it should be said here that the one truly unique characteristic about The Kill other than its view of the river is its locals. They have magically remained resistant to the usual flow of townie doldrums and fought off the ever-enticing urge to embrace laziness and become inhumanely boring. The lot of them being some sort of aspiring artist or musician helps their cause, but it is more their expansive knowledge of the city (and henceforth, the world) married to a sense of social duty that helps deliver a level of wit and cultured taste normally unheard of outside the city limits. Most of them have proudly detached themselves from the world of trends and turned, wisely, I might add, toward the world of classics – the world that endures. Making the brave decision to leave the city behind had forced everyone here, that is to say if they wished to remain somewhat interested, or at the very least, a part of the Peekskill hub-bub, to take up arms and interests in tid-bits of culture that have staying power – things that aren't so subject to flop and fold like that of the cyclical nature of urban culture. The result has led to an admirable mosaic of talkative townies, ex-urbanites of spires and squires, and native tongues that all speak a well-curated and open-minded language. If you take all of these young-blooded, smart and well-adjusted attributes and let them ferment a bit, you'll earn yourself a solid reason to believe that the Brewery is one of the best drinking spots outside the city every Friday-Saturday night.

And this Friday was no different.

Except in one way – it was my birthday. And Jack, that two-bit bastard of a friend, had lured me into a trap. A surprise birthday trap, something I never would've been down with had I known the man's original intent.

"SURPRISE BEANS!" They rumbled as I opened the door.

I could barely let go of the handle before the roar thundered strong against my chest. Shock took me in two ways. First, from the sheer amount of faces smiling at me and second, from Jack and just how that awful fuck went about getting me to this celebration in the first place. (Who the hell tells a best friend he's sleeping with his ex just to get him to *his* surprise birthday party? *Jack, that's who.*) The shock soon gave way to elation, finding it was impossible not to mirror the joy of the faces that stood before me; the bright and warm mugs that were perfectly content just to see me. *Moi.* *Yours Truly.* I started to get a little weepy-eyed myself. Not in the overly dramatic sense, but my eyes watered. There was some definite watering. I choked the rest of them back and took a mental snap shot of the scene. The vast amount of people there, some whom I had known over twenty years and had to travel far distances to be at the Brewery that night, was a little too much to handle. I drank it all in and slowed everything down – the collective happiness in the faces there was somehow a reflection of me and that was a remarkable thing all on its own. It was probably the closest to nirvana I'll ever get; that rushing roar of happy faces. There were old faces, new faces, faces from high school, faces from my youth. Faces I hadn't seen in years, faces from work and college, faces of happenstance, of fortune, of strangers who had become friends and friends who had in turn, become family. They were, collectively, faces of my past who were certainly to be faces of my future; the faces of a bond that would never be broken and tonight reinforced the feeling.

"Surprise Beans." Jack whispered in my ear, as the rest of the celebrators started to break ranks and make their way forward. "I'm not really sleeping with Carla, by the way. How's that for kickers, you gullible twat."

I glanced back toward him. His eyes went as wide as an owl's when he realized just how convincing his performance had been. I didn't quite understand it at first, but as his gleeful boyish mug digressed into a crack-fiend's smile that had just finally caught the dragon, I knew it for sure.

"Dude, you're sick man." I said. "Like really sick. Like, *Jesus*. You need help."

"Ho-HOAH!" He boasted, letting out a hyenas cackle of a laugh. "Goddamn, the screen is calling me! Won't be long now before you're askin' for ole Jack Thornhill's Hancock, everyone...or maybe just his cock!" He paused for a moment to take in his triumphant performance, and then, under his breath grittily mustered: "Enjoy your night buddy. Now let me get you that beer."

He slapped me on the back and made room for the others coming my way. I felt thankful for that piece of shit and laughed at him as he congratulated himself to the crowd for getting me to the brewery on time, yelling "I AM ALL THAT IS MAN" while hoisting his hands to the heavens in celebratory grandeur.

What a true piece of shit, I thought. But the good kind, ya know? The kind that doesn't stink and barely calls for a wipe and always leaves you feeling better, lighter after it's gone.

They came and they came and they came. The Faces: red-cheeked and buzzing, squinty-eyed and content, all of them filled with history and hope. These people of my past, these people of my future, these people with ear-to-ear's, all offering hands and hugs and kisses and inside jokes and looks and laughs and language ungraspable to the public and history unfathomable to a loner...they offered the sense that life was actually worth the struggle if you knew this was what surrounded you. It was an aura of easy love and quotes and comedy. Every person in there was more than a friend, they had defined a piece of my life, and more importantly, a piece of my personality and that, my hermitted wallflowers, was the ticket. My god, their light had now become a constant source of energy, one that is refracted back on to everyone I meet solely because these people were kind enough to shine it on me in the first place. I can only modestly attempt to return the favor. The hands kept coming throughout the night, as did the glinted eyes and full-hearted embraces and drinks and stories. Sweet Jesus, did the drinks and stories continue for hours on end. And from the memories came the laughter and through it, the electricity; a good-natured buzz that filled the walls of our very own brew-ha-ha. The low humming sizzle of happy hearts and hopeful spirits made me think, this wasn't my night, this was our night and I can't even tell you how glorious it was. The real magic of it came from a shared history between everyone there due to years of drinking bouts and stumbling tours of cities. This traveling circus of cronies quickly turned debauched menagerie and a resulting learned familiarity arose. Slowly, by similar forces of magnetism and of course, humor, it claimed the many different cliques here and galvanized them into one unholy armada.

I thought briefly about how I had no family there and re-gretted it. The subject had never brought much good to any situation anyway and over the years I had learned to repress it – especially during high points in my life. So, I did as I al-ways had and shook it off and tucked the thought deep back into the shadowy recesses of my mind. Fortunately, the peo-ple that filled the brewery offered me something more valua-ble than gold. They offered me a sense of solidarity in my times of solitude, a sense of grace in those ugly pernicious moments when having a family was essential yet absent. These folks have been a real sense of encouragement in my times of despair – they offered to me the belief that I was never truly alone.

That's what family is for, after all.

Isn't it?

There was Slim Jim Dean (whom we called Dean, but also Mini-Jimmy on account of the junior size sausages and his man-parts being of similar make-up) and Tommy Briggs (whom we called Two-tone with regards to his inability to sing and that he loathed the pop classic "867-5309/Jenny" by Tommy Tutone) and Levenson (whom we called by his last name because living with his first, Shmuel, seemed like enough punishment for a lifetime) and Killjoy (because he embodied his last name) and Shortstack (who saw fit to dub himself this nickname because A) he likes women who are "tiny and thick" to quote the man and B) his original calling card, Stephen Dunklemeyer, wasn't cutting it cool with compact little women) and Beau (recently dubbed "Bae from the Bayou" for reasons that need no explaining) and Pretty Ricky (who constantly checked himself out in the mirror, a narcissist of narcissists, who to everyone's supreme enjoyment, never got laid) and Sean and Jay (whom we called by their actual names because The Twin Twinks wasn't going over smoothly) and Big-Mugsy and his brother, Lil-Bogues (yes, they split their name on account of the famous point-guard from the Charlotte Hornets – based on looks and their corresponding heights of course). The list of faces and names went on and on and their re-imagined story lines, their persona-non-gratas were ever evolving, clever as hell, ball-busting to the point of tears and always, always a thing to behold.

Half of the boys had now landed significant others and sadly, their presence had become more and more of a rarity come reunion time. It was an understood arrangement though, and a key part of growing up (which many of us still had to do), it was just tough to see the slow natural separation of a group start to happen. We were all of sound agreement however that it *needed* to happen when family life arose: letting go of youth is never an easy thing to do, but it was something that had to be done, absolutely essential in order for the next round of carefree to thrive. On this, there was no question.

The other half of boys at the brewery, the half which I myself was still a quasi-proud member, were more single than they cared to mention and extremely happy to be at the brewery this Friday night for it was holding up its end of the bargain: high standards of aesthetic value. Yeap, the ladies of the night were out and about. So, quite naturally, we drank and drank to quell the nerves most men suffer from when surrounded by beautiful women. The challenge was not to drink too much. There is an ongoing war that takes place between man and bottle, and only woman possesses the power to play peacekeeper. Eastern Standards were the choice glass – it being the brewery's response to the West Coast's style of IPA – and I have to tell you it has outdone the Californian recipe in style and zest and that's not hometown pride talking, that's the beer talking.

Two A.M. came and went and the doors remained open with the owners yelling from the bar top, "last call will be with the last man standing!" They poured full pints down their gullets. They saw me swaying near the bar and after wiping away the beer that dripped from their beards, decided to pull me up along side them. "And it better not be with this fucker!" They were all sorts-a-twisted. They motioned to Timmy, the youthful bar back who was now running the entire show for the night, to cut the music.

"A TOAST!" A voice bellowed from the depth.

"YEAH TOAST!" Another rumbled.

"TOAAAAST!" More came clamoring in.

I held up my hands in a gesture of submission, nodding along to their madness.

"Ladies and Gentleman!" Ted, or Boss Tweed (he had a thing for professorial blazers), took the reins. "I give to you, Frank Gently. (Some cheers, some boos) A man who frankly won our hearts all too easily, and of course, the last man we'd ever call a gentleman. But, that's why we love you, you big knob. So, get over here Frank and give the people what they want. Here's to the big three-two!"

I shook hands with the two of them and they hopped off the bar top and gave me the floor (which in this case was still a bar top). There was a cheer and some whooping and beer slugging and slopping sounds from beer spilling topped off by a few cutting jibes and taunts. I normally thought of being in front of a crowd as the most life threatening of spaces; one that was inclined to produce arrhythmia and sand-papery tongues and fleeting states of consciousness, but there, in front of those I cared for most, I imagined it was what a womb might've felt like. That is, if your mother was a drinker.

"Thank you, Ted, for that delightful introduction. Alls I can say is, it takes a knob to know a knob," Crickets rubbed their legs together. "So, umm, yeah. Thank you for that. Everyone, what can I say? I'm completely taken aback and humbled that you're all here tonight...lord only knows what kind of blackmail Jack pulled on you to force you to make the trip! Just know I have plenty on that scuzz-ball so if you're looking to settle the score please feel free to hit me up when the night's over. (Slight laughter. Jack flips me the bird and I return the favor). But seriously, I look out and I see all these faces and in them, all these great memories . . . memories you all gave me. Just know I cherish each and every one of them. It's really the greatest gift a guy could ask for, so thank you all for that. I don't know what the future holds, but if it is anything like the past I'm fixing it's gonna be one hell of a ride for all of us. I mean, who ever said thirty-two couldn't be a banner year? Am I right!? ("Hells Yeah!" "Myeaasss." Takes a long drink with crowd.) Okay! Okay. And on that note, I have a toast for every single one of you here, including those I don't know. Yeap. So everyone raise your glasses. Oh Christ, Beau's is empty again already. ("Fahck you!") Dan, will you please be a gentleman and pour some in his glass. Now Bae, you have to wait before the toast is over to drink it. Ya got that, sweetheart? (Slight laughter, "This man is a cuckold!" More laughter.) Okay. Okay! This one is to Character Flaws, for without them, I certainly wouldn't be friends with all of you. Cheers!"

"Cheers!"

"Fuckin Right."

"Shitch-Yeah."

"Alright." I said, climbing down off the bar, "Can someone please put the music back on? 'S-a-goddamn snooze-fest in here."

I was met with a couple of manly daps and hearty handshakes and of course, more forced beer slugging. I looked around and realized, with the beards and slurring roars, all we needed was a couple of kilts, an axe or two and a bagpipe player and it would've looked like your average Scotsman's gathering. A highlander barnburner.

And then there was a voice.

"Nice speech." The voice whispered. It was raspy, booze-worn and had been hushed so softly and intimately that I almost didn't make it out over the music. "How'd you know I had a character flaw?"

I turned around to a pair of eyes I had never seen before. A pair of eyes you could lose yourself in. 'My god, the blue.' I thought. They were Robins egg blue. Never-to-be-forgotten-blue. They weren't cutting or out of this world but pale and sweet and inviting. The edges had a constant glint; an upwardness that allowed what would've normally been a sexy, too-cool-for-anyone pair of cat eyes to be warmth and comfort...to be home. I fell right there and then. I fell so freaking hard it's not even funny. Everything else that came to me in those first moments only made my cause that much more hopeless: the jet-black hair thick and flopping. The creamy, drinkable skin. Her voice. Fuck. *That voice.* How can anyone refrain from sentiment when their world changes in an instant? When a couple choice words and a soft-sweater-smile remind you what it feels like to be alive, isn't sentiment the holiest and most called for of responses? Finding sentiment in her was worth every ounce of cheesy sop and revolting gush I could muster. Her beauty seemed to match her character and rare as that was, it was all too apparent in the way she carried herself. Her slightly tilted sense of humor was worn on her shoulders that were relaxed and canted to one side. There was a playful, if not flirtatious quirk to her head and jaw line that allowed her cheekbones to pop and catch the light just right. All this accompanied by a confident, almost waggish repose in her posture and let me not forget...the curl of those protruding crimson lips...*toof.* It all provided sound argument that this invitation to chat wasn't just with any girl. It was with thee girl – a woman of value, of intuition, of care and, hopefully, a woman of that most sentimental of virtues... love.

Ahem, if there is such a thing.

I regrouped and pulled my jaw back up off the floor and finally made some sense of the vision that stood before me. I gulped down drunkenness and stammered into a rather desperate focus, a faux-sense of sobriety. I felt my head reel at the attempt to iron out all the usual giveaways that define shitfaced. I think I somehow managed to pull it off:

Outside: calm, cool, collected...smooth. Dare I say witty?

Inside: Light-headedness backed by illiterate inarticulate slop. A whirling madness of stupidity sure to top out at a category five.

"Oh, I – I actually practice astrology." I said, pulling out nonsense from nowhere. "So. You know – *I know everything.*"

She smiled.

I smiled.

"Do people actually *practice* astrology?"

"Umm yes. In the Alps."

I had no idea what the fuck I was saying.

"The Alps?" She waited for me to break character but I was too drunk. I stuck to my guns.

"Yes. The Alps. It's like the Tibet of Astrologists."

She chuckled a little, "You're ridiculous."

"You're right."

"Okay, so what are you? A Cancer?"

"Well, seeing how that was my birthday speech and this is October...I think that makes me a Libra."

"Oh, right." She dropped her eyes embarrassingly and took a drink, somewhat ashamed that she didn't know the right sign.

"Don't worry, I *love* that you didn't know that. And besides, you were right anyway. Astrology is a cancer."

She laughed, this time full-hearted. She had a sense of humor. She had more than that — she had me. "So what's your fortune cookie say, oh wise one?"

"Well, I asked Siri this morning except she answered me back in Spanish. Never did get around to changing my language settings, but, what I think she said was: 'Birthdays are only worth celebrating if you have someone to celebrate them with.' Or perhaps she said, 'don't dip the cookie in the tea for fear of sogginess?' Who knows! I'll have to follow up with you on that."

"Well, it certainly looks like you have a lot of people to celebrate with...what are you, the Mayor of Peekskill or something?"

"Actually yes, but only in its establishments that serve alcohol. Every where else, I go by my other and much more suitable title..."

"BEANS!" Dean interrupted.

"Beans?" She said, raising her eyebrow in concern.

"Well, I was going to say Peasant, but — yeah. Sorry, can you excuse me a second?"

She nodded and began to laugh as I had no choice in the matter — Dean had pulled me back from the bar. The boys had organized yet another beer drinking contest that required minimal motor function and zero brainpower. I was set to lead the one group of teetering cronies against the other. I glanced back at her, mouthing 'one second' while flashing my index in the air before being ripped backward by Dean again and shoved head first into a solo-cup. A couple rounds of uproarious flip-cup went by cup by cup, each one more painful and muddling than the next. It is a game that if foolishly played that late (or shall I say early) in the night, especially by bodies of a certain age with beer of a certain alcohol content, will always see to it to end the night abruptly, sloppily, greenly. We were just about to make our way into the fifth round when I looked over at Jack and told him I was out.

"There's a girl." I said.

"There's *always* a girl, Frank."

"Not like this, man. Not like this."

"Dammit Beans," Jack continued, his eyes half-lit, his hand on the table for balance. "It's time to stop chasing women and start chasing dreams."

"What happens when they're one in the same, brotus?" I looked over at the mystery lady and was happy to make eyes with her once more before approaching. "Besides, flip-cup-champion ain't the dream anymore — even you know that you big buffoon."

"But it's your birthday, maaang."

"Exactly."

I had already left the conversation and his lazy eyes before I let the news sink in. He'd eventually come around to reason, whether it lacked oxygen or not. The buxom silhouette that had already bounced in and out of my mind, sweaty and naked and panting, was now standing by one of the large floor to ceiling windows amongst a crowd of strong females. This was not about to deter me. Hell, I would do well to remind you that it was my surprise birthday party and like I said, for better or worse, liquid courage is still a helluva thing.

"Excuse me gals, I'm afraid I need your friend here a

moment."

"Oh yeah? What for?" The tallest, snootiest and most re-pugnant of the clan retorted.

"For baby-making, what else? We keep cots in the back. C'mon you." I quietly nudged the beautiful lioness away from the threshold of her pride. I apologized for leaving so abrupt-ly, "I'm sorry I had to leave you earlier, Miss?"

"June. You sure about this guy?" The snoot brought down her hammer of disapproval once again.

"I'm fine Paula." She cut off her friend who actually looked like a Paula. "And Juniper," she said quietly, as she turned her attention back toward me. "It's Juniper, but every-one calls me June. And you? You're what? Beans? Or Frank? Or what was it...Peasant?"

"All are welcomed here m'lady."

"Well you seem frank to me. So Frank it is."

"I think I am, therefore I am. Or somethin' like that."

"You're a bit of a kook, aren't you?"

"If that's a compliment then yes."

"Well it might be – I'm not sure just yet. But before you buy me my next drink, I think you're gonna have to explain to me why the hell they call you Beans? That's like the worst nickname ever."

"Hm. I happen to believe Boner is the worst nickname ever but that's just me." She nodded adoringly. "But I think I'm gonna need to get you that drink, anyway. It's a bit of a long story, ya know? It starts back in fifth grade around a camp fire...and you know how fifth grade camp fire stories go...it's all farts and franks and beans and you know, toilet humor. Murder she wrote, Beans is what stuck."

"Well isn't that gross."

"Hay. Everybody poops."

"Ew. Everybody doesn't have to talk about it."

"I guess so, but I'm into honesty and well, sometimes the truth iddn't pretty...that is, unless we're talkin' about you."

"Oh lord."

"Errr." My vocal chords were at war with my head. Just what the hell was I doing!? What rank bowl of cheese did I just serve up!? Porridge came curdling from my mouth. I made a desperate attempt at recovery, "Sorry 'bout that. Little drunk. My birthday night and all."

"It's okay. I kinda liked it." She finished her beer. "I mean, it was pitiful. I don't think you could-a-had a worse start. You did just go from poop to pretty in two seconds...but I still kinda liked it."

It was my turn to hang my head and wallow behind a tipped pint glass.

"Seriously, it's okay." She said, warmly. "Perfect starts are for the big screen. Catastrophes are more real anyway."

"Suppose I can only go up from here."

She nodded. "So, Franks and Beans, huh?" She smiled slightly and swaying her hair away from her face, took two tiny steps closer as a means of encouragement.

"And June, yeah?"

"Yes," she said. "Franks and Beans and June."

"We'll call it Frank and June for short."

"I think I'd like that."

"I think I like you."

"I think you're a fool."

"So! You knew my true sign after all. C'mon, lemme get you that drink."

"I think I'd rather have some air..."

She made for the door but before I could fret over my sad and rather basic performance, she stopped half way, turned back toward me, threw on her jacket and waited for this drunken Libra to read between the lines — *she wanted me to follow her.* Well holy hell, it was my birthday night after all! I needed to sober up and dry out the plumbing fast so I ran to the bathroom and quickly upchucked inside a urinal. The acidic froth of half-digested beer hit the blue-pad with tremendous force. I was glad to get some of the leftovers from flip-cup out of me. I wiped away the tears, threw in some gum and bee-lined it outside where June was already showing off her oral skills…with a cigarette.

There's nothing quite like Irishing your own birthday party.

Chapter 2

Snowy Warmth
On the Waterfront

"You know a gin martini is actually my drink of choice?"

"No. How would I know that? I just met you."

"Right. I mean, with a name like Juniper…oh screw it, I'm sure you get that a lot."

"Actually, most guys don't talk to me much. They tend to go for the Paulas of the world."

"The Paulas?"

"Yeah. You know, the tall, fast, fluorescent ones with too much eye-shadow."

"I take it you two aren't close?"

"No way." She looked at me like I had just insulted her. "You couldn't tell? She's a friend of a friend…of a friend. I just met her tonight and have been contemplating throwing myself into the river ever since."

"Well I'm glad you didn't do that. The river's much more enjoyable from above."

"I could see how that might be accurate."

We walked leisurely through the street-lit, tangerine afterglow that accompanies a large snowfall at night. High-stepping over what was easily a half-foot of fluffy powder, we made our way to the river and the frozen docks just off the Peekskill train station. Despite the biting cold, the spirits and ales held us warm and upright, and guided us cozily to the riverfront. It would be hard to speak for her, but by my telling, we wanted for nothing at that moment in time. Well, maybe a kiss or two, but out there in the lustrous charm of the Hudson Valley, everything felt right. Its beguiling whisper of crisp air allowed us to carry on like a pair of grade school kids who knew the following day would surely be a snow day — kicking snow piles and sliding to and fro, stopping like professional hockey players on the unplowed road. We landed on the docks and took in the placid view of the river.

It was intensely quiet.

I was immensely happy.

I pointed to the snow covered mountains across the way that sat there winking at us with white eyelashes.

"Winter's so underrated." I said, opening my mouth, thirsty for snowflakes. "It's absolutely perfect out right now."

"It certainly is." She cocked her head at me. "You know snow is ridiculously dirty, right?"

"Yeap."

"And yet you still have your mouth open."

"Yeap."

"Okay. I guess this is where I should ask 'why?' but I'm not sure I want to know the answer."

"I guess I'm just a kid who still likes to play in the dirt."

"So you ate the dirt when you were a kid?"

"Well, no. But it was a metaphor."

"I'm not sure, but I think it fell flat there, stud."

"How so?"

"Well, playing in the dirt doesn't mean the same thing as eating the dirt. Unless you were the dirt-eater?"

"Nah, nah. Worms were more my style."

"Don't be cute."

"Can't help it."

"Alright smart ass, let's see what you think of this metaphor: Did the pretty girl in the sandbox ever kiss the kid with mud on his lips?"

"Well, no." Her question forced me to close my mouth, drop the fuckery and confront the nervousness I had been sloughing off our entire walk. "No, I can't say the dirty boy ever really got any."

"Well, that can still change…I've always had a thing for dirty boys…metaphorically, that is."

I leaned in and so did she.

My heart thumped a deep bass that hit so hard I hoped she couldn't hear it. When our lips finally came apart, like magnets unwillingly peeled from one another, I told her how I actually felt about her. I told her how glad I was to have met her and how thankful I was that she had said hello earlier. The sobering authenticity of my rambling hit her, I think, where the hitting counts – somewhere below the neck and just above the belly button.

"I have to admit, I was shocked." I continued. "I know you say boys don't talk to you much, but lord, the girls don't talk to me…especially ones that look like you."

"Like me?"

"Yeah. Like you."

"And just what does that mean?" She asked, raising her voice in an almost insecure fashion.

It was out there, on the borders of cheese and sentiment and the solid ground of insecurity and intrigue that I finally broke through and found some semblance of realness:

"Remarkable."

Our lips found each other once again and we kissed for so long that little lumps of snow started to accumulate and melt on our cheekbones. When I pulled away from her the melted snow resembled tears. As I looked at her again, this time with a more primal and downright bothered instinct, I noticed that her full-figured body matched what my hands had just devoured. And her lips, her lips were inflamed by my drunken nibbling. I apologized to her and she laughed for mine had embraced the same swollen effect.

"So why on earth did you say hi to a fool like me?" I joked.

"That's easy. People seem to like you…and I like people."

"Hm." I once again took in the fortune of the surprise party and all of those who made my entrance to thirty-two one for the books.

"And besides, I couldn't stand one more minute with Paula."

"Ah. Now comes the truth."

"You didn't think it was because of your dashing good looks and fleeting charm, did you?"

"Well, yes. I did, actually. Ahem – did you say fleeting?" I threw my hand around her hip and we gazed longingly at the Hudson.

Her eyes were married to the serene waters, "is the river always like this?"

"Yes. Yes it is."

"Mesmerizing."

I nodded but she failed to notice that my view was now only of her. We kissed once more and enjoyed the orange cream-sickle hue of the streetlights a little while longer. The aura of fallen clouds enveloped us and when our senses finally had their fill, we gave into the night. She grabbed my hand and refused to let go until I unlocked the door to my apartment.

It was a beginning.

Our beginning.

Chapter 3

Buds & Distraction
au Château d'if

(Present Day)

"I'm not fucking around, man. That shit is true." Dean's trumpet echoed defensively through the other room.

I presumed he had gone off on another one of his tall-taled tangents again, and the boys, as per usual, were calling him out on it. I was on beer detail and had walked a good twenty some paces beyond the "parlor room" to get to the kitchen. From there it was another ten paces past the laby-rinth of hanging-cast-iron pots and pans and another five past the hexagonal marble island – adorned with expensive wine bottles and cheapo beer cans; the majority of which were now empty and dispersed in such a violent manner it looked as if a fraternity had taken over the premises and was now deep into its fifth day of bingeing. Mind you, this was every trip to land at the Sub-Zero fridge. I couldn't even bring myself to look at the niceties most of the time, the actual decorum of this grandiose dream of my departed father (or whatever I should call him) – it had been only two weeks of living here, but all of the high-browed, well-quaffed niceties just weren't me and they, along with the entire Garcon de Garrison (or Chateaux d'if, as I affectionately referred to it these days), stand only as unwelcomed reminders of pain and deception and things I'd rather not get into at the moment.

Since my move to the d'if, I'd been left with hardly any alone time. The boys, as nice and as caring as they could be, have seen to it to work in shifts (not that it has been too painful for them to take up residency in this gaudy fortress) to keep me company throughout the move until I sort of find my feet again. Granted, I didn't know I had lost my footing, but I guess that is what happens when your world is turned upside down. It is apparent to everyone except yourself that you are no longer…well, you. I loved them for the support but at the same time their hanging around and the constant partying that followed made me feel even worse. It's hard to explain, but their presence, like any other unnatural amount of attention after a funeral or tragedy was just another reminder that something had gone afoul in life…the worst part being I had to put on a face while they were around, you know; an everything-is-fine-even-though-it's-not-fine face. This is not to say that I didn't enjoy their company, truth be told I fucking loved it. And hell, I could even find a smile from time to time and occasionally, muster out a laugh. But, simply put, I couldn't escape the obviousness of having other shit on my mind, that's all. I'd never really grieved over anything before. Perhaps disassociating myself from my mother but there was some justification there. She was crazy after all. Whatever grief is, I'm guessing this is what it tasted like. As far as the boys go, I think they could tell that the solid ground they were providing didn't really matter while I was off floating around in the outer regions of my mind. But they were still here and so was my gratefulness. The mansion, on the other hand, was the kicker. It doesn't need mentioning but I don't think anyone could ever find their feet in a place that feels bigger than a strip mall and colder and more meticulously curated than a museum.

I muttered something out about how "I should've never moved here in the first place" while opening the fridge. Again, I was drunk, and again, I was talking aloud to myself. I grabbed a half-rack of Buds and made my way back to the massive leather sofas and wingback chairs where all of the lads had comfortably parked themselves. Foil and aluminum from breakfast sandwiches and empty beer cans had been building steadily over the past few days on the Nakashima coffee table as well as rolling papers and other degenerate devices. I chucked everyone beers while the conversation clamored on:

"Dean. You lie through your buck teeth," Jack was flippant, twisted, enjoying every ounce of joy to be had from nipping at Dean's ego. He handed Dean a freshly packed one-hitter.

"I'm telling you man," Dean went on, "one of my buds who still works in the industry is doing a mini-documentary on it. It's like, a whole real underground thing. Like *8mm* but for women."

"What thing?" I asked, as I sat down on the hideously waxed, mauve leather sectional that made a noise relative to a fart when you moved around on it. "What on earth are you on about now, Dean?"

"High powered business women liking to be spanked and shit. That's what I'm on about. Like paying big money to have candle wax burnt on them and to be stepped on and weird shit like that...I *know* it's real so fuck everyone here."

Everyone laughed, more at him than with him.

"Dude, pass that bat, I think you've had enough." Killjoy's favorite pastime was prodding at the holes in Dean's stories.

He reached his hand out for the one-hitter but Dean swatted him away like an annoying fly. Killjoy winced and began to start physically manifesting signs of fatigue and annoyance from Dean's current charade — these two might as well have been sworn enemies in another life. But for now, it was just another fifties sitcom and when the gloves were off, it was entertainment of a very high order.

"Oh yeah?" Dean snapped. He was flushed and a tad aggravated at the crowd's lack of enthusiasm. "Well, just think about it: Women are on the up and up today...soon to take over the world if they aren't there already."

The group grumbled cohesively offering Dean one big yawn.

"Okay — I can tell by all the vapid faces here that I'm dealing with fuckin' cavemen so let me drop some knowledge on this vacuum. Does the name Sheryl Sandberg ring any bells? Oh yeah, *that's right*, you all have no bells to be rung. Well, she represents this mass movement of women that exude power and strength in the business world today. Yeah? *Lean In, anyone?* Hello? McFly? Beuler? Finally, two nods from the only two people in the room who read — thank you. Now don't get me wrong, I'm all for this movement. You know me, I've always said the world's one big sausage-fest at the top and who the fuck wants that? When it comes to the ruling class, I'm pro-egg-salad. But what I was getting at earlier is like, now that there is this high amount of women being forced to front the same ridiculous amount of power and testosterone in the workforce as men...the same reactionary shit is startin' to happen. Think about it – it's unnatural as fuck: and just like all those American-Psycho-wall-street-shmucks who need to get their kicks by having their nuts stomped on by women in stilettos or being spanked as powerless, helpless boys...women are now having the same sexual fantasies too. It's like the most ironic one-eighty of fetishes you could ever imagine. I mean, I can't speak to specifics – but I guarantee ole Sheryl's got a whip in the closet and she ain't the one usin' it, ya feel me? And don't even get me started on ole Margaret Thatcher's dungeon, I'm sure the skeletons in that bag-o-bones' closet go on for days...are ya'll pickin' up what I'm puttin' down? 'Cuz you still look dumber n' dirt. I suppose that's a genetic problem."

"*Meanwhile back on earth.*" Killjoy interrupted. "Seriously Dean, do you purposefully sit around and think up stupid shit all day or does it come to you naturally? Like a gift. Like some rare, extraordinary talent for idiocy."

"Fuck you. I doubt you even know what tang smells like."

Killjoy sat back in his chair and ignored the childish response with a smug, do-I-really-have-to-listen-to-this-shit? eye-roll.

"Yeah. That's what I thought." Dean said. "And what, nobody else believes me?"

"I believe you, Dean." I said. "I just don't believe whoever the hell it was who told you this nonsense."

"Okay. You know what? Fuck it. You wanna know how I know? 'Cuz I know, *alright*. I KNOW."

Everyone's head perked up at the tonal change in his voice. What was usually snarky and rather immature had suddenly dropped into a more assertive, borderline confessional baritone.

"Believe whatever you blow-jawbs want too, but *I* know it's real."

"Wait. What are you saying Dean? How do you know?" I asked.

"I'm just sayin', *I know.* Okay?"

"Dude. Are you saying you're a male escort?" Jack chimed in, coughing up smoke and confusion in the process.

There was no response.

Dean nodded faintly and looked downward, fiddling with his beer tab.

"Dean. No offense, man, but you're ass ugly." Killjoy interjected. A few chuckles lightly bounced around the cavernous room. "And one tall-drink of skim milk. I can practically *see* through you for chrissake. You're like a skeleton with a white sheet draped over you that's been pulled taut from years of rampant masturbation and cocaine abuse." Dean was slowly unwinding his middle finger from his fist. Killjoy continued unaffected, "Unless women are into anemia these days, I think you're full of shit."

"Whatever." Dean snorted.

"You really expect me to believe that women pay to have sex with you, let alone attractive powerful business women?"

"Yes." Dean said, dead-eyed.

"You're off your gourd."

"That's fine. Believe that then."

"Look at him," Killjoy motioned to the rest of the guys in the room who had been enjoying these usual suspects and their cerebral fisticuffs. "Do you guys believe ole Casper here? Either I'm losing it or this micro-dick has a twelve-pound tongue 'cuz there's absolutely no way in hell you are getting more ass than me, Dean. NO. WAY."

"Is that jealousy, I hear? No. No wait. I think it's insecurity. It always does tend to come with an air of douchebaggery attached to it, doesn't it?" Dean was playing to the crowd, we enjoyed it. "Don't put your virginal shit on me, bro."

"Fucking prove it then, gimp!"

"Oh Okay. Since this is something that's *so* easy to prove. How 'bout you prove your dad fucked your mom for me." Dean smiled savagely. "Oh wait, we have the most wretched display of *fact* sitting right in front of us. You and your bullshit, Killjoy."

"Coming from the king of fertilizer himself...go 'head, buddy, spread it on thick. We know the smell all too well." Killjoy huffed and puffed. His chest was now sticking out and matched the apish, mental chest-flexes being tossed around the room like hot potatoes. Everyone else was feeling way too good from the Buds and bud to pay any real attention to the jousting on display. Besides, the awesome news of one of their friends possibly being a man-whore had turned them all into silent mummies anxiously waiting for Dean to seal the tomb.

"Alright! *Alright then.*" Dean said, realizing he was going to have to say *something* to keep the group from going full blown catatonic. "Her name was Leslie. All right? She was in her late forties and works as a high-powered consultant for one of the top firms in the country. That's a pretty big deal for all you anti-corporate poofs in the room. She lives in Midtown."

"Go on." Hymned the group.

A symphony of beers cracked open.

"Okay," Dean took a gulp and fired up the one-hitter. "But everyone here has to fucking swear on something they worship, like something that is holier than holy to them that what I say here doesn't leave the room. Got it?"

"Got it," sang the drunken choir.

"Now swear it and swear it aloud."

"Women and alcohol." I said.

"Same." Said another.

"Drugs." Followed the second.

"All three." Laughed the third.

"Food." Said Beau, tragically holding his pronounced gut.

"The pursuit of truth." Said Killjoy.

Jack was just about to add his two cents to the well but could not keep himself from blurting out laughter at the dullest man in the room. "If truth means pussy, I'm with ole Killjoy over here."

"Okay." Dean gathered himself, leaning forward while taking another swig of his fat-weiser, and placed both elbows intently on his knees. "I work for a small agency that specializes in this sort-a-thing, ya see. I get a call sayin' that I fit the description of what this woman likes. So to your asinine comment, Killjoy, this broad happens to like tall, skinny men with Fage-colored flesh. It's called a *fetish*. I suppose you're in need of a bunch of schooling on the matter, but *alas*, no one here's got the stamina to put up with you so I hope you enjoy a long life of celibacy, you mongoloid. In fact, why don't you do the world a favor and put your sacrifice to a good cause and become a priest? Anyway, like I was saying. This Leslie broad would get my number through the agency, right, and then set up a time and place for me to come over and I'd take the train down to her high-rise apartment. Meanwhile, the agency would text me things about her likes and dislikes and safe words and all that. You know: Light-spanking, break-in-burglar erotica, latex, cuffs all the usual B.S. you see in movies. Except some of these women are into weird, like I-wouldn't-even-consider-it-kinky-type-shit, I would consider it a reason for therapy. Stuff that goes beyond just the mommy/son role-play and watersports stuff."

"The fuck is watersports?" Beau asked, completely puzzled.

"Peeing on people." I said.

"What! *Mleuch*. That's straight up nasty."

The group laughed at his innocence. "Thought you liked the Yellow River, Bae." One of the guys cut in.

"Tip-o-the-iceberg, my man." Dean continued. "I don't do it but people do, a-lotta-people, half of Germany, in fact. Anyway like I said, some of these masochistic-mavens are into weird mind-fucking shit, that's like truly unexplainable; where they just want to be straddled and breathed on in guttural grunts while having their arms held down or others who just want female organ shaming, like 'make fun of my sagging tits,' the one lady told me." Dean started to mimic the lady's physical movements bringing his hand down from his chest to his ass. "'Now what do you think of the cellulite on my ass. *Tell me!* Okay good, now touch my unshaven pussy. Yeah, rub the hair. Rub it up and down and tell me how much it bothers you that it's not shaven. *Good.* Now, smell it and tell me what it smells like.' I tell her Pantene Pro-V and her eyes roll back in her head."

The group boomed with laughter.

"Just insane shit, guys…and that's where I tend to draw the line though…when it gets to the mind control, like actual skull-fucking, 'Hey-I-want-your-hump-your-brains-for-lunch type stuff, that's when people need help. Either way, Leslie was into light playful antics so with her, when I walked in she was just standing there – not beautiful but certainly not ugly – she had a nice body and a bobbish haircut and was completely decked out in full business attire. I'm talking corporate to the nines, as if she had just got out of a meeting or something: Beige skirt-suit, nylons, heels, make-up and earrings...the whole shebang. She told me to 'stop right there' when I walked in the door and told me I was to be in charge from now on and that she wanted me to rip her clothes off as hard and as fast as I could. I mean, I obviously nodded to her – it's pretty much my job to nod and do whatever it is they say – and try to keep in mind it's all a fantasy, but there is a second or two where you have no idea how serious they are or what exactly they want or just how hard and forceful they want it. I think that is the turn-on for most, the uncertainty of it all. She was dead serious so I complied. She said 'I mean it, the second you take another step I want you to throw me on the bed and rip my clothes off till I'm bare assed and then do nothing. Got it?' I nodded and then she said, 'Good, now go!' So I ran up to her and I shit you not, buttons were flying. I grabbed her legs forcefully and tore the matching beige pumps from her feet. Her skirt ripped from seam to seam but the nylons weren't so easy. The internal and external struggle of keeping her *into it,* my ripping of the nylons from her flesh, meanwhile failing miserably with that indestructible sheen of spider silk made the whole thing an hysterical failure...but, I bit my lip and finally, I got those things off...and in turn, so did she."

"Maybe it's a sign you should get in the gym." Jack barked.

"Shh!" Said Killjoy. "Fucking get to the fucking part!"

"There was no fucking you dunce." Said Dean. "I told you already, some of these women only want to be breathed on wrong."

"So you're an escort that's not an escort! *A hoax.* I knew it!" Touted Killjoy.

"*Sometimes* it happens. *Sometimes* it doesn't. It all depends on the woman."

"Bah-loney."

Dean whipped out his phone and scanned through it for a couple of seconds and when he found what he was looking for, paused for a short moment — a little unsure of himself — and then showed us all a photo. It was a girl with her rack out, smiling on a bed.

"Everyone, this is Leslie."

There was a ripped beige suit jacket lying on the sheet beside her. Everyone's mouth sat gaping open, their mandibles unhinged.

"I'm pretty sure you shouldn't be showing us that." I said.

"You can't tell me you believe him!" Killjoy screeched. His words fought hard to get through the heavy air of disbelief hanging in the room. "That's obviously a stock photo. Where'd you pull this from, Google Images?"

"I don't know," I continued. "I just know if she is real she probably wouldn't want us all slobbering over it. Know what I mean?"

"You're right, Frank...discretion is right."

"Fuck discretion!" Somebody boomed from the back.

"Naw-naw. I shouldn't have shown you guys. But now that you know, you keep your traps shut. Yeah?" Dean tucked the phone back in his pants pocket. He stood up and stretched his back. "Now if you'll all excuse me, I have a train to catch to the city...got another appointment."

The group sat in a smoky, buzz-fueled hush as Dean threw on his jacket and made his way to the door. He walked out of the stained and leaded glass entry way but just as it clicked shut, he immediately came barreling back inside, practically kicking the thing open, yelling:

"GOTCHYA YOU FUCKS."

"Shit."

"Lame."

"Fuck I knew he was lyin'."

"Me too."

"I'm the only one here who knew it all along!" boasted Killjoy. "The rest-a-you inbreds actually believed him!"

I had to hand it to them. The boys were pure entertainment. The gimmicks, the jibes, the blatant immaturity – all of it was a welcomed distraction and helped make the painful days seem much shorter. Yet still, late into night, as the drive and humor of our conversations began to fade, so did my spirit. I always ended up crashing earlier than everyone else. It became an *understood* or *necessary* thing for me to the guys. I don't know why I even attempted it really – I couldn't sleep for shit. I guess, when you're genuinely suffering, being alone somehow feels just as appropriate, if not essential, as being with a group. You would think most of that alone time would be spent in some remorseful, angsty state of disillusion. You would think it'd be chalk full of anger and resentment toward the cursed course of events that brought you to where you were in life, but, you'd be wrong. When the drugs wore off and the fumes from my liver finally evaporated, there was only June. Hell, she was there when I was three-sheets to the wind, too.

Alas, tonight hailed much of the same result. Before heading up, I briefly whispered to Dean that I knew he wasn't *actually* lying about being a male escort. He looked at me uneasily. I told him it was okay and not to worry because I wouldn't tell the guys. I told him 'from one storyteller to another,' nobody can tell a tale that well without somehow knowing it first hand. I gave him a half-hug, half-drunken-embrace and went up to bed. I lay down for a bit but had chosen not to take my clothes off. Out of laziness, I guess or, maybe, I figured tonight might be the night I get around to finally unpacking all the boxes from 112 Hudson that still sat, unopened and stacked in the corner of the bedroom. I looked over at the daunting pile and thought 'maybe not.'

Lying in bed could be absolute torture. More often than not, to avoid wallowing in my own despair, I would turn to fantasy...escapism. I stared at the matte ceiling and tried to picture June. The cream paint matched her lovely fair skin and if I fuzzed my eyes just right, her adorable face would come to life. If I connected certain cracks, if all the right creases and grooves fell into place, her generous smile would appear. My brain would add in the striking color of her eyes and the darkness of her hair and those unforgettable smile lines would start to animate and...shit.

I rolled over.

Pipe dreams.

I still couldn't get over the fact that she had left me so abruptly the morning after my birthday. I know it was well over a couple-a-months ago now but I couldn't shake this feeling that something wasn't right, that I had somehow missed something important. It's true, I was severely drunk that night and I'm sure I've missed out on a lot more than that, but still. I have racked my brain over it a hundred times now and the rolodex of events from our night together just don't add up: Why'd she leave so early without saying goodbye?

She had a blast, didn't she? Or was I too blasted to see otherwise? No. She had a good time – a great time. And so did I. Hell, we were magnetic. And she approached *me*, for chrissake! Or does that mean something? Like all she was looking for was a one-night-stand or something else, something worse? No. No. No! Not possible. So why on earth did she bail without leaving a way for me to see her again?

Listen. I know this all sounds pathetic and I should've moved on by now but if you were there you would've seen it, you'd have known too. It wasn't supposed to go down this way. We dug each other, man. There was a thoughtfulness there. A mutual, unspoken affection. It was something you feel when you realize that one night together wasn't only going to be one night – it was the beginning of something. Something special. So much so it bothered you, drove you to a point of madness. You yearned for it and needed it all the time and had to start this new adventure as soon as possible – together. You want as many of those nights as you can get and you want them now because they're so damned easy. I think that's what really did me in – just how easy it was. Not in the sense that she was easy, of course, but because we fit so snuggly into that lofty dream of a relationship where nothing requires work. Absolutely nothing. Things just were, and they were easy. From our banter to our ideals to bumping pelvises late into the AM, none of it required 'work.' And yet, I've got nothing to show for it except a memory.

I stood up and walked over to the window. It was glazeless…lifeless. I cared not for its crown molding and venetian blinds. I cared not for the French door way and the spiraling staircase to the widow's walk above, either. I cared not for anything on the premises. I cared only, just as I had for the past decade at 112 Hudson, for what lay beyond –

The Hudson. The Mountains. The West. *Anywhere but here.* I took one last look at the river and couldn't help but wallow in how wide and dark and empty it was.

It looked lonely.

'Don't worry, old friend.' I thought. 'I'm alone, too.'

Chapter 4

A Stir in the Night

The watch-hand finally struck two-thirty in the morning and I could hear the rumble from the guys carrying on downstairs begin to trickle and lull. The remaining stragglers quieted now by a sudden urge for munchies. I had been lying there for the past three hours doing nothing. Meditating without the meditation. Thinking without the brain activity. I couldn't bear the burden of trying to focus on a TV show and reading was out of the question. I had given it up for the time being because it made me deadly jealous of the writing...and well, I wasn't writing.

I hated it when I wasn't writing.

Words began to piss me off and the people who used them even more so.

Writers. Don't even get me started.

One hot air balloon more in need of a prick than the next.

Whenever I stopped writing, what usually followed was the terrible T's: Terror, Self-Torture, and a weird, mentally manifested strain of Tuberculosis. Yes, I would literally get sick to my stomach from the lack of output. The longer it went on the more and more it seemed like a rat had taken up permanent residency in my innards. The little vermin saw my gut as the perfect place for feeding and there was, admittedly, a fair amount of storage to live off. But the continuous gnawing would burn and deteriorate to a point of such self-loathing that it often made me dyspeptic and absolutely miserable to be around. It was a horrible cycle. I felt poorly so I wouldn't write, but when I wasn't writing I felt even worse. The hollow pain grew more insufferable with time and had peaked this last week when I totaled up the number of words I had produced since the funeral: Zip. Zero. Zilch.

Squat.

A poop-stick amount of words. (Which I guess if a poop-stick was accurately represented as a digit it would equal 'one' so that would make it a lie.) I can't even lie – I've been living up shits creek without a paddle to poop on. I had written nothing. That's not even the worst part. The worst part is that I was just being a lazy piece of shit and I knew it. I could write if I sat down and really got to work, I was just blaming my ineptitude on grief and how sad is that?

'What's the use?' I'd say, in an attempt to justify my slothful state of mind. 'Jean-Luc Wharm has officially gone cold since the funeral and the disappearance of June.'

It was right there where my internal monologue ran into a brick wall. I literally experienced a mental car crash. It was a collision of epic proportions. The title of my latest book was slammed back into my prefrontal cortex and knocked everything loose. It set my neurons on fire. Like an ember, smoldering a distressed signal of smoke from the notebook buried in the desk that now sat upside down in the corner of my room. The title I had haphazardly scribbled down months ago bellowed and swirled around my head like flames out of control:

My Red Hot Winter in June

I jumped up. My heart raced. The world is full of coincidences. Everything, I thought, was a coincidence. Everything that's ever been lauded: divine intervention or karma or 'energy that always comes back around' seemed, to me, to just be one big whopping bunch of coincidental nonsense. Faith, for what it's worth, wasn't worth that much to me. It was all just a belief hopping on the right bandwagon at the right time, I'd say. An odd but obvious form of spiritual capitalism, that's all. *But this.* This little tidbit of using June's name in a book title *the night before* I met her threw me for a loop. How something so obvious could have evaded me for so long, I'll never know (insert drink of stale beer and a solid hit from the hash pipe, here). Fortunately, for both our sakes, I was too wound up to dote on the boring gripe that comes with Fate vs. Chance.

Instead, I was already rummaging through the leftover pile of stacked boxes from my studio in the corner and began heaving them off of the tiny wooden desk. And then there he was; upside down and dismal — I don't know if there's any more depressing a sight for a writer than an ignored desk. I flipped the thing over hurriedly and rummaged through the drawer for my notebook. Buried beneath a good pile of rejection slips and 'do keep us in mind for your next project' return letters was the little journal. I got to the last page quickly and there sat the title, loud and telling:

My Red Hot Winter in June
By: Jean-Luc Wharm

It screamed do something, you waste of space! You've been doing nothing for four months except sitting around and feeling sorry for yourself. Do something! 'This is some sort of sign,' I thought. 'Just another coincidence,' I rationalized. *So realize it's a fucking special coincidence and react rationally!*

So I did. I carried the desk over to the window and unwound the modern crank frame to let the cool air in. With a solid view of the river, the new workspace was reminiscent of 112 Hudson and made my headfirst dive into the shallow end of the pool that much more horizontal. I broke open the laptop and decided to continue right where Jean-Luc Wharm would've left off:

Butt-play in the morning.

No. This isn't a radio program. This is every morning after a tango with the spirits. It was almost a guarantee — I would be severely horny in the waking hours after a long night of drinking. Perhaps this was because drunk sex was more like two frogs leaping at each other in a dark, muck-riddled pond than anything resembling tantric-orgasmo-perfection (although the sauce always made it seem transcendent). I rolled over to a view of her back. It was curvy, elongated and neat. Ballerina-esque. It took my breath away. I gulped at the slight curve of her hip half-covered by the sheet. My eyes moved downward to the dimples of her lower back. The sensual sight immediately forced me to remember how I couldn't finish the night before. It was no reflection on her, of course. I was proud of myself for even finding wood after the amount of liquid we'd consumed. But now, I couldn't keep the throbbing pain down. I wondered if she felt the same way when hung-over; the throbbing aches from both north and south poles. There was only one way to find out.

I started to rub her back. She exhaled deeply as she woke and I could tell she was enjoying it. I gradually pushed her over on to her stomach and climbed atop of her. I rubbed her entire body; from her shoulders to her calves and all the way back up again. I did this a couple times. Hell, I think I enjoyed it just as much as she did. Blood was starting to pump south of the border. The swell grew larger and harder as I moved fluidly across her skin stopping religiously at the rump. Oh boy. The Christmas hams sat there and desired glazing. They were a big, double-bubble that longed to be burst. Two plush tulips patiently waiting to be sniffed. Her ass was rotund and more edible than an apple. The entire mass started to rise off the mattress and she arched her back in such a way that made me feel more animal than man. I rubbed round and round slowly grazing her forbidden parts in the process. Her backside was now bending backward and I thought how if I had a beer I could've poured it down her spine like an ice luge and lapped it up like the dog I was. She tilted her hips in the air, begging for more, and I found full-pine when I caught eye of the juice seeping from her peach. I licked it from behind, placing my nose in her canal and my tongue playfully on her holy nub. The over-zealous move had caught her off-guard. She jumped slightly and her ass knocked me backward, catching me solidly on the forehead. I laughed and told her she kicked like a bull. She apologized but I told her to shut it and kept after the nectarine of the gods. I *was* dehydrated after all. I spent a decent while down there, slowly moving upward to the tanned edge of her asshole, and then, just when she thought I'd turn back around, I'd let my tongue off its leash and go for a walk around the park.

"God! Do it already!" She yelled into the pillow.

I grabbed hold of the redwood and brought it to her. I rubbed the entire area with it, refusing to give in to her at first. I moved up and down teasing her with hogshead meat. I'd start south of her swollen nub and bring the rod the whole way up through her, spreading her lips apart moving north to the top of her ass and back down again. The entire area was wet so the movements glided nicely. She started shaking with enjoyment. I'd wash, rinse and repeat. I could've lived there for chrissake. But I was still hungover as hell and instead, decided to throw the pipe in the thread and get to turning.

She was sublime and I, of course, couldn't hold it for too long. A few seconds went by like hours and that was long enough, I thought. I pulled out and ruined her back and some of her hair but I didn't care at the moment: The aches and pains finally went away. I felt light for a little and then I felt worse. Light-headed. Woozy and hot. *Too hot.* I apologized for going so soon. She just laughed me off and hopped in the shower. I was sweating and nauseous but half of me figured it was well worth it. The other half ran in to the bathroom after her to decorate the toilet with vomit.

"Jesus Christ. Are you okay?"

"This normally comes first."

"You sound like you're dying when you do that."

"I think I am."

"Well, get it all out and brush your teeth when you're done — my kitty likes fresh breath when you're lickin' her clean."

"You've got to be shitting me."

"Chop. Chop." She pulled the curtain halfway open and threw her leg up on the side of the tub to show me the little cat, purring. Her lips were engorged. She started to play with it and put on a face that made me forget I was green.

"Fuck me." I said, eyes-wide, falling to one knee in front of the toilet. I started to rub her thigh.

She whimpered a slight moan.

"Alright. Alright!" I yelled and reached for the toothbrush.

I took a step back and reread what I had written. It infuriated me. *Might as well be writing for a goddamned skin mag.* How the hell is this romance? I figured I was too frustrated all around in life to pump out anything I'd consider quality and then made my way to the bathroom to beat my cock into submission. When I came back, I sat down and reread the little ditty again and found it somewhat entertaining. A fresh perspective always helps, I guess. Or maybe I was just relaxed and didn't care anymore. In about a half hour or so I would always find out it was the latter.

I found a small bic lighter in the desk drawer and lit up a Toscano and noticed the Gently Envelope still sitting in there, staring me in the face, untouched since the first time I had read it — almost five months ago now. I thought about how when I first saw it I almost pitched it in the trash just by the look of it. I wondered then if I would've been happier never knowing the disturbing contents that lay inside. Then again 'what the fuck is happy?' I thought. 'Ignorance?' That wasn't me. That could *never* be me. I always needed to know — wanted to know. I guess I was like Killjoy in that regard, what with his obsession with truth and all that.

I wondered then if too much truth leads to a joyless life, or, at the very least, a cynical life. I wrote it off with the reassuring knowledge that cynics still had sarcasm and satire and there was plenty of joy to be found there. And with that thought, I opened the envelope back up and reread the well-crafted message. As one might expect, the words hit me differently this time around. I hadn't any want or desire to find out who my father was until that exact moment, when I reread the man's words. I looked at the purpose lying behind the letters, the careful, innocent language involved that cast no blame toward my mother. The real lack of hatred. The palpable hope for a family lineage. There was a tenderness there, an open-ended love bereft of ill-will that only a man facing the end could've found in so few words. The trunk of my body started to shake with deep, harrowing grief. Raw stuff like that just comes out of you – there is no control. Especially when there was no sense to be made in any of it. The lack of reason behind everything that happened just made it all the more terrible. I guess that's the worst part about truth – it never comes with a guarantee of reason. No answer of 'why?' included.

I felt deeply tired. Rereading the letter unearthed a sense of fatigue in me I had not thought possible. Breathing became arduous, as did holding up my head. I had finally let demons float to the surface. Their release took the form of an opiate in the bloodstream. The colossal amount of energy it takes to keep an emotion repressed, hidden from plain view, let alone a memory from coming to mind, was finally relenting and so with it came the paralysis. As my catatonia came full swing, I felt much of the animosity brewing toward my mother begin to dissipate. My eyelids felt like they had weights on them. My shoulders, my neck, my entire body could not be held upright without enormous amounts of effort. I felt like I hadn't slept in weeks. *I hadn't slept in weeks.* I placed the envelope back on the desk and laid my head down on folded arms for a second.

When I snapped back up, my neck was sore and I felt large indentations on my forehead and cheeks that mirrored uneven knuckles. I had dozed off. It was almost five in the morning now. My eyes were crusty and dehydrated from the booze but as I massaged sand from lids, my vision cleared. A small yellow sticky-note that was stuck to the backside of my father's envelope came into focus. It was folded back up over itself, obscurely – it seemed accidental, as if the envelope had brushed up against it and took it along for the ride. I started to peel down the note and couldn't help ripping it off completely when I noticed a woman's handwriting:

Frank, Beans, Peasant,

"OH GOD!"

Thanks for the lovely night. I'll most likely be in and out of the city these next few months so Peekskill won't be on the radar but I expect you to call me. OR ELSE!

Xo, June
646-555-6879
PS. If you don't call,
I will purposefully forget
how good you were in the sack.

"OH MY FUCKING JESUS."

I scrambled. I stood up. I sat back down. I stood back up again. I didn't know what to do. I started to sweat and my mouth went arid in the confusion. I looked at my watch: 5:15 AM. I gave it two seconds worth of thought before figuring that she'd most likely be up for work anyway and called the number. Wait a second. I didn't even know what she did for work. I hung up immediately. What a hot mess I was! What the hell would I say to her? Is there even an explanation?

YOUR NON-EXISTANT FATHER DIED!

WHO GIVES A TIT.

JUST CALL!

I dialed again and a telemetronic woman's voice, that whorish Verizon voice – the goddammed Strumpet of Bad News – came on directly saying the number no longer existed.

"FAAAAHHK!"

I collapsed backward into my chair and sulked. My fist slammed down on the desk. Hard. The wood cracked under the force of the blow.

"JUST UN-FUCKING-BELIEVABLE."

I looked at the envelope and cursed it. It alone had been the reason for my discontent. I threw it out the window. I got up and kicked some of the boxes around out of mere frustration. I grabbed June's note and started to head downstairs to loathe the sunrise with a bottle of Makers. Just then Dean and Jack came clamoring through the door.

"The fuck's goin' on in here?!" Jack yelled in his Superman underwear. He was wearing a classic *INXS* t-shirt and wielding a bed table lamp that was cocked back behind his head like a Louisville slugger. The chord dangled at his feet in yellowing tube-socks.

"We heard yelling." Dean said, his face dropping back into its casual gleam when he saw the room was intruder-less. His gaze turned to his sidekick's apparel, "Nice tube-socks, Jack."

"Read and weep, muh'boys." I handed them the sticky note. "Read and weep."

I threw the cigar in my mouth and continued on past them. I had my mind fixed on finding the bottle, ingesting the contents that lay inside and asking a yellow star, soon on its way to cresting the horizon, to roast me alive. I was already down the stairs and on my way to the kitchen before the boys could do the math. They would follow suit but Jack had to return the lamp first.

"Hey, Superman – *Keeper of the Peace.*" I heard Dean yell. "Don't forget some pants."

Chapter 5

A Goose. A Chase.
And Many-A-Feather
To Rustle

"Maybe thirty-two means something in Greek. Like hor-rible luck or the Year of Oedipus or something." Dean said, playfully albeit painfully.

He had just laid my father's letter back on my lap. He'd seen it laying in the yard and I watched him pick it up as I took a gag-worthy amount of bourbon down my gullet. I nodded to him, thankfully, but there was no response. I was quiet, interminably quiet and Jack was yet to fully open his eyes. It was barely 7am. Granted, we were all very tired but this morning I couldn't even conjure up the usual energy required to put on the it's-all-good-face that made everything okay in times of distress. Things were not okay.

We were out on the edge of the empty reflecting pool with our legs dangling over the side. It was quickly becoming the best and worst place for reflection. I figured that I felt lousier now, more depleted and beaten and downright cheat-ed than when I had learned of my father's passing. The fresh slew of cheap beer in my stomach combined with some of that harder stuff had fixed much of the physical pain that dwelling on such sludge can deliver, but the majority of my frustrations — the inherent failure to be and feel real — couldn't be snuffed out and righted by anything...until now.

"Dude. Oedipus slept with his mom." Jack whispered to Dean. "Are you saying Frank's year is going to get worse?"

"How the hell do I find her?" I sighed, loudly.

"You look for her." Jack answered, prickly.

"*Jack-ass*. Now's not the time."

"Sorry man. But you gotta admit," Jack felt profound wisdom coming on and needed to share it. "This is so you right now. *Your life, that is*. It's fuck-all. When you just gonna accept that shit and move on, ya know? Throw your middle finger up to it all and just *do you* already?"

"Haven't I been?"

"Getting wasted in the family mansion is a middle finger, I suppose. But more toward yourself, not life."

"And just what are *you* suggesting?"

"I don't know. *Obviously*, I don't know. I just know that this shit iddn't you and it isn't cutting it."

"Hmph."

We sat and drank some more.

Birds chirped and carried melody but there was no song to be heard.

The sun rose and I soon became carsick. It happens to me sometimes when the sun crests the horizon. There's a hard rewire in my brain and I finally realize that we are the ones in motion, not the sun. It's only for a brief moment and then I settle back down, but there is a strong minute or two where I can actually feel the earth spinning round. It is violent and dizzying and I wish gravity would just finally let go. But it doesn't, so I stay there and drink, and so do the boys.

We lingered on despite my not wanting to and, in a forced attempt at distraction, absorbed every ounce of goodness the early spring sunrise had to offer. Globs of sunlight that had bypassed stray clouds claimed Bear Mountain for their own. They lit up the melting snow, casting it golden against the dark slits of barren trees that marred the flowing, vibrating wave of white and bronze. Garrison was a beautiful place; there is no denying that. With its enormous abounding wealth, it would be tough to call it charming, and yet there I was, smiling for a split second at its beguiling wonders, reeling and transported by what could only be accurately called a champagne-breath, splash of spring. I guess this chance enjoyment shouldn't be surprising in any way, there is, after all, a reason why so much money from the city had found its way up here over the years. The view of West Point, the United States Military Academy that sat across the river, made Garrison's particular perspective a painter's wet dream: Inviting and nostalgic and filled with romance, its subtle offerings are remembered dreams of another time. Yes, nestled in those mountains across the way is a history, but a history that extends far beyond the times of Washington and the Revolution. Appalachia, it seemed, though less spiritual and much more subtle than the natural wonders of the West, had its unique way of getting inside you. Owning you. *Home*, some may call it. You see, the mountains here are millions of years old so their roots grow just as deep and as penetrating as any sequoia or cascading waterfall has to offer...if not more so. These rolling mountains and their humming river valleys are sustenance. They are life and their gift, as approachable and undervalued as it may be, is nurturing. It is not so obvious but if you ever meet people from the area you will quickly recognize that their pilgrimages back to this Promised Land normally tend to come without reason: "Why here?" you could ask. "Well, I dunno. It's home, I guess." They might answer. However profound or lost their statements, if any critic were to experience one full cycle of the region's soft hills and epic changing of the color guard, I doubt even the most judgmental of pricks would not succumb to its beauty, its quaint wilderness. It is the same reason why the strong majority of those who leave always find their way back to its small towns and coal-driven cities. These mountains' flowing ripples resemble a communal living space and its wild warmth echoes throughout. Its supporting pillars and inviting climates sing a siren's song to life – a hard life for almost all who bear it, but still, a life worthy to be called North Eastern. A life that commands return. A beautiful life.

This all said, as I sat there and drank in its gifts and comforts and all the awesome fortune that comes from the restorative nature of home, it felt oddly appropriate for me to remember how these deep-rooted qualities can keep us planted, stunted from a full and realized life. Though not unwanting of growth, but unaware that it can't even happen unless we leave in the first place. Yes, we can't circle back, we can't *remember what it was like here back in the day* unless we've experienced the new, the different, the strange and bizarre – all things we deem foreign. All things that serve to remind us what was so special about home, why we crowned it holy and domestic, the place ever-deserved of return.

It was in this short breath of a view from a home that wasn't my home but a river valley that was, did I start to believe that a house is only given meaning and importance when standing outside of it...looking in and wanting, ever-wiser, ever-readied to slowly climb back into the womb... different yet the same, better.

And that viewpoint could only be seen if I left.

I now knew it was time for me to go. I now knew that the answers I longed for were not to come to me in these mountains. Nor were they to come in the cursed Garcon De Garrison – the debauched Chateau d'if of personal history I never had the privilege of knowing and a lineage I wasn't quite ready to join. No, the answers would not be found here. Nor would they reveal themselves in Peekskill or the brewery or in the attic of 112 Hudson. It had been a solid decade of drunkard scribblings and lost-cause-love-affairs alongside the river with nothing to show for it except a failed book and a failed love-life. Throughout it all, I never, not once had the courage to float my skiff down the main artery of adventure and see what might come from the chase. It was hard to believe, but I never chased that which deserved chasing – yes, I'm talking about love. Nor had I ever mustered the resolve to cross the channel and see what might lie on the other side, beyond the mountains…could it be a woman? Happiness? Both? Perhaps the right words my books so desperately called for?

I now had to find out. I now knew it was time for the next adventure…and finally, it didn't stem from internal but external factors. Factors that all started with a warm name and a staying smile that all followed spring…

June.

"I think this means I'll be leaving for a little while guys." I said.

"I had a feeling." Dean gargled out over half-swallowed beer. "But where?"

"I'm not sure yet. I think that's what makes it an adventure."

"There are no adventures anymore." Dean said.

"What?"

"There just aren't, man. I mean, what you gonna do? Use your phone to find her? Gonna log into some geo-locating device and track her down? Gonna Facebook stalk all the girls named June till you're barred from all the internet? How is any o'that an adventure? No. The last adventure that existed was turning your back on all-o-that crap. And that dude from *Into the Wild* already beat you to it."

"Didn't that guy die at the end?" Jack said, still groggy.

"Nice, Jack. Real nice." Dean said.

"Well fuck I don't know." Jack puttered around, sifting pockets for cigarettes. "Pass me that bottle, would ya?"

I passed Jack the Makers that was now half-empty and he knocked it back. He blew out fire and quoted one of our favorite lines of Jim Carey from *Dumb and Dumber*, "Don't you go dyin' on me!"

We laughed and I quickly returned to my mission statement.

"I am leaving this place — that is the adventure," My all-knowing arrow was aimed at Dean's forehead. "What lies ahead doesn't matter. The choice to go is what matters."

"Hm." Dean retired himself, unmoved.

"I don't even care if it's a *grand* adventure or not. I just want something different than this. Okay? Call it *Frank's pathetic attempt to discover himself through a long lost love* if you need to Dean. Christ, you're turning into Killjoy."

"Take that back."

"When your balls drop."

"Hm." Jack huffed, eyes wide off the Mark. "Forget him. His input is equivalent to that gook that gets stuck between the bottom ridges of your boot...personally, I just never would've thought you'd take me seriously."

"Whadd'ya mean?"

"I mean with leaving all this behind."

"Whoa Jack, easy. Let's be clear here, I never ever take you seriously. I just have a highly functioning built-in filter for horseshit...or I guess, you're more-a-donkey but the smell's all the same. *What is a mule again, Dean?*"

"Any of Jack's illegitimate children."

"That's right. But duhddn't that mean he had to screw a horse or something like that?"

"You seen the women Jack's been bringin' home?"

"Dean." Jack said, pressing his lips in anger and raising his thumb up in the air as if to give the universal sign of approval. "Why don't you sit on that and spin for a while."

"You've got a knack for gay jokes even when unintended. I'm starting to question this one," Dean threw his head toward Jack.

"Oh you didn't know?" I played along. "Jack batted righty and lefty in little league all the way up through high school. It was only when he was cut from the team that he figured out he didn't have to swing both ways. Much to the first base coach's dismay."

"Oh yeah?" Dean asked.

"Yeah. He missed the sight of Jack's ass wiggling up to the plate."

Dean and I were riotous and I felt surprisingly happy for a moment. Every group has its jester, ours just happened to be named Jack to boot.

"Ha. HA-HA. *Anyway.*" Jack huffed. "I was tryin' to say somethin' serious if you two would shut the hell up a moment."

"Alright-alright. Serious faces, Dean."

"I guess what I wanted to say is...we'll miss you."

"Oh."

"Yeah. I mean, of course we will. Right Dean?"

"Meh." Dean shrugged his shoulders.

"Okay, then *I will.*"

"And to think, for a second, I thought you were actually going to try to *change* the subject of you being a homo." Dean cackled, leaning backward and chuckling into the bottom of his empty beer can.

"You constantly redefine lowering the bar." Jack snorted.

"Finally, something we agree on."

"*Whatever.* So, hoss." Jack continued in a rather serious tone directed my way. "It's *June* right? What's the next move?"

"I don't know actually. I guess I'll try to retrace some steps to find my way forward again. I think the best place to start is with my birthday night…since that is really all I've got to go on aside from this note."

"Christ! That was like a *year* ago." Jack said, somewhat seriously.

"Dude, if it were a year ago, that would mean it's his birthday again. And it's obviously not." Dean was shaking his head in disbelief. "They should do studies on you. Like, how you make it through your day to day with such negative brain function." He poured on some salt. "They'd probably win a Nobel."

"You're a miscarriage that survived!" Jack yelled, slightly red. "If only your mother's uterus would've spewed you out when it was deserved, you gremlin."

"Tell me about it." I said, pulling both of them back around to the problem at hand. "It's not like *I'm* the guy who can remember too much from that night anyway. One of the last things I do remember before leaving is covering a urinal pad with bile."

"OO-ALCH." Dean gagged at the thought of it.

"Well who was there that *might* remember something? Anything?" Jack offered, generously.

"No idea. But I know if I go around asking the fifty some-odd people who were there about a drunken night that happened almost half a year ago, they'd just laugh and ask if I changed medications."

"Yeah..."

"Yeah."

"Hm."

There was a break in the conversation and the sun finally rose tall enough to leave the enchanting angle of easy orange behind us. The clairvoyant sky that always follows a crisp spring sunrise was about to hit us, bright and clear blue.

"Wait. Jack is gay! That's it!" Dean burped out.

"Not following." Jack said, too tired to be mad.

"I'm kind of following." I said, laughing at Dean's drunken wizardry.

"Sean and Jay." He said, clearing his throat and speaking with his hands like a maestro who had had one too many. "Sean and Jay were there and they weren't drinking right? They were doing a cleanse or preparing for an Ibezan cruise or something, 'member? They were talkin' about it. It was one of those all-inclusive trips with all you can nibble ding-dongs and all that jizz."

"OH YEAH. *That's right.*" I mustered out. My watch read 8:12 AM. I had about thirty minutes before Sean and Jay were to be on the train down to the city for work. They were assistant directors for some of the most highly revered photography houses in the city. I was still drunk and admittedly, rather stoned off the thought of finding out more information about June, but I knew there was no time to lose. I would get on the same train that they took in the morning for work. I would ride the commuter rail down and find out all there was to find and start my adventure *now.*

"Who is the soberest here?" I asked.

"Not me." Said Dean.

"Me either. And *soberest?* You inventing words again, Beans?" Jack corrected. "Are we climbing Mt. Soberest today?"

"Fuck. I guess since I had the wear-with-all to even ask that makes me the most light on my feet."

"*Lightest.*" Jack said.

"Thank you, *School House Jock.* Do I really look like I give two-shits about grammar right now."

"No, you look fine, you just sound dumb."

I shot him a look that all but said fuck off.

"And the *lightest,*" Jack continued. "Is ole skeletor here, Dean-the-dinosaur-from-the-Natural-History-exhibit. *Weighing in at a sopping 145!*"

"What ever you say, twinkle-toes." Dean flopped his hand over, highly effeminate in manner. "Gimme one-a-those, will ya?" He turned his palm to the sky and waited for a cigarette.

Jack popped him out a Parli. As they smoked and carried on I figured I was legitimately the most sober of the trio. I figured that more than anything it was the past few weeks of insomnia that had been magnifying my insobriety. I figured right then and there that I should stop trying to figure shit out and got up and made for the car. I left the two of them poolside and told them not to burn down the place (although at that exact moment, I wouldn't have been too upset if it happened).

"Bon Voyage!" There was a harsh G pronounced.

"Yeah. Break a leg! And if you need anything, call Kill-joy!"

✻

The drive to the train station gave me a few minutes to pull my head together and get the newly stumbled-upon itinerary in line:

> *Make it to the train station.*
> *Don't get arrested.*
> *Find Sean and Jay.*
> *Find June.*
> *[Doesn't have to be in this exact order.]*

I landed at the Peekskill station at 8:29 AM. I had five minutes to locate my favorite gay couple on their way to work. I sprinted down the platform and was set at ease when I saw their juxtaposing outfits outlined against the dull mass of corporate-commuter attire huddled nearby. Standing out like a pair of Waldo's in a desert of uniformed corporatism, my horrified ex-neighbors guffawed at my disheveled presence as I approached. They, of course, were always well put-together and this morning was no different. They were wearing dark jeans, brown shoes without socks, oxford button-downs and casual leather-jackets. Add on top of this anal-retentive approach to self-presentation that they were also holding hands while reading books; their visual cues all but screamed individuality and intrigue and allowed them to float effortlessly atop the drowning sea of blue and grey suited gentlemen buried in their devices.

"What the hell are you doing here?" Puzzled Sean.

"You look like absolute shit." Observed Jay.

"I haven't slept in thirty-six hours." I said. Wheezing took hold and a sharp pain found my left-kidney.

"That doesn't excuse anything." Sean leaned inward and sniffed me. "Thank god. He's not pungent yet."

Just then the train howled against our ears and came barreling through the station.

"I can't imagine you are getting on with us?"

"That I am, fellas. That I am."

"Did you buy a ticket?"

"No."

"Do you have any cash on you?"

I pulled out my wallet and realized it was empty.

"Of course. The middle class supporting the uber-rich." Jay said, pulling out fifteen bucks.

"Ah, man. You know I'm good for it."

"It's fine. I know you are."

"I'm not even rich, ya know." I said. My shyness about the topic couldn't be avoided. "I just live in a large house now."

"If you can call that thing a *house*."

"You know how I feel about it."

"Yeah. Yeah. *We know.* Your dad didn't leave you his money, just the mansion." Sean rambled on as we boarded. "And all you have is the house now and the land but you still have to work if you want to live and all that. Blah-blah-blah – *I'm poor still.*"

"Right."

"And if you sold one of those sculptures sitting in the front yard you could probably solve the poverty problem of New York."

I sighed, he was right. "I guess . . . it's still not *mine* though."

"Calm down, I'm just fucking with you." Sean sensed my drunken defensiveness coming on. He wasn't the type to deal with any shit like that, particularly when it ended his prying good time. "Good lord where has your wit run off too? Excuse me miss." He motioned to the lady-conductor collecting our tickets. She raised her head to him. "Yes, I'm sorry. I'm looking for an admirable, handsome young man by the name of Frank Gently. Have you seen him?" She shook her head no in sheepish confusion. "Hm. A shame. Neither have I. Tell me," he continued the barrage back my way. "Has Garrison ruined our delightful neighbor? Is it true? People do get dumber as they get richer?"

I shot him a half-smile but had nothing to follow up with — I was too focused on June and the reason I was on the train in the first place.

"Listen guys, what I'm gonna ask you might sound a little off but hear me out."

"No. I will not hear you out." Sean said. He could be a stubborn prick sometimes. "Not until you've said something on behalf of your mental absence this morning."

"Sean." Jay said.

"No. No. It's fine. I'll wait."

Jay sighed and shook his head.

I pulled something out of my ass.

"And I always thought gay men got to skip out on the whole pre-menstrual thing, ya know?" I winked at Jay modestly without breaking character. "Lacking the proper equipment and all. I guess there's exceptions to every rule."

"Okay. Good. See, I knew he'd come around." Sean said to his lover, happily content. "Well done. *Now*, you may continue."

I talked and talked and talked and hiccupped and then talked some more. I stumbled into a slight hangover along the way and they looked at one another dizzily as I rambled on but I was determined and kept it moving. It took about fifteen minutes before they came around to understanding just how mad I had been driven by June. And just how pissed off I was at Reason and Logic and Fate and how all of these bullshit abstract terms don't hold water when it comes to what kept me from seeing her these past five months. We blew by the Tapan Zee Bridge and I finally made it to the point in the story when I heard the Verizon call-girl's voice message informing me that June's phone number no longer existed. I then made it clear to the two of them that they were my only sober hope to putting anything together that might resemble clues for finding her.

"Why didn't you just call us?" Jay asked, rather smartly.

"Don't ask questions there are no answers to." I said, spouting off faux-wisdom with the speed and grace of a hairy-bellied Buddha. "I need to find her so I am following my gut." I grabbed the flub with both hands and supported it like it was just about to enter its third trimester. Jay laughed. Sean revolted in disgust. "And my gut said 'get to Sean and Jay before they made it to work.' My head has dealt me a whopping pile o'shit lately so I am goin' with my gut from now on. Okay?"

"Okay-okay. I was just trying to make your life easier."

"No, no I get it. I do, and I appreciate it...I just know my life won't be any easier making phone calls from the d'if in the dark."

"This is true."

"So do you guys remember anything? I mean *anything*: What she was wearing? A possible career? The gals she was hanging with before we left? I can only remember one – a Paula – and she was miserable and not really her good friend. She was one of those loathsome Westchester Italian birds. You know the type, she had drawn-on eyebrows and a spray tan and fuck-off stamped across her forehead. A forehead drawn taught by a hair-sprayed pony-tail – the symbol that marks them all to the public as they should be seen...*bonkers*. She did have nice legs though. Got to give them that, they all have nice legs."

"Oh *her.*" Jay said, his memory perking up. "I do remember her actually. Very well. She was a legit homophobe. Not like you, she doesn't *choose* to be a wretched inbred," I smiled. "She was like, authentically backward. Like a time-capsule of down home, small town hate. You remember her?" He motioned to Sean. Sean shook his head no. "Of course you don't. You were too busy eyeing up the bar back." Sean rolled his eyes. "Sean and I had just ordered drinks and she was standing right next to us, swaying out-of-control with her eyes rolling around like pinballs. This was a while after you left. We were just standing there with our hands around each other's hips and that is when she said it was a shame that the both of us didn't have penises because we were very attractive. I kissed Sean right then in front of her and she made a loud noise of disgust. She said that God would see to us and make sure we paid for our sins. I then asked her if she was on birth control and she didn't answer – I think she knew what I was getting at and then she walked off flipping her hair at us in the process. I think I might've found God right then."

"What!?" Sean croaked, deeply offended.

"Yeah. I even said a little prayer. I said, 'God, please let this bitch be on birth control because we don't need any more-a-that coming into this world.'"

I lost it and Sean couldn't be contained. Neighborly businessmen twisted and turned in their seats, seething with annoyance from the good time being had on a Thursday morning. To put it lightly, the commuter rail stank. I think it was the pleather seats; their smell reminded me of work and unhappiness. There was plenty of that to go around in our cart, that's for sure.

"That sadly sounds about right." I said. "She was appalling, as most Paulas are."

"But. I do remember one thing, she was flirting with the young and strapping bar back...what was his name again, Sean?" Sean rolled his eyes again. Jay smiled and continued. "You know who I'm talking about, Frank. The kid who was running the show at the brewery that night? Timmy? Was that his name?"

"Yeah! Timmy. That's it."

"I can almost guarantee she went home with him. I know an easy-bake-oven when I see one and she had her cupcake primed to be eaten."

"Damn. I didn't know that." I said. "That's—that's great news...for me at least. Hope Timmy made it out alive."

✢

We pulled into Grand Central just as the news of Paula and Timmy's relations was brought to light. We joked how Timmy was easily five inches shorter than Paula and how we hope he gave it to her in such a manner that it might've fucked the bitch out of her. He did resemble something of a pit-bull and I knew he served three tours in Iraq and Afghanistan. Not that that would've made him a good champion of grudge-fucking, but his hardened persona seemed to be the perfect handle for Paula and her incorrigible, Type-A whorror story. I drifted for a minute and thought about what I would say when I called him as not to offend. Timmy was a peculiar cat. Anyone else I would've dialed up straightaway and blared my problems outright. But Timmy had a knack for not letting people get too close and calling him ass early in the morning just didn't feel kosher.

I didn't know Timmy before his time in the war but it was clear-cut that it had changed him...he seemed inherently quiet, eerily unapproachable, almost incapable of anything past small talk. A smiling ghost. Despite this, I, along with everyone else at the brewery, knew he was a good man. A hardworking man. Just inaccessible was all. The wall was permanent and impenetrable. I knew this because I had attempted to scale it many times – offering up conversation after conversation starter when we shared shifts. To no avail, our tete-à-tetes only lent themselves to sports and beer and food and nothing else. The second something deeper, like feelings toward women, or beliefs, or anything resembling an opinion or pain would be touched upon, Timmy would quietly resign until the conversation meandered back around to the more superficial. I let it be. Lord knows I wasn't trying to change the man. Hell, I had my own shit to worry about. I just wanted to know him, that's all. Unfortunately, Timmy kept that knowledge at arms length and left any attachment for friends to be just that, kind of friendly. I couldn't understand it personally, and I don't think I'll ever be able to. I didn't serve. To be honest, I felt insane amounts of guilt over it. It was a constant source of unease in my life that I didn't enlist or do ROTC, especially after 9/11 but I also knew I didn't believe in war. That may have been a luxury of mine – a choice, an allowance of freedom that comes from others at the cost of their own lives – but I also knew that I needed to be able to write. And if war would've done to me what it'd done to Timmy, limiting my ability to communicate about anything…it would've killed me. Whether I survived the war or not, I would've been dead. I wondered then if Timmy still felt *alive*.

Jay gave Sean a bit more of a runaround, teasing him that Timmy was most likely hung like a horse because, apparently, short compact men can be just as big, if not bigger in both girth and stature than their taller, lankier, long-limbed brethren. I swayed the convo away from cock-talk and we chatted only a couple moments more about June and this wild hair I was going off of to find her.

"Can you believe it Jay?" Sean said. "Our little boy is all grown up, chasing after a woman, letting go of the cynic…*I'm touched*."

Jay agreed it was admirable of me…and necessary. The train pulled to a halt and we were off. It was in the middle of the station; under Grand Central's beautiful cerulean star-lit vault ceiling, just a few feet from the central clock-tower that I hugged the both of them and told them it might be a while before I saw them again.

"Go easy on ole Doris, will ya?" I said.

"When Doris goes easy on us, we'll go easy on her."

"Fair enough."

"Speaking of Satan's sister, she asked about you."

"Oh yeah?"

"Yeah. She asked for your new address because apparently, you owe her for the cleaners she brought in to take care of the cigar smoke."

"Bah! Gotta love that woman. Constant as the North Star."

"We told her you died and moved on. Pretty sure she bought it." Sean said.

"Jesus guys. That's evil."

"Hay. We saved you a couple hundred bucks."

"Yeah yeah. Thanks, I guess. You two take care o'each other, all right?"

"We're pulling for you."

I gave them both a double pat on the ass and sent them on their way. I called Timmy directly but his phone went to voice mail. I figured he might've closed up shop last night at the brewery and if that was the case he was probably still snoozing. I left him a short voice mail and a text message just asking for a call back and said it was kind of urgent but no one was dying so if he was on the john with his knees cracked, he had my approval to finish up and wipe before hitting me back.

*

Real people. People with jobs and lives and *things to do* were flying by me at cosmic speeds. Crisscrossing as if they were some sort of preprogrammed computerized pattern, the whirling madness of bodies combined with the last two hours I endured without a single drop of booze made my head start to pound. I hit up a local vendor for a big twenty-four ounce Bud, and like the true piece of homeless scuzz I was, parked myself on the floor along side one of the walls in the main corridor and fantasized about June. I cracked open the beer and thought of something my mother used to say about Budweiser: "S'a headache in every can, Frank." I toasted and drank every ounce of it to our unhappy relationship.

This headache's for you, Ma.

The marble floor was cold on my ass but the brown bag felt good in my hand and I was drunk again in three gulps. I leaned my head back to take in the enthralling architecture and art of the Grand Central ceiling. I had never really sat down and enjoyed it before. It was spectacular. It had all of the Astrological signs sprawled out over the bustling trans-portation-hub and looked as if they had been scraped, almost etched out of the fading cerulean night sky to reveal nothing but gold underneath. The imagery reminded me of June and our first conversation: 'Astrology is still a cancer,' I thought. 'But I guess it can be beautiful.' I hoped to one day show her this, the wonderful blue-green vault and let her know she somehow still surrounded me. Even when she wasn't there…she was still with me.

Ahem.

I'm lame, I am aware of this.

They say the first step to fixing shit is to stop saying, "they say the first step is to…" I had no intention of address-ing my lameness so I tucked this twelve-step nugget of gold into my pocket and kept on keepin' on. I drank some more of the Bud and the sentiment, along with the headache soon faded. I hadn't really given two cents of thought to my looks but a couple of the jarring faces I received by gawking tour-ists made me think about going to the bathroom and freshening up. I'm sure all I needed was a cardboard sign and an empty Dunkin Donuts cup and I would've fit right in with the rest of the urchins scattered on the marble floor. Just as I was about to get up to head to the restroom, my phone buzzed out of my pocket and fell to the ground. Timmy's hoarse, cigarette-stained voice grated over the airwaves.

"Yo. Beans. Gotchyur-message. What's up?"

"Timmy, what's good mang? Sorry for wakin' you. You close last night?"

"Naw-naw. You're straight." He made a hacking noise followed by a mouthful of yawning words. "I just can't sleep *period*. What can I do for ya?"

"Alright. Well this is gonna sound out there but..."

I went at it again, riling off tit for tat the same story I had just polished off with Sean and Jay. Timmy was a good sport. He chuckled at the times that called for it and offered slight condolences when the off-colored beats weighted and thickened the air between us. I appreciated him more now than I had ever done as a bar back. I guess I was just too busy pouring drinks and trying to make tips or, let's be honest, chatting up women, than giving this stoutly stack of a man his deserved due. He was a hard worker and I should've thanked him more for slaving over dirty glasses and tending to empty growlers and refilling ice bins behind the bar. It was shit work and he always did it with a smile. The more I spoke the more selfish I felt. I needed to get to know Timmy better. And then I finally came to the part of the story about Paula. His voice jumped up a couple of notes at the sound of her name and that's when I knew — he ate her cupcake.

"So. Yeah. I think Paula was sort of friends with June." I said. "You have her number or anything? Pretty sure she's my best bet for finding her."

"Man. Whew. That Paula's fierce, man. Like... Damn."

"Oh yeah?"

"Yessirp. You bet...*Shew.*"

"Go on."

"Shit man. The girl was out to prove something. She had like a permanent chip on her shoulder. *Freaking hot.* I think she's got a love-hate relationship with men."

"Don't they all?"

"Yeah I guess. But shit-fire-and-apple-butter, she was feisty – *whoo-doggie.* Man. Either way, I got her number and I'll dig it up for you...I know she commutes down every day from Poughkeepsie to work for some head hunting firm in the Metlife building so I doubt you could call her right now though."

My heart took a long solid drag off of my adrenal gland.

"You mean, the Metlife building in Grand Central?"

"That's the one."

More adrenaline. More beating.

"You know the name of the firm??"

"Ah shit. I was a little sideways when she told me and it's been so long. I think it had two first names. It sounded like the name of some British-dude. Think it was Richard Russel or something like that. Gah, in all honesty," Timmy paused and I could hear a tussle over the phone, "I should've called her after we hooked up and never did. Just got nervous or something. Feel real bad about it now if you know what I mean."

I thanked him and told him not to worry, I'm sure she'd come around if he called her again. I told him to text me her number when he finds it and that I'd have to call him back. I was already up off the floor now, walking across the station and up the escalators to the MetLife building. I pounded the rest of what was left in the can and felt the blood vessels in my eyes ease and find focus. I quickly searched for consulting firms in the Metlife building on my phone and there it was, as pompous and British sounding as ever: *Russell Reynolds.* There was no time to lose. This was it. I registered myself a guest and was on my way up to the 23rd floor before you could say "Jesus Christ what the hell are you doing! You look like shit and smell even worse!"

*

I hadn't worked out what I was going to say but I was always better without a script, anyway. Half of all improv is confidence, right? I caught sight of my reflection in the mirrored steel as the elevators closed. The shock of my sunken eyes, ragged hair and scraggly beard made me realize it would take a miracle to get past reception. Especially after riding up along side three other well-coiffed, Brooks Brothers whose power-tied, pin-stripe suits ebbed and ached with the sort of self-absorption you can only find in Reality TV. 'That's the ticket,' I thought. 'Be self-absorbed. Be an asshole. Be a client. That'll get you through.' A horrible plan, I know, but the three D-bags' conversation made it seem a viable option. They were vehemently discussing a dumb client who they were getting one over on. They laughed at themselves with a successful, schemer's pride. They were openly using racial slurs and the prevalent slime in their dialogue lead me to the easy conclusion that to these three egocentric men, I was completely invisible. Less than invisible, I was nothing. I didn't exist. My presence in the elevator didn't make one inklings difference to them and the way they spoke. It was weird and horrible and suddenly, I didn't feel so bad about myself. I guess that happens when you're around truly bad people. The elevator chimed and they got off at 10. Almost instinctively, I dove into a manic state of primate grooming with my hands. I buttoned up my shirt, tucked it in and made my hair look as artsy and as purposeful as humanly possible – whatever that means. There was a ding and before I knew it I was out and in the lobby.

The receptionist was attractive and I had in my hands a new way in. Thank god, being an asshole would've never worked for me. My poker face consisted of calling all in and then losing everything directly. This new plan was gold though: I'm not the client anymore. I'm the boyfriend.

"You're seeing Paula?" The receptionist asked, quizzically.

"Of course." I said, pearly whites aglow.

"You'll have to excuse me but you don't seem like her type."

"What? Well I guess that's why you haven't heard of me." I winked at her. I was debonair, flowing in and out of unconscious charisma. "Look, this is really important, I wanted to surprise her – it's our two month anniversary and I know she'd be thrilled."

"I don't know."

"Hey lady, this isn't some joke." I said, turning a grayer shade of serious. "I've met her family already. This is the real deal. I could easily just call her up and let her know I'm here but I wanted it to be a surprise and take her out for coffee. Can you help a guy out and just tell her she has a guest waiting in the lobby?"

"Where did you guys meet?"

"What is this, twenty one questions?"

"Well we get a lot of people in here trying to talk to head hunters, faking their way in. I don't mean to offend you but this is my job."

"Do I look like the guy who uses a head-hunter?" Her eyes squinted at me. "We met upstate, alright? She hated me at first. Actually, she despised me. Her first words to me were 'get lost, creep.' And now she loves me. That sound about right?"

"Yes...surprisingly."

"Now, please. Would you kindly..."

"Yes-yes. Of course. It's very sweet of you. I'm sorry."

"Thank you.' I smiled long and hard.

I was baffled by my own performance.

"She'll be down in a few minutes, you can have a seat. Sorry for the confusion."

I nodded and helped myself to some breath mints and the waiting room water cooler. I heard the clacking of heels coming down the hall way and then she was upon me. A tall, tan-legged specimen rounded the corner and the relentless woman was there in full effect. I was staring into the very fires of hell. It took her but a moment to recognize me:

"You!?" Her eyes wreathed in flame but her eyebrows didn't move, couldn't move. It wasn't that they were drawn-on so much as her forehead had just enjoyed a fresh dousing of Botox.

The Appalling Paula

Her body, an homage to plastics,
Her attitude a tribute to Kudjo.
Her attire an active, living testament
To the fashion-backward.

It was the cross strung out on
Tanned skin that hit me.
And there, the gold plated,
Diamond crusted ornament sat.
Pious, Penitent, Pornographic Plagiary.

The gems twinkled in between
A pair of twins that were
The only thing worth remembering.
Soft, Succulent, Sinfully Sweet.

All of which were fake,
But looked good,
Like the woman
Who proudly
Supported them.

The Plasticine Figurine. . . Wolverine.

"What are you doing here?!" She cried.

"Surprise!"

There was dead silence.

I was cheery-eyed. "I missed you babe!"

"*Excuse me.*" She said, "I am not your babe. Now what are you doing here?"

"Wait, this gentleman isn't your boyfriend?" Asked the receptionist.

"Janine. Don't be gross. And call security."

"Wait—wait. Okay! Okay. I'll leave peacefully – but I'm trying to find June. I've been trying to find her since for...forever ago. Since the night we met!"

"And why should I care?" Paula was fiery. "Janine. What are you gaping at? Call security."

"I'm sorry okay? I'm sorry, but I didn't have any other choice."

"No other choice than to show up at my work looking like... *that.*"

"I know. It's not right but you're my only hope." My tone changed, desperation was pouring out in all directions. "I literally just got off the phone with Timmy and he said you worked here."

Her brow lost its furrowing intensity and the botox magically relented. Her shoulders, too, lost to a sweet memory drew backward and rested easily after hearing his name. "Timmy told you to come here?"

"Well he said you worked here."

"Did he say anything else?"

"Well, yes, but.."

"*Like why he never called?*"

"You know. Actually he did mention that. He said he got nervous and that he messed up. You—"

"Well he *did*. He did mess up, *big time.*"

"Listen, I messed up too...with June," She pressed her lips together. "I mean, we're guys. That's what we do. We mess up. I think the good ones are the ones who at least know they messed up and try to make up for it...Timmy is a good guy. He's gone through hell and back."

"I know." She said, irritated. "He told me."

"He did?" I was shocked. Timmy doesn't tell anyone anything. "Well you would know he's one of the guys I'm talking about then. One of the guys who's worth giving a second chance, ya know? To make up for it."

She huffed a little bit at my limp-dicked sentiment. "And what about you. Are *you* one of those guys?"

"I think I am. I dunno – *listen,* I've gone through my own personal stack-o-shit lately. Please, I don't know what to say to make you believe me but I just know I need to find June."

"Well I can't help you."

"Paula. I know Timmy likes you. I could hear it on the phone." I truthfully couldn't tell. The sheer language Timmy was using when I mentioned Paula had thrown me off. His "wowed, fierce, chip-on-her-shoulder" type-talk made me think he had actually found a match in the most unexpected of places. I didn't want to lie to her but at the same time I wanted to find June.

"Don't patronize me." She cut me off. "If he likes me, *he* will do something about it."

"Okay."

"And don't give me that damaged goods routine either. We're all damaged in one way or another." I was taken aback by Paula's dexterity with life. Perhaps she had had it harder than I assumed. "But really. I can't help you. I don't know June."

"What about a friend? A mutual friend or anyone who might know her whereabouts or last name or *anything...*"

"Oh...yes...No wait. *No!*" She shook off the conversation and what looked like thoughts of Timmy and grabbed my elbow and forced me toward the elevator. "Oh my god, you reek of booze! This is ridiculous!"

"Sorry." I said, practically giving up. "I'll go now. You don't have to do that."

She let go and I Charlie Browned it to the elevator and hit the down arrow.

"I just wanted June to know why I hadn't called her.."

"A half a year later? There is no excuse."

"No. No. I get it. You're right."

I was fully defeated. In every avenue, in every way...the world had won.

The door chimed opened, I matched its emptiness and got in. Just as the two metal doors formed a seamless wall of failure, Paula threw in her stiletto and it kicked back open. She walked inside and hit the button for the lobby.

"So." She said, crossing her arms, unable to look me in the eye. "What *is* your excuse?"

Her interest in me could only mean one thing. That Sean and Jay's predictions were one hundred percent accurate: Timmy had inherited a mighty gift between his legs and Paula was a girl who liked gifts.

Chapter 6

Celebrity Sightings At JFK

The fluorescent lights at JFK terminal struck my eyes mercilessly with the authority of a club to the skull. The ceaseless banging and searing noise would not give way until I found the bar. The airport was massive so it took a while and TSA blows-a-fat-donkey-dick but just when all felt lost, the seas parted and *Tigin's Irish Pub* was before me. The rosy hue of dimly lit cattle that surrounded the wooden high-top bar made the watering hole feel like a traveler's home away from home. 'Lighting is everything' I thought, shimmying up onto a barstool. 'Well, lighting and scenery.' There was a glowing, brown-eyed forty-plus-feline across the way with her rack hanging out over the bar. She was definitely sending intrigue my way, or *someone's* way. A rack just doesn't hang out like that for no reason. She was a looker: buxom, blonde, beautiful and she knew it too. But still, no June.

I ordered a Bloody Mary and whipped out my credit card and kissed it. It was the same card that had just bought my one-way ticket to Los Angeles. *LAX, that is.* I couldn't tell you what it meant or what it looked like nor did I care to know that the X stood for international. I was a man on a mission and that mission was now headed out west. The

West, as it has been called since the country's founding, had always felt so foreign to me that it may as well have been another country. So, that international X started to make a bit more sense the more I thought about it. I tried to imagine what it might be like – surfer dudes and plastic-bodied-blondes were all that really came to mind. When an easterner recalls the usual imagery bolstered by poor Hollywood blockbusters and Reality TV horrors that now claim lordship over the land, it only made perfect sense that this other world was near the bottom of my "Places I Need to See Before I Die" list. In fact, people who told me LA was their dream destination often frightened me, like someone telling you their highest aspiration in life was to be a custodian (or play a custodian in a movie). However, in a mere matter of seconds La La land was thrust to the very top; the new found supreme dream destination of Frank Gently.

Unbelievable, right?

I know. I know. My thoughts exactly.

It had only been six short hours since my embarrassing rendezvous with Paula and I was still in disbelief that I was actually flying out to LA and doing it – actually finding my balls. Not only finding them but grabbing them firmly and showing them off to the world and going after the girl. The world was not yet impressed, but it would be.

The red nosed and white-haired bartender brought over my bloody. I downed the delicious painkiller, slurping at the spicy salt with loud gulps radiating from my neck and gut. My cheeks drew taut and my head warmed and cleared. I felt easy again. They had used olive brine and pickle juice in the mix, two of the best ibuprofens an admirer of the drink can afford. I glanced down at my ticket and was immediately consumed by a deep sense of worry. What at first offered a promise of adventure and hope — traveling and being brave and finding the girl and all that other bullshit that goes into doing something your skin isn't used to — now unleashed a sharp pang of doubt that could be felt all the way down in my butt-hole. The worry spread slowly, creeping into my innards and rotted me from inside out. Thoughts of June's negative reactions to seeing me wouldn't stop coming and soon overwhelmed me. I drank harder and faster and finished the first tallboy strong. It drew the attention of the man sitting next to me but I paid him no mind. Knowing that the chances of June deeming me, well, a psychopath, wouldn't be too far from the truth — what with the vast amount of time that had passed since we'd last seen one another — well, I needed another heavy-handed splash of distilled V8 and needed it quick.

I flagged down the bartender again. He was not too happy with the old drunkard sitting caddy-corner to me at the elbow joint of the bar. As I waited for him to wrestle through the man's slobbering dialect and fraying golfer's cap, I thought of everything I had already been through to get to June. Anything that might make my case seem a little less batshit. Yes, I was building an argument, so to say, anything that might make my chances with her seem a little less *One Flew Over the Cuckoo's Nest* and a little more *An Affair to Remember*. I thought of my parents — my mother, my father, my insomnia, my perpetual insobriety, my sheer rotten luck and my distaste for all of it. I then thought of Paula and my bones shook. The very marrow rattled around and finally settled back down when my second bloody appeared.

The Appalling Paula.

Holy fuck.

Dealing with her alone had to show June that I was serious about her...*if not - her loss!*

I was drunk again already.

Paula and I had talked for almost twenty minutes in a small café in Grand Central. She asked the barista for a latté that took more than two minutes to order. I got a coffee. She was less interested in my story and more interested in if I were genuine or not – and therefore upping Timmy's chances of being genuine, too. After much ado about my family and loss and June's elusive note and everything else one should consider self-pity, Paula finally caved and agreed to give me Chloe's number (Chloe was the friend of the friend who was also at the brewery that night). She kindly prefaced the digits with the warning that Chloe would be less happy to hear from me than Paula had been when she saw my disgustingly sad face in her office lobby. She used the words 'disgustingly sad.' I thanked her for the backhanded warning and texted Timmy and told him to call her – she was legit into him. From what I could discern from our short convo, he seemed into her as well. And hey, if he had managed to wring out just an ounce of sympathy from Paula, enough for her to help my cause, and if she had brought out just an ounce of deeper communication in him, more then I ever thought possible in Timmy, I felt the two had a decent shot at making it. And making it for the better.

*

Chloe remembered me, fortunately (or unfortunately depending on what she witnessed at the brewery that night). I called her up directly from Grand Central. She was surprised and cold and off-putting as all hell, but still she heard me out. She said that when June was hurt she never really opened back up to people after that, so my chances were *"with the birds."* Chloe went on for a little while; weaving together a pride-scorned monologue, the likes of which would've given any modern day feminist chill-bumps, about how June would not want to hear from me, *"like, at all,"* and that she'd be doing wrong by her friend if she helped me out. Despite all this and despite my ensuing hangover, I was able to pull yet another sympathy card out of my ass and procure some answers as to why the hell June was so unreachable.

"She's off the map." Chloe said, condescendingly through the phone. "So it doesn't even matter if you want to find her. She's incommunicado right now. You can't find her. Got it?"

"What on earth do you mean, off the map?"

"I mean off the map, the grid, the universe. She doesn't use her phone or anything when she's touring. She gets too tired and yeah, she doesn't want to have to deal with any distractions. And that is all you'd be...*a distraction.*"

"Touring?"

"She didn't tell you?"

"No?"

"Hm."

"Please, I have to know. She has to know why I haven't been able to reach her!"

"Well she *did* like you. And that's past tense, buddy, but I guess you should know. She's a front woman for a band."

"Whaaa." The majority of blood in my body left my extremities and found its way to my loins. I got light-headed.

Chloe silently waded through the five-minute torrential downpour that came tumbling from my mouth. The pitiful Ringling Brothers display of tearful backflips and self-explanatory aerials was on, the heavy content of which made

Sophie's Choice seem like *Child's Play* when compared to what was going on between June and me. Our situation was dire and I got the desperation across. Perhaps a little too much so, for just when I thought the show was getting good Chloe stopped me abruptly.

"Alright! Jesus! *I'm at work.* I don't' have *time* to play therapist. I've got my own shit to worry about."

"Sorry. I'm just battling all the odds right now."

"I'll say. You're a long shot, all right. But, it's still kinda sweet."

She told me that *Lickity-Split* had a residency all through the month of March at the Silver Lake Lounge in LA. I hated the way she said LA, but I loved the way she said *Lickity-Split.*

A front woman!

Whew.

Hot damn, can you believe it?

I couldn't. I had no idea what Los Angeles had to offer, nor would I know what to do when I got out there but I did know one thing – I was going and I was going that very moment. After a two hour nap on the A-train and a few missed beats of groggy dialogue with the ticket kiosk manager, (something to the tune of "How the hell does this thing work!?" "Well, you follow the directions, sir.") I now found myself with only a half-hour to kill before boarding a flight to the land of the lost.

Hence Bloody Marys one and two.

*

"Hay. Hay." The harsh faced man with the fraying wool golfer's cap started tapping the bar for my attention.

"Whadd'ya think?" He flashed a toothless half smile at me and waved his hand a couple of times over his face as if to say, *not bad, eh?* Actually, he was saying more than that, he was saying, *pretty damned good lookin', right?*

"Clint Eastwood! Yeah?" He continued on, wiping drool away from his lip with his soiled polo jacket sleeve.

"I'm sorry. What?" I didn't want to acknowledge him but it was now beyond my willing.

"*Clint Eastwood,*" he said. "Get him all the time. Whadd'ya think?"

I didn't have the heart to tell the man that aside from the rare times when Clint entertained a golfer's cap, he looked about as far from the rugged sexual icon as the present day skeleton of Clint Eastwood looks from the Outlaw Josey Wales Clint Eastwood. I should've nodded along and laughed with the old fool – he was joking around after all – but instead I just shrugged. I was too tired for gimmicks and flattery.

"Bah. Yur all soft!" He yelled, slightly offended that his joke had fallen flat. He placed his top pair of dentures back in and I finally got the joke. I made like I didn't hear him. He was a little too worse for wear even for my liking.

"You heard me." He continued. "What are you twenty, twenty-five? You're all soft! Can't depend on the lot of you for nothin' these days. Clint's right. A whole generation-a-pussies."

"We are a sensitive people." I snubbed.

"Yur damned right-chu are. Probably couldn't even tell me what an alternator was if you tried."

"Oh sure I can."

"*Sure you can. Let's hear it, then.*"

"What? Right now."

"Yeah. Go on! An alternator. Let's hear it!"

"All right: an alternator is that thing they put in old people so their hearts don't switch off or start beatin' crazy when they walk past a microwave."

His eyes shot wide at the irreverent tone aimed at his temple. What can I say? The man was a true drunk and I didn't have time for him. Especially his particular brand. You know the kind, the kind who could talk a mile-a-minute on a head full of sauce. The kind of stammer-free fool who reveled in confusion and ill-minded variables, yet still kept it together. The kind of scummy low-life who could be sent spiraling, uncorked and out of control – ranting, raging, positively maniacal – all over something as little as a bumped elbow. The worst part being, and much to the discontent of anyone who might fall within his ten-foot radius I might add, was that in spite of the incredible amount of poison coursing through the man's veins, he still remained painfully lucid.

"Are you fuckin' with me, boy?" He was now eyeing me up. "I hope yur not fuckin with me 'cuz I'll sock you! I'll sock you right in the jawl!"

I smiled at him. He didn't like that. A smile at those heated, toe-to-toe times of life tends to be the most insulting of gestures.

"I'll drop you like a pancake!" He yelled.

I wanted to inform the man that unless he was insinuating he was a clumsy grill worker at the local diner, I think he meant *flatten*. The bartender came over. He glared at the elderly man now standing up on his stool's foot supports, knees wobbly, practically shaking with indignation at my apparent lack of respect for the elderly.

"Sir, is this man bothering you?" The bartender asked me.

I looked at the old coot. He was slowly sitting back down in his seat. His face had quickly slipped from rage to defeat. A sour whimper hung there for a moment, it was a flash recognition of wrongdoing, like a toddler who could barely admit flooding the sink while standing in two inches of water. I could tell he didn't want to leave the watering hole and I didn't feel like playing lifeguard. Hell, something in me admired that withering sack of bones and his gusto for life. It should also be mentioned that he was frail and couldn't break a pair of chopsticks in half if his life depended on it. So, any socking or dropping or flattening for that matter wouldn't have done much harm anyway. My attention swung back to the bartender, "No, sir. Not at all."

The gentleman behind the bar made like he was going to unleash a verbal assault on the decomposing wino and then, in sudden disbelief, performed a rather funny double my way. I reaffirmed what I'd said was accurate with a head nod and he sauntered off down the bar, highly annoyed at the new odd couple.

"Yur still soft." Clint Eastwood muttered.

"Where you off to old man?" I said, intrigued.

"Los Angeles."

"Awh-yeah? Me too. Never been."

"You ain't missin' much."

"Oh?"

"Yeaah...ARGGH." He burped out his last four beers.

"What about The Pacific? Heard it consumes you."

"Just a bunch-a-water."

"And the sunshine?"

"Too bright."

"What about the women?"

"Not bright enough."

He slugged his beer and threw his hand up for another. The bartender submitted, unwillingly.

"Sounds like you got it all figured out, then, eh?" I said.

"How you think I got this pretty?"

"Well, I know there's one gal over there who's brighter'n you and me put together."

"Shit. Don't tell me you're one-a-*them*."

"What's that?"

"A shit-headed romantic."

"Well yeah. I guess. Sounds like the slightly more colorful version."

"Hold on, let me get a violin."

"What are you on? Aren't violins for sad songs?"

"Exactly."

"Not following ya, Dirty Harry."

"You woudn't."

"Hm. Must be a generational-gap-thing." I said, smartly sucking down my second bloody.

"You'll figure out why it's a sad story sooner or later."

"What? 'Cuz we're talkin' about love?"

"Bingo, Rico."

"I take it a man as good looking as Clint Eastwood's probably had his fair share of affairs."

"And that's all they were," he said, struggling through what looked like congestive heart failure. "Affairs."

"I'm sorry to hear that, Mr. Eastwood."

"Knock that shit off."

"Naw. I feel bad for you – if that's truly how you feel."

"Listen pal, I got your number. You think love is real. What kinda asinine shit is 'at? You know what? I take back what I said about you all bein' soft. Yur just dumb. And to think alls I wanted to do was sit here and drink beer and have a joke or two and now you're all down memory lane and feelin' sorry for people and shit. Christ O'Friday, if you wanna talk why don't you stick to a topic you might have a tits chance-a-knowin' somethin' about. Otherwise, move the hell on."

"Hay! You started in with me!"

"Kid, I don't *start in* with nobody. You looked like you were about to have a heart attack or somethin' (this must've been when I was worrying over what June's reaction to me might be like) and well, I'll be damned if I was gonna sit there watch you keel over."

"Alright-alright. I got it. Thanks." I checked my watch. "I've got to be getting to my gate anyway. Nice talkin' to ya, *Gran Torino.*"

"Pahf!" He sneered at the reference, "Be careful out there. Bunch-a-softies runnin' the world now. Who knows what could happen. Know what I mean..." He had turned and continued the conversation on to his next unassuming victim, an elderly lady with bifocals. She was drowning out the world one crossword puzzle at a time and was enjoying a white-wine spritzer until I got up and left. I don't suppose she enjoyed too much of anything after I high-tailed it out of there.

✳

The plane was large and had six seats across. Drunk and clear-minded (which I know sounds oxy-moronic), I was afforded with a couple of minutes before take off to think about what old Clint said to me about love – it being a fantasy or not. Though I was not about to be deterred by some old drunkard, I wondered just what affairs the man had endured, how bad things must've gotten and if indeed the obvious was true: alcohol had got in the way. Or maybe it was the bad teeth combined with bad jokes, which all still, were probably worn away and worsened by the drink. The road signs all pointed toward an unapologetic man, who had convinced himself by his ability to *handle* the alcohol that it wasn't a problem. A functional unrepentant. His face and his teeth and his turning away from that which makes everything worthwhile made for a very strong argument against — *he couldn't handle it.* Mid-thoughts, I saw the same fraying golfer's cap come walking down the isle toward me followed by the same beady, blood-shot eyes and wry half-smile. I couldn't believe it. The man was going to sit next to me the entire flight. AN ENTIRE EFFING FLIGHT OF CLINT EASTWOOD. No-no. Not possible — not livable! I didn't know whether to act asleep or address him. I was still drunk enough to entertain the latter.

"Hay! Hay! Whaddya know. Clint Eastwood everyone!"

The son-of-a-bitch acted like he didn't even know me.

I was astonished. I had never been ignored by a bum before. Usually it's the other way around, which probably makes me sound like an asshole but hey, sometimes bums deserve a cold shoulder too. I turned in my seat as he passed and looking over the headrest, I felt an odd desperation to catch eyes with him. He finally fell into his seat, stumbling over an innocent couple in the process and that's when I saw it — he was gone. He must've tipped the threshold back at the bar because now that function, that ability to handle everything, was nowhere in sight. All that was left was a blue glaze, a sad weariness so fraught with despair that it frightened me to death. It was the same look of a deadhead who dropped acid a little too much, a little too often and couldn't find his way back – it was a look of no return. It was a look of giving up. *It was the look of the lifeless.* I spun around quickly and made a promise to myself right then that I would not become him. I knew that I was on his path and certainly would've stayed on it had I remained at the d'if. And there was no time to waste. I would sleep the drunk off on the flight and deal with the hangover on foreign ground. Of course, it wasn't the best of plans, but June. She deserved me in a better form.

I deserved me in a better form.

It didn't have to be perfect – no one ever was – but it certainly wasn't going to be like this and for damned sure wasn't going to be like Clint Eastwood.

Chapter 7

The Lost Boy Meets the Sun

"Sir, this is Silver Lake."

The man's voice sounded tired.

I was tired too. I was more than tired, I was still asleep. I dreamt that the man was describing a magnificent clear lake surrounded by palm trees and pearly sands, a reflective oasis with magical powers that could cleanse the toxins pouring from my pores. This natural healing pool was filled with skinny blonde people who had tans and skimpy bathing suits. Even the men had on skimpy bathing suits. The sight of it made me wince. *Yeesh. Dreams are weird.* Everyone had perfect bodies and everyone was smiling. All they did was smile, in fact. No one was talking really, just smiling and looking at one another. It was eerie and I wondered how their mouths kept from drying out. I licked my lips and they felt chapped. Everything was dry. Dry. Dry. DRY. The sun was bright, too bright and drying. Then, a man next to me started talking again. He was ugly and had a cartoonish, ear-waxed mustache that extended out past his cheeks. He was the taxi-driver:

"PLEASE WAKE UP SIR. This is the lake."

The cabby had pulled to a halt just outside of the Silver Lake reservoir, which may as well have been the epicenter of a hipster mecca. I peered out through the window and quirky creatures walked by like they had never left the fifties. I mean, I wasn't one to talk. I looked like I'd just stepped out of a Brawny man commercial. That is, if the Brawny man were an alcoholic and over weight by twenty-thirty pounds. Give or take a few.

"This is the lake?" I asked, barely awake.

There was nobody swimming. There was no beach, no sand, no hope! But there were swimsuits and blonde people, tanned and smiling. That there was plenty of. There were also tattoos, lots and lots of tattoos and a few mustaches... and sunglasses. I needed sunglasses, dammit. I felt barren and milky and sickly.

All three were accurate.

"How am I supposed to know?" Said the driver, impatiently. "You said Silver Lake. I asked where in Silver Lake and you said 'The Lake.'"

"Fine. Fine."

I paid the man, got out and rubbed my eyes. They were painful and had dried severely while I slept in the cab ride from LAX. I was now in what could only be best described as full-onset Delirium Tremens. Any one who knows their worst hangover ever knows a fraction of what a couple weeks' bender can deliver: all superfluous conversation magnifies the pain. Forget nausea and headache. It was full body ache. Muscles start out shaky and soon deteriorate to a state of full out rebellion. My ability to make easy decisions and perform basic motor functions was on the brink of collapse. Everything hurt. The sun hurt. Water hurt. Air hurt. I was death on legs. Death-risen. A pale green ghoul. A flash of one of my favorite quotes of all time bounced back into my head. I think it was Jefferson but at that exact moment, it could have been Jeff Bridges for all I know. The only thing I could remember were the words, the mantra to which I knelt and prayed to as I sat down on a bench on the outskirts of the reservoir:

"Life is the art of avoiding pain." I said it aloud and grasped my thighs and put my head between my legs.

The theory was fact in my book, but what that genius forgot to mention was that most of the ways life chooses to avoid pain brings heaps upon heaps of it later on. And sitting on that bench, watching strange looking cats stroll by – extremely healthy looking cats, bizarrely healthy looking cats, the type of cats who drank only green juice and worked out often and tanned 'just enough' – I sank into denial. My brain receded in a futile attempt to disprove how much pain I was in. It was a fight to the death. Mind vs. Pain. None of it worked. The pain won and rubbed its victory all over.

Still, none of this compares to what I felt when landing at *LAX*:

I had slept the four hours and forty-five minutes out of the entire five-hour flight. A blessing in disguise, it was the first time I had slept more than three consecutive hours in three months. We'd begun our descent when minor turbulence shot me upward. I was disoriented, delirious, decomposing. My clothes were soaked in sweat. My brain had shrunk to the size of a peanut and was slowly disappearing into nothingness. It hated me. It rattled around and pummeled the inside of my skull with vicious heartbeats...it wanted out. I wanted out, too. I could smell myself and it made me sick. All the sudden I had to vomit and had to do it *now.* The seat-belt light was on. I looked for a vomit bag but there weren't any. I got up and ran to the bathroom. Both were locked! The flight attendant came trucking back toward me – big lady that she was – and told me I needed to take my seat.

"But, sir.." she started.

"Vomit bags!" I yelled. "PLEASE GOD ANYTHING."

I must've been green because she ran, or shall I say, furiously waddled back to the front without saying another word. It was too late. I was banging on the door for someone to let me in. It wouldn't budge. I didn't care if they were shitting out Benny's Burritos in there, I would've gladly used the sink while they carried on. Nothing opened up except my mouth. Then it came. It came hard and fast and punishing. I tried to cover it up and pinch my lips tight with my hand. A huge mistake. What happened then I'll never forget, and neither will the rest of the passengers on that flight: The pressure of both my lips pierced tight combined with the sheer force of what needed to come out created a geyser; like when you put your thumb over the open end of a hose. Everything shot out yellow and red, spraying wildly, violently covering the door and much of the floor as I bent over to shield passengers in the back row from my wrath. It was horrible. Gruesome. Utterly humiliating. No one else threw up, thank god, but there were still ten minutes left in the flight. The descent had taken such an angle that much of the liquid began to run down the front of the plane toward the passengers' feet. I walked passed the rear rows and noticed they all had their feet up with their noses covered or buried in their shirt necks. They were scowling, painted red with contempt. I should've felt shame but I didn't care. I felt *that* bad that shame and embarrassment were out the window. If only

I could've been out the window too. I sat back down and hoped for a crash landing.

We landed safely.

Rats.

✻

I waited for everyone to get off for I was holding in yet another round of puke. At least this one was more manageable. All the passengers filed off, one by one, none of them ever looking my way. The brave and most disgusted let out loud sighs and huffs as they passed. And then I saw Clint Eastwood walk by and look back at me. He shook his head and mouthed "soft" right before walking off. 'THAT PLAGUE!' I thought. 'THAT DISEASE OF A MAN!' First he ignores me and then he has the brass cahoneys to kick a man when he's down! I was livid. I was pissed. I was sick again! All anger left my body with the rest of the battery acid that came out in the second round. I apologized to the one flight attendant and asked for an orange juice before leaving the plane. You would've thought she'd kick my ass right out of there, but something in her facial expression – perhaps a reaction to how horrible I looked – awarded me a complimentary OJ. 'Free juice' I thought. 'Things aren't so bad.'

Crawling out of the airport, I found the taxi line where I was immediately hit by intense sunlight. It was unlike anything I had ever experienced before. I guess more so because it came with a balmy seventy-six degrees and a light wind that acted as a perfect counterbalance to my wavering soul. I became steadied by the breeze and could think clearly for a moment. I then realized I had given zero thought to the temperature difference out west. It was forty-four degrees when I left New York and that was a warm day. I had on flannel and jeans and boots and so, the sweating and the hangover, or let's be real here – alcohol poisoning – continued without interference. Then a familiar voice came over top of the sun, assaulting my personhood. What was left of it:

"Welcome to the Land of the Lost, muh boy." The voice was cajoling.

It was Clint Eastwood. For the second time in our short time of knowing one another, I acted like I didn't hear him.

"Be careful now son," he continued. "This is where it gets real…or weird as they say back where I'm from."

"And where on earth are you from?"

"Venice."

I was too sick to put together that 'back where he was from' was only fifteen minutes away. He was being a smartass-delinquent-fuck. Nothing new under the sun there. There was only one thing new under the sun – me. I brought my hand up over my eyes to form a makeshift visor, "Is it always this beautiful out here?"

He smiled at me as he put on a pair of sunglasses. That smug son-of-a-bitch! HE KNEW. He knew you needed shades out here and I didn't. I questioned my potency as a human being and wept inside.

"Yeap. You know what Meraz says about LA, right?"

I actually didn't. I had heard of the poet, Mike Meraz, but didn't know his work. I shook my head and felt myself squinting harder and harder as the power of the sun set in.

"Yeap, he says you can rot in LA and never *feel* it."

The words were stirring, considering that I was rotting at the time (and feeling every ounce of it). I asked him then if he thought it was true.

"Only a bum would ask another bum if somethin' like that were true." A cab pulled up. "See you in Venice, Rico!"

"Who the hell is Rico?!" I yelled.

He rolled down the window and hung his arm out in the breeze. "It's You. Rico Suavè! Good luck with the love lust — don't let it bite you on the ass on the way out."

I never met another man who could make so much and so little sense in the same sentence. The cab pulled out and he was off. Good ole Clint Eastwood, homeward bound to Venice. I didn't know it then but I would eventually learn he was a real-deal Dharma Bum. The last breed of Kerouacian knaves who stuck to the rhetoric of drug-induced literature. One of the wild, the mad, off-kilter dreamers who thought they were *most* alive. They were The Beat Children and Clint was one who never found his way back out. And let me tell you something, it is essential to find your way back out. Out, after all, is reality. Otherwise, your star burns out just as Kerouac's did; and all that is leftover is frightened and alone and a liver failing you before the age of fifty. I would meet Mr. Eastwood again but that is a story for another time. A time of *High Plains Drifting*. Now was a time of survival.

The next cab pulled up and I was fast asleep.

*

I sat on a bench on Silver Lake Boulevard for a couple of minutes looking left and right, trying to decide where to go and instead, stayed exactly where I was and empathized with the mentally retarded. A man passed by with a dirty blonde high knot with both sides of his head buzzed. Tribal tattoos crept up his neck and down his arms out of his baggy cut-off band t-shirt and it was hard not to notice that the dude was sculpted. I glanced down at my gut and then back up to the man of steel. We were walking-talking case studies. The difference between ten years spent in the ocean and a decade spent behind a laptop (and a bottle).

"Excuse me." I said. "You know how far away the beach is from here?"

"Which beach?"

"THE BEACH."

"Well if you take Santa Monica or 10 West you'll hit Venice or Santa Monica."

Was this guy purposefully trying to confuse me or was I just severely hurt? I figured I was too messed up to make sense of anything so I went along with him. The guy seemed decent enough. Apart from the sun-scorched high knot, he had an artist's nose, a brow and jaw-line that screamed The Ideal Man and an air of confidence about him that made one assume he'd never known what it was like to be considered unattractive; let alone feel the lashings of an ugly stick. Still, he seemed decent to me. Quiet and mysterious but good-willed and helpful. Like any of that mattered, anyway. I had zero room to talk about aesthetic value – I smelled like cow cud and probably looked just the same.

"Okay. Thanks. Wait." I said. There was an intense struggle but bearings were nowhere to be found. "So you said if I take Santa Monica I'll get to Santa Monica?"

"New here?" He asked.

"Bout two minutes worth."

"Right on, man." The guy *actually* said 'right on.' I couldn't believe it. I thought right on was what they said out here in the sixties? "Welcome-welcome. Just so you know, you're on the East Side, man."

Okay, now he was definitely fucking with me? I couldn't tell. Could there really be an east side in the west? I put everything on me being too hungover to function, and therefore too hungover to communicate so I just went along with whatever the man said. Nodding. Sweating. Burping. Squinting. Shaking. I was getting nowhere fast and then suddenly, I remembered that there's a west side in New York. After that obvious conclusion, I became the man's loyal subject.

"You lookin' to get to the Pacific?"

I nodded.

"You surf?"

I shook my head.

"Got a car?"

I shook my head again. I was a lost cause. Perhaps I belonged out here.

"Alright man. Well, if you're lookin' to get to the ocean, I'm headed there in a half-hour...if you wanna ride?"

"Really? That'd be amazing."

"Straight up, that's how we do 'round here."

I winced at the man's language, but he was being nice. I would wince once more when he put his fist out and asked me for a pound. I don't know what it was, but when a grown man is so laid back that a handshake or a DAP doesn't cut it, I become lost. I know that's just me being a rigid old fart, but either way, I agreed to go with him and before I knew it, we were off.

I needed the water.

Needed to see it, be in it.

Be reborn and what not...or maybe just feel less shitty about myself.

They were now one in the same.

I hopped in his car and was fast asleep again.

"This is Venice, bro." He said, parking in a side-lot. I snapped to and looked around for Clint. He was nowhere to be found, thank god. "And *that*," he pointed to the horizon, "is the Pacific."

And there it was, life in blue.

The Atlantic had much. But the Pacific, the Pacific had a style. And I am not talking about the lifestyle that surrounded it; they were just *people* after all. I am talking about the sun that kissed its lips every night, the westerly winds that sat savory on the soul and the smell of salt that made you long to return...and the vast, vast blue. It was a blue that reminded me of the Hudson. It had an eternity to it. An immensity that promised it would always be there, long after I was gone, long after we were gone. It was a resigned coolness, a sense of absolution that was fearless and affected all who paid it homage. The hope of the Pacific would've normally held me transfixed for minutes, possibly hours on the shoreline, but not today. I was too miserable today.

Today I was going in.

I didn't even pause to think about how there weren't too many other people in the water or that it was March. I was ripe and had to get the stink off me. It was more than just physical stink, it was something else. I needed to shed the past few weeks of my mind, the last few months of my life. And so I did. I shed clothing faster than a hot-rodded teen post-prom while booking it to the tide. Thankfully, I was running too fast to realize I was diving into fifty-degree water. The head-first plunge into the icy oncoming waves shocked and paralyzed my body. When I hit the surface I was hyperventilating. I felt high and good and my muscles seemed to thrive from the water's numbing effects.

"You need a wet-suit you kook!" Shouted my high-knotted friend from the shore.

I waved at him, proudly. *Look at me dad!* I didn't care; my boxer-briefs were handling the job just fine. Sure, my man parts had now gone internal but I was invigorated. The tang of salt water on my tongue was a memory from childhood. I was splashing around and jumping, diving, tumbling under-water like a two year old in the tub. I hadn't felt that good and free in months. It lasted maybe five minutes before my body gave into the cold but it was damn near perfect, I tell you.

The Pacific was exactly how I imagined the West to be:

Adrenaline on High
Life on Chill

...it was both those things.

Chapter 8

Lickity-Split Tomorrow
The Affable Looneys Tonight

The Affable Looneys are not another ridiculous band name (although I can't say I'm one hundred percent sure on that).

The Affable Looneys that I am referring to are Jon and his uber-laid back, disconnected pack of loons that all live (or squat) in a communal house on the border of Silverlake/Echo Park in East LA. They were an odd bunch to put it mildly – each one speaking a nuanced dialect that had the pacing and cadence of a southerner, but the bro-man slang and peyote-induced drawl of one Keanu Reeves. What was more astounding than the way they talked was just how marvelously nice everyone was. We're talking incredibly nice here. Jon, my new high-knotted and good-hearted friend, had even gone so far as to have a couch made up for me before we got back to the house. Who does that for a stranger? Let alone one reeking of Boone's Farm?

The Affable Looneys, that's who.

✻

I had spent a few hours on the beach, lying in the sun, taking in the sound of the waves; dying happily. I was entering into that third and final stage of alcohol withdrawal – remorse. No one ever really tells you but it is much, much worse than the physical manifestations. The self-loathing. The guilt. The shame. They come on slow and unexpected and in their suffocating stillness, the sand I lay on turns quick. I cannot even begin to express what sad, imaginary childhood delusions of "mom and dad and son as one big happy family" consumed my mind over the next twelve hours. The disheartening thoughts of "what I missed out on" were pervasive and though I ought to have sat down and wrestled with them; truly ruminated on how these apparitions of dreams never shared are probably some sort of healing necessity, some proper exercise in coming to grips with reality…I'm sorry, but I just can't. It was too painful then and I don't have the strength to revisit it now. Call me weak. Call me a poor narrator. Call me anything but a man without pain.

Jon had left me sprawled out on the sand a good while ago. The good news was that I wasn't alone on the beach. A seagull had come and parked himself beside me. We made friends. He was a chipper little guy. I asked him what his deal was with parking lots but he just blew me off. I realized I was being impolite and apologized. I then informed him that I was just happy he wasn't a crow or a turkey buzzard. His little coos and caws as he preened his wings reminded me that I was still alive and though I couldn't communicate it to him, I think he knew I appreciated the company.

I lay there zoned out for a long while and soon wondered if Jon would indeed come back for me. He had had plans for Venice – some things to do, people to see, drugs to deal – who knows. It was all very general and vague to me. I would soon learn that this was the way with everything to everyone out west: general and vague. Some might call it laid-back but that's not really it. The conversation feels empty, almost hollowed out, excavated of substance. This is not to say that people didn't like to speak deeply about topics. On the contrary, many a convo was quote-unquote *deep*:

"Yeah, man, that's the problem with politics today, it's the ruination of civilized society. Can you pass the guac?"

What was disconcerting was that that depth always lacked a certain clarity, detail, coherence…and more often than not, meaning and common sense. The hazy communiqué produced a dialogue that evaded any real connection between listener and speaker. Not that this is in any way news to you, I'm sure you've heard all about these superficial stereotypes that have consumed the city for decades. And though it is alarming and at times to this easterner, terrifying, it has become increasingly more difficult for me to find fault in any of it. For only after a few short days of blissful weather, I too felt a change coming over. A laziness in speech. A weakening of dialogue. A change that is in truth, nothing more than a byproduct of too much sun.

And can you blame them?

I couldn't.

Why spend time getting down to brass tacks, meditating on the actual, when it's so much nicer to speculate about the theoretical, ideological, mildly political. I mean, why get upset over anything when tomorrow was certainly going to deliver the exact same thing? Another gorgeous day. So, the people liked to float in some sort of Simpletonian Splendor. Some surfer's home-grown Duderonomy. Who was I to try to supply anchor and weight to conversation? From what pedestal in Peekskill did I preach? How could I honestly lay claim that the easterner's approach was that much better? Sure, we talked about real shit and real problems back east and in its greatest moments, employed a flare of snark that made life worth living, but tell me, is that any better when every single person I know is now in need of a therapist to make it through the day? I guess when it comes down to it, this whole east vs. west approach to life, we need only ask ourselves if ignorance is indeed bliss? Or, is bliss, in fact, a pill from your psychiatrist to take the edge off? Or a Budweiser for those who can't afford the pills? *Who knows?* All I did know was that as much as I wished, and would continue to wish that people spoke differently out west, it would be an aimless endeavor. The bubble remains intact and suspended in air for a reason: the sun will most definitely come out again tomorrow and with it, the hot vapid air of Los Angelino language.

Remaining the poor narrator that I am, I forgot to mention that Jon was nice enough to invite me to tag along with him on his Venice excursions. I gave it some thought but seeing how I turned into a birthing water buffalo as soon as I hit the sand, I told him all movement was out of the question. I told him I'd be right where he left me till he got back, should he decide to come back. If that was the case, he said, he'd give me a ride back to Silver Lake and if need be, a place to crash. I thanked him continually until he left and then spent the entire day recuperating on the beach. My seagull buddy had now long since flown the coop. People walked by while I baked. I roasted evenly like a slow-turning turkey stuffed with a beer can slowly seeping out its contents. When I started to sweat, I'd jump in the ocean and start the whole process over again.

What felt like twenty minutes must've been a couple of hours for Jon was back and sitting next to me in no time. He'd brought with him Gatorade, water and pretzels. I was humbled by his thoughtfulness. We watched my first Pacific sunset together in a pleasant silence and for the first time in a long time, I tasted sobriety.

It tasted good, warm and ultraviolet.

Who knew an orange disk disappearing over a far off line could always come so damned original. Say what you will, but I tell you now and I'll tell you fifty years from now, a sunset isn't cliché. We try our damndest as a species to make it so, but it remains impervious to our demeanings. It is perfect, in every way. It is better than perfect…it starts the night.

✿

On the way back to Silver Lake I was startled to realize that Jon and I had yet to exchange names.

"I'm Frank, by the way," I said, nonchalantly. "Just realized we never did the 'formal introductions thing.'" Jon nodded but a little. "You always this nice to strangers?"

He shrugged his shoulders at the word 'strangers' and said, "It's Jon." He was forbearing over the exchange. Cramped red taillights went on ahead of us for miles and miles and I thought it was the traffic that had him ticked. It wasn't. It was something else, "What's a name anyway but something your parents gave you?"

I couldn't tell if he was being rhetorical or sarcastic so I played both sides of the field safe. "Don't mean to offend you or anything." I said. "I can't tell you how nice this is, you doin' this for me. This just wouldn't be kosher back home. Lettin' some random dude crash a couch or whatever."

Jon was silent for a bit and I didn't know what to say so I said nothing at all. Another violent wave of a headache was coming on and I felt anxiety rear its bastard head. The unease of relying on a stranger for help was setting in and I sharply remembered how submitting control has always been my toughest of challenges. *To let go.* To not only let go, but to sit back and smile as the reins whipped around in the wild, wild wind.

A couple of long minutes went by and then Jon found his words, "The way I've always seen it man," he canted his head slightly down and to the right, the tail-lights splashing a red glow on his face. "Is that everyone we ever meet is a stranger at one time or another. So, if everyone is a stranger...no one is."

"Hm."

"Where is home?" He asked.

"New York."

"Ah. The Yin to our Yang. Makes sense."

"What's that?"

"Aw nothin' man. There's no strangers in my house. That's all you need to know. You look like you need some more rest. We're almost there."

"Thanks Jon. Really, man. Thank you." There was another silence and I felt nervous and awkward. I saw him notice my hands shaking so I quickly clasped them together. 'He must think me a junkie,' I thought. I reached out instinctively for a mundane topic, "So I hear you guys have to watch football in the morning out here?"

"No need for small talk." He waved his hand across the wheel like a Jedi knight. "I can tell you're burned out."

"Okay."

"Don't really take you for the football watchin' type, anyway."

"My beer gut would argue otherwise."

He smiled and kept the wheels between the lines. The highway that had been all but jammed on our way home, flooded with cars of every class and color, was now moving fluidly. I dozed off again and then he was nudging me awake. We were there.

The Looney Bin.

✢

Jon's neighborhood offered much to be taken in by. The first and most obvious was the terrain – it was unbelievably hilly where Jon lived. Not that I knew what LA was supposed to be like, but his neighborhood looked like a snapshot of San Francisco. Except, instead of wealthy Painted Ladies and BMWs galore, there were ill-maintained bungalows and dirt-filled yards with burnt grass and rusty pickup trucks; it was a mug shot of rundown real estate, one plot more unappealing and helpless than the next. There was also the unavoidable smell of dog shit in the air. I wanted to believe that it was mulch or fresh-spread fertilizer but I would've been kidding myself. A low hum of a thousand flies swarming nearby gave me the willies. The house was located in the poorer section of Echo Park; the part still untouched by the oncoming wave of hipster gentrification and the part that would remain untouched, according to Hector, the most talkative of Jon's roommates. Hector's words would take on a whole new meaning later that night when I woke to the sound of gunshots and helicopters circling overhead, spotlights like laser beams casting down authority into the deep dark.

Note: megaphones ring out clear in starlight.

This might be a good time to mention that Jon and Hector and the rest of the Affable Looneys were not hipsters. They were something else. A big wacky hybrid of something else: World Class Surfers, Joshua Tree Campers, Burning Man Dancers, K2 Climbers, Nature's Wild Men and Greenpeacers alike. Spiritual descendants of a Native American wandering tribe whose souls were constantly adrift and only steadied by the sudden onset of adrenaline. Nomad doesn't quite capture it and Gypsy doesn't do it justice either. Traveler is the opposite of what these guys were. They were at home wherever they went. Their ease and casual assuredness about the environment and ideology they operated within commanded my respect and I felt lucky that Jon was the first person I had spoken to in LA. And staying there in that house, under the halo of the world traveled, amongst a group of people bereft of insecurity, I experienced a mindset both foreign and peculiar. It was some weird fusion of New Age spiritualism. They were all on a Buddhist-like kick that I could never even fathom being a part of and yet, for that short time, was a part of it. Swaddled in it. Perhaps they knew how badly I was hurting, or perhaps they were this nice to everyone. Whatever it was, it was appreciated tenfold.

Upon entering their two-story ranch, I couldn't help but notice the mass of works by Muir and Thoreau piled up in the corners of their living room. Eastern philosophy books were spilling over onto the old Mayan throw rug on the floor while other stacks of spiritualized literature covered the coffee table. Someone had painted Ram Dass's *Be Here Now* circular symbol on the wall and the burning of incense made my nose wiggle. 'At least it's not patchouli,' I thought. 'Thank god.' There was also a smattering of large photography art books lying around and then, playfully, like a true tease — a couple of vintage Playboys. My gaze naturally held there a moment longer. The 60's cover girls were cheeky and humorous and completely out of place and yet somehow fitting. I adored those tasteful covers, adored 'em good. What was most remarkable was how truly unrevealing they were. I mean, not even a nipple. Just cleavage and legs. The mystery of what wasn't shown made it undeniably more sexy and provocative than any of today's photo-shopped shaven-mavens.

John had gone into the kitchen while I got my bearings in the living room and came back with beer in hand.

"Here," he said. "This will help."

I shook my head no. Actually, I think I said "please god no," but he only pushed the beer out further as if I had no choice in the matter. He didn't say much but I was figuring more and more that when he did talk, you listened. "It's homemade with agave and herbs," he told me. "Full of nutrients," he said. "Will help with the shakes," he went on. "Your appetite too."

I cared about none of that crap if it meant drinking a green beer. He waited and stood there till I cracked the damn thing so I drank of it what I could, making little whimpering noises with every sip, absorbing the rest of the Affable Looneys' sanctuary as I puttered along...half alive, half very much something else.

Despite every window being wide open, there was a dusty smell about the place. It must've been the furniture: old, recycled couches, futons and wooden chairs faced one another and there was no TV. Then came the kitchen or what I

affectionately referred to as the botanical gardens. The green-
ery in that room was too much for me, too much to even
attempt to lay down an accurate portrayal here. 'Botanists
don't have green rooms like this,' I thought as I sauntered
about, treading lightly amidst the plant-life that easily took
several years to nurse.

"Everyone is out right now but they'll be back in ten or
so. " Jon said. "I just let 'em know we landed. You'll like 'em.
Good peoples."

I nodded to him gratefully and continued looking
around. Vines were growing up the walls and cracking paint,
rooting themselves to the infrastructure of the house. I probably use the word too much, but the kitchen was perfectly
absurd; like something out of the last scene in *Jumanji*. And
don't get me wrong, I love me some nature, but these guys,
they were *in touch* with nature. So much so, that after any
conversation we had that revolved around the *disappearing
wild*, I'd find myself puzzled and completely turned about.
Sans sense. And not in a good way, mind you. It was a little
discouraging for I, too, wanted to be one with my surroundings, but not if it meant sounding like Mathew
McCahoney after a long waltz with the local Shaman. This
all said, it was highly amusing to listen to them jaw. At one
moment, they'd be touching on transcendental spiritual one-
ness and the next; they'd all be caught up in the grooves of
their palms discussing vibrations and light (this was where I'd
bow out or kindly plead for a bullet to the brain). It was pure
entertainment is what it was:

"See man." Hector said, poking at the fire pit while we
smoked in the backyard. I had offered him a Toscano and he
was all too happy to join. "What those guys were talking
about...that shit's the *then* man, the *then.*" He'd pull drag

slow to let his next-level parable take flight. "And where we're talkin', man...this shit is the *now*. See?" He held his hand up in front of me and turned it around. Back and forth. Back and forth. "*The now*. But what we talk about man, what we talk about in this house, around this fire," he stoked the red coals a little more to emphasize his genius to come. "That shit is *the future*."

I nodded along. What else do you do with that? Nod. Smoke some more. Nod some more. I didn't even know who 'those guys' were nor how he got to telling me this whimsical story of wisdom and shrooms in the first place. Once again, it didn't matter. The vagueness was a key part of the storytelling, an essential factor in it all making sense. Besides, I didn't give a shit about the particulars – I now had a place to stay, a place to rest, a place to find myself again. In many ways I imagined the house to be what rehab might've been like: a strange place full of strange people all rallied behind a strange new dream.

There were about seven or ten of them in all who crashed at the house, a couple girls, mostly young men. Always coming, always going. Everyone there was lean-bodied, easy-eyed, and unfettered by stress with skin drawn taut and colorful by the sun. They all resembled the peak of health. The gals, too, were incredibly fit, attractive inasmuch as you can find someone attractive who only washes their hair twice a year, and also extremely quiet and south Pacific. They had names like Reiya and Miho. They smiled often and swooned at the guys of the house like they were immortals. Everyone was very content with just being and the silence that came attached to its backside didn't bode well for the socially inclined like myself. Wit and banter were a lost cause in the house – an extra effort that wasn't necessary. It was all weird and wild to me. A trip. The girls seemed to be smitten, completely in love with Jon but they seemed to only shack up with other guys there, who of course, all looked damn near identical to Jon. It was tough to keep their names straight. Hector was the only one who didn't seem to fit in with the lot. He was round faced, round bodied, and roundabout minded. I naturally felt more at home next to a man who didn't have veins popping out of his biceps and found good company there. I left them all by the fire pit before nine that first night and thanked them again, graciously, for the hospitality.

✲

I slept for what felt like an eternity. Noon came early the next day and with it, the realization that I was now in the same time zone as June. I was sweating yet again.

A two-day hangover.

Jesus. Fuck.

I sat up and could tell this one wasn't as bad. Manageable. And plus, today was the day. *My day. The day I'd finally find June.* When I made my way to the kitchen table, I found to my surprise that Hector was the only one left in the house.

"They're all out on the water." He said, his eyes steeped in a large hard-backed, art book.

"You didn't go?"

"Don't surf, man."

"Oh yeah? Me either. My balance is shit."

"My balance is good. My swimming…not so good."

"Oh?"

"Yeah. I'm much more of a floating device than any-thing."

His humor was unexpected so I laughed unduly hard at him.

"I'll remember that if we're ever ship-wrecked together." I said.

"Do it to it. See these arms?" He held up one pipe in classic bicep-flexing fashion and flapped the flub of his tricep back and forth. "Natural floaties."

We laughed together for a good bit. I was heartened by Hector's good nature and wanted to befriend him immediately. Some people just have that gift. Some call it magnetism but it is more than that, it is disarming. And talking to Hector was to talk without weaponry, shields cast aside.

"Whatch'ya got there?" I asked, peering over his shoulder.

It was a massive art photography book with beautiful black and white images of naked women all smoking the devil's lettuce. He flipped it over to reveal its cover and it read *CONTACT HIGH*. A perfect title. I was fucking jealous of that title it was so good. He saw how much it agreed with me and opened it back up to where he was before.

"Well if that ain't perfection I don't know what is." I said.

The girl was sprawled out on some sort of bench with one leg in the air, toes in perfect ballerina point, extending all the way to the ceiling and nothing but a white sheet draped over her body. Everything was elongated but round. Supple. Inviting. Magnificent. Almost regal, in a dirty underground royalty sort of way. She was allowing smoke to fall out of her mouth in such a manner that it sat salaciously on her lips and I felt immediately out of place looking at such a book with Hector by my side.

"The lighting here is *to the moon.*" He said.

He was admiring the work. I was dumbfounded. How could he fondle himself under the table while so absorbed in a shooting style? I had never looked at such a book for lighting. I had never believed there could be that much technical work behind nudie polaroids. I was wrong. Hector saw me squirming internally for the lighting quality he'd just described and took the reins:

"Look here." He pointed to her hipbones and the indentations that ran the whole way from her ribs to her happy place. "See how he holds the shadow faintly on the front of her body. You can see every groove, every curve, every... thing. *The dude's painting a celestial goddess with a lens, man!*"

He was right. You could see everything. I was getting a semi. I needed to avert my eyes or go to the bathroom so I made my way to the cupboards.

"Ya got any coffee 'round here?" I asked.

"Nah, just tea. Water's still hot though if you wanna make some." He pointed off to the opposite direction without pulling his head from the page, "Mugs are over there."

"Ah, that's okay." I looked around for a bit and fought off the urge to go park right next to him and stare into the skin mag till my little man was content. "So, how'd you wind up here, Heck?"

"In LA?"

"Nah, the house. How'd you end up livin' in the botanical gardens of Echo Park?"

"Oh. Like everybody else, just wound up stayin'."

"Yeah?"

"Yeap."

"Well you didn't just stumble in did you?"

"Nah nah. Happened to me same way it happened to you."

"Jon brought you in too?"

"Yeap," he was still focused on the same image, literally unable to peel his head from the book. "Him and a couple others. Must-a-been almost five years ago now. I was on the beach with my camera one day when I saw Jon and some of the guys out on the water — just crushing wave after wave. Next thing you know, I'm shooting all these guys for a living."

"Just like that?"

"Just like that."

"Damn, that's great." I poured myself a glass of water and sat down. "You travel with them and stuff?"

"Any chance I get."

"You must love it."

"It's the end-all." He finally perked his head up from his book and lowered his voice, dropping into a sincere and breathy whisper. "These dudes won't tell you, but they're fucking legendary. Zev just got back from Hawaii last month with a video of him on a forty-foot monster. You should-a-seen him on that thing, like it was just another day at the office."

"Jesus."

Hector smiled. He had a knowing glint in his eye that made me think his own work must've been of high quality, the likes of which worthy enough to capture a tiny figurine on a forty-footer, and he too, wouldn't talk about it. I liked him all the more for it. His sly modesty, his humble heart. He withdrew and refocused his gaze back toward *Contact High.*

Damn, that's a good title.

"Say, Hector. You wouldn't happen to know where the Silver Lake Lounge is, would you?"

"Well that depends...how much money ya got?"

"Um."

I just looked at him.

"Nothin?" He asked.

"I got a credit card..."

"Well that won't get you too far 'round here Chico."

First Rico. Now Chico. What the hell's goin' on around here? Does everyone give people cheap nicknames out west? And why are they always Latino in nature? It's true, coming from Hector's mouth, Sport or Slick, would've seemed downright condescending, but Christ! Can someone cut me some slack here? Up until now I hadn't even mentioned June or my reason for being in LA to anyone in the house. Jon hadn't asked in the car rides to and from the beach and obviously never felt the need to. I guess, to these guys, no one needed a reason to just up and go visit a city on a whim. I guess, to these guys, that *was* the reason to go.

"You need to have dat greeeen, *hombre.*" Hector put on a malignant Mexican accent, which was quite possibly the most ludicrous thing ever, since he himself was Mexican and well educated and his English rather sharp.

Again, I just looked at him.

"Bro. I fucks wit you!" He grabbed the side of his belly and cranked out a laugh that lasted far too many Mississippis. "If you're gonna be out here, first thing you need to learn is how to give zero fucks."

"Okay." I said, tartly.

I didn't like being told how to make it in America.

"Look at your face! HA-HA! You're still giving fucks!"

He laughed harder and longer this time around.

"Hector." I was serious. "This is me giving all the fucks in the world. I need to get to the Silver Lake Lounge, *tonight.* Can you help me out or not?"

"*Aye. Chill chill.* You'll burn up out here with an attitude like that. The Lounge is only eight blocks away. Not even. I'll roll with you. You gotta loosen up your life, Frank. You gotta live for the day! Things are never as bad as they seem, they just aren't."

If he pumped out one more cliché I was going to scream. He didn't, however, and was kind enough to walk me to the lounge. He offered me a pair of sunglasses before we left. They were massive, damn near animated with their neon green frames and smelled of Hawaiian Tropic sun tan lotion but I took them anyway. If I were to run into Clint Eastwood again, I would be dammed if I had to look at him through squinting, unprotected eyes.

"Those are my burning man jams." Hector said, proudly as I placed them on. "Those things'll get you laid out here, mang."

There were no mirrors in the house so I was left to my own devices to imagine how silly I looked.

"Lezz go, lezz go!" He barked. "I'm gettin' pretty gringo these days. The sun calls me home!" He lumbered out the door, adoring his two forearms that were easily a shade or two darker than mahogany.

✿

"HOLY SHIT. THAT'S HER!"

As we rounded the corner to the main drag of Sunset Boulevard, I saw a big wheat plaster ad on the side of a building for *Lickity-Split.* It was legit awesome. (Listen to me. I sound like a teenie bopper from the 50's going to see Peggy Lee or June Christy. God, kill me now. Why didn't I just go for gold and call the band poster 'pretty neat.' Oh well, the hell am I gonna do? I'm a fan before hearing the music, shoot me. You would be too if you saw the poster.) The whole representation fit right in with the retro-wave of graphic design in the haps this past decade. Hazy, sunny imagery washed out a distant group of band members on a tall grassy knoll in the background. And then there she was, Juniper. Alive and real in the foreground, trail-blazing front woman glory like a badass-brunette-*Blondie*. She was decked out in all black and shading her eyes from the sun with tousled hair that swayed consciously in front of her face. She was just as beautiful and fierce and endearing as I remembered.

"No wonder you give all the fucks, bro." Hector joked.

We chuckled a bit and I carefully took down the sign. Just then a girl walked by and I stopped halfway, worried that she might think I was vandalizing. She was a tiny blonde with a tanned hide and a belly shirt that read, "LIFE SUCKS AND SO DO I." It was the statement that had me captivated more than anything. She caught eyes with me and smiled. I smiled back and felt boyish and transparent. She passed by and both Hector and I admired her backside as she made her way up the hill. Her white denim cut-offs were so short and tight that they might as well have been swimsuit bottoms. She looked back and smiled our way again. I raised my hand to wave to her like an idiot and Hector slapped my hand away. She laughed and was gone up over the hill.

"Burning man jams," Hector said, nodding in appreciation of the moment. "Burning man jams."

I had completely forgotten I was in clown glasses. I got back to work on the poster and finally finger-nailed it off.

"What are you going to do with it?" Hector asked.

"I dunno. It's important – might be worth something someday, ya know?"

Hector sighed. "New Yorkers. Always tryna turn a buck."

"I meant as value, Hector. Like, to me. *Valuable to me.*"

"Oh." He smiled. "Right on."

I read the set time aloud. "*8 P.M.*" I looked at my watch and became frazzled. Less than eight hours away. "You want to check it out with me?" I asked Hector. "I'm not gonna lie, I could use the company. I'll be more nervous than a born-again in the Red District."

Hector looked over June once more as I rolled up the poster.

"She the reason you out here?"

"Yes. She's the only reason I got right now."

"*Aye.* You gringos and your melodrama."

I forced a smile at him but my lips lost their will. He sensed then the deep, insecure need of support that lay hidden nervously behind his sunglasses. It was a need of friendship.

His tone changed, "Well o'course I'll come man. I luh me some new vibrations. I know some of the others will check it out too. *That's how we do, bro.*"

I thought about offering him money to stop talking that way but, once again, I bit my tongue and rightfully so: both he and the entire lot of Affable Looneys would have my back later that night and be in attendance for the show. Though it pained me greatly at first, I finally started to care less about how they were talking and more about what they were saying. That sentiment may sound lovely, but it is still much easier said than done.

*

The hour hand on my watch spun around eight times in four seconds and 8PM was upon me. The whole house came along and we walked the eight blocks to the venue together. I trailed nervously to the rear, feet stumbling one over the other in unsettled anticipation of the events to come. As my mind reeled, I looked at everyone's shoes and noticed they all had on the same brand and makes – it was either Toms or Vans black classics, the low-ankle boys. Nothing else. Every-one, every single one of them had a calf tattoo and it made me laugh. My favorite was Miho's; it was of Betty Boop bent over with her ass staring you in the face while she pulled out a simmering cooked head from an oven. If you looked close enough, you would see that it was Hitler's head steaming on the platter.

We made it to the lounge early and I had a second to check out the scene: it was your average, dimly lit sidebar venue. A place where up and up performers came to work the kinks out of their set or pray, by random chance, that a talent scout might be in the crowd that night. Time sped ahead on fast-forward and I cannot tell you a thing about the opening act. I was incoherently nervous and sober and no longer hung-over and needed a drink. Badly. I held off... for a little. It was useless to hold off. I knew a Green Flash West Coast IPA would help with the nerves that came with approaching June. I ordered up and down it went. It worked its magic for the most part. Except, I still had no idea what I was going to say to her. All of my pre-thought-out storylines and excuses had left me and wouldn't come back. I was blank, gone white, like an empty page out of this sad-sap book.

I stood there in the back of the bar, waiting impatiently.

I hoped the sight of her would help...

...it did.

...And so would the sound.

The lights went up from darkness and fell again, landing on a cool gel blue that would remain throughout the set. Then *Lickity-Split* was on and June walked out to the mic like a woman born for the stage. Her presence was paranormal, effortless and cool. They might've only stood there for five seconds before the first chord was struck. Then June lit off like a firework, dancing and jumping around enthusiastically, embodying the sound waves that pummeled the crowd, gyrating her powerful vocals from somewhere down near her pelvic region...and the audience responded in kind. The confidence of her first long, jawing note soared clean and true and retained its raspy sensuality that all but sealed the deal for me: *Lickity-Split* was the real thing. And June, good-god! June! She personified that charming soul a performer either has or doesn't have. It is not something that can be worked on nor learned and is much more than just talent – it is something inherent, something that just comes through you. Much like conducting electricity, to be a performer is to be the handler of a current, a maestro of emotion, an amplifier whose performance ebbs and flows with the audience, where the heartbeats of all in attendance start to thump and bang in perfect harmony with the act on stage. She was only a quarter of the way into the opener and my heart was already railing against my chest, on the brink of leaping from my ribcage and spilling my embarrassing love for her all over the floor.

I glanced to my right and saw the Affable Looneys dancing. They were vibing it hard. Swooning unabashedly with limbs flowing all about themselves, hippie-like in their arrhythmic carelessness. They could hardly keep a beat but then

again, swaying doesn't really need to be on beat. I saw Hector
up toward the front. He didn't dance. He did more of a jolly,
bop and a kick with each leg. Back and forth, kick. Back and
forth, kick. Everyone was along for the ride and the entire set
flew by. They killed it. *She killed it.* Her voice, booze-worn
and alive, was exotic, like hot white coals that danced upon
unexpecting irises. You combine all this with her zealous
presence on stage and what you got was an entire performance that echoed a refreshing take on garage-slanted indie
rock: The *Yeah Yeah Yeahs* meets *Metric* with fluttering,
sun-drenched guitars and progressive, syncopated beats rec-
orded in a tin can.

Mm. Hot.

I wrote a poem right there on the spot in honor of their
performance. It's called *Good Shit, Goddammit.*

Good Shit, Goddammit

I'm a fan.
I'm a fan.
Fucking kill me now,
I'm a fan.

As you can tell, it still needs work but it is truest to the
emotions felt at the time and therefore, a ditty to be shelved
alongside Byron or Keats.

It was a huge relief, of course, to adore *Lickity-Split's* set.
I don't really know what I would've done had the whole
thing gone horribly – if the talent wasn't there. If they out
and out sucked. I'm sure I would've still been supportive and
taken that shitty low road where you don't say it was bad but
you certainly can't say it was good either. Tell me, is there

anything worse than loving someone whose dream might not ever come true? Apparently there is: loving someone *knowing* their dream would never come true.

The lights of the Lounge went down to a round of loud cheers and applause and any of my inner-biased doubts toward the quality of the show were laid to rest. I downed the rest of my beer, scrounged together some flimsy courage and forged my way to the front of the stage. I caught eyes with Hector who gave me the hang-loose sign as I passed by.

"She's killer!" He said, smiling like a goon. He was on Molly, I think. If that were the case, *Cher* would've been killer to the man. "Go get her maaaan." I gave him a reassuring nervous tick and he, in turn, knocked me on the shoulder hurtling me toward the stage. "Git up 'dere, honnes!"

Lickity-Split had begun packing up their own gear, which I loved. They were so small that they didn't even have a techie yet. I glided up to the mic, sliding forth on a plane of confidence and bold moves, retelling myself again and again that this was all meant to be. *But was it?* Yes. Yes. *It had to be.* It was all now or never. Six months and three thousand miles later and I was finally doing it. June turned around and just as I was about to yell her name a man came bee-lining from the opposite side of the crowd, his eyes fixed adoringly on June.

"Rocked it!" He yelled.

He looked like Adam Levine.

Fuck.

When she caught eyes with him I knew he wasn't just another fan. She walked up to the edge of the stage and threw her arms around him. He hoisted her from the platform and there they were, holding each other on the ground floor, no more than five feet away from me.

"Absolutely killed it!" I heard him say again.

She smiled deeply, genuinely and their lips locked.

My heart dropped.

I couldn't move. The blood had literally left my body and I went cold, frozen in time. He was kissing her like a freshman out to prove a point and there I was watching every slobbering miscue. It was gross. Too much tongue, not enough charisma. Why the hell was she with this punk? His hair was easily super-glued together and he had a chain hanging from a carabineer on his belt that was attached to his wallet like a middle school Misfit for chrissake. 'This is bushleague,' I thought. I couldn't look anymore but I couldn't move either. I used my peripherals to glance back toward where Hector was standing and I must've looked like I was having a heart attack because he was already by my side, throwing his massive bear paw around me and pulling me back toward the bar.

"It's okay, man. It's okay." He kept saying. I must've looked sickly because Hector's inner-nurse was now out and on full display. "Plenty-a-women out west. Pah-lenty... Forget-about-her, man..."

And so on.

I'm pretty sure he continued sooth-saying for a minute or two but the adrenaline had taken full grasp of the wheel and I couldn't really remember anything. Cloudy thoughts and disbelief danced around upstairs, their steps all-wrong, their choreography gone volcanic, their music a concerto of lost souls.

"I flew three thousand miles to say something to her... *her*, Hector. *HER*. And now I can't say anything..."

I was beside myself. My mouth was dry and speaking was difficult.

"It's been a while though, hasn't it?" Hector asked, setting me down on a stool, searching my eyes for signs of mental edema.

There was no answer.

Catatonia slumped on a barstool.

"Frank." He shook me a bit. "You said it yourself! It's been a *long* time, right?"

"It has…but still. This was my night." I was too let down to feel sad or even empty. "What the hell do I do now? What the hell am I gonna do now?"

"We'll figure it out. We always do."

I was fed up with life and felt another one of his golden clichés coming on.

"*Cuz' that's how you do 'round here?*" I said.

He choked up a half-smile at my petulant sarcasm and motioned to the bartender for two more beers. I pulled the little yellow sticky note from my wallet and hopelessly eyed its contents once more. I started to feel sorry for myself. *I hated feeling sorry for myself.* I tried to think of the bright side. The adventure of the West. The excitement of going places far and away. The learning curve of the new and for-eign. The promise of good-hearted people like the Affable Looneys. The fact that the world is full of women and how getting laid with strange tail is bar none the best thing ever and on and on and on.

None of it helped.

I looked at the note once more before deciding that I needed to leave the lounge.

"Hey Hec-"

I had turned to where Hector had been standing but he was no longer there.

"Frank?"

It was June.

Holy fuck it was June! Up close and beautiful. Her eyes large and confused, her hair radiating pheromones, her cheeks flushed, her brow beading with sweat. She was fucking gorgeous. I wanted to kiss her right then and there but I couldn't even blink. Time passed and I still had the note in my hand. 'Do something!' My body screamed. 'Say something you shmuck!' My brain wouldn't listen. Nothing came out. My heart puttered like an engine freshly jumped.

"Wha—what are you doing here?" She asked.

I couldn't speak. I was petrified. Someone had jammed an iron rod in my throat and I was figuring how to pry it back out again.

"Are you okay?" Her eyebrows smushed together.

"You remembered me." I said, a remark worthy of a toilet flushing.

"Of course I did. Obviously."

Again, I couldn't speak. It was maybe the first time in my life I had ever endured an awkward silence and said nothing. I just sat there, silent and stupid, each millisecond a millennia.

"What are you doing here?" She asked again.

She was slow moving.

But I – I was a goddammed glacier.

"Uh. Yeah. Sorry." I paused. I glanced down at the little yellow note in my hand and gave it to her. I didn't know what else to do. "I came here to give this to you." She looked at it as if she were looking at an eighth grade boyfriend's yearbook entry. Except that the decade-old-ex now worked at Wal-Mart and kept calling her on their anniversary. "And to let you know I found it only a couple days ago." I wanted to stop talking but I couldn't. "And well, it's a long story and you know how school-boy campfire stories go...but yeah. Listen. I know you've got someone. And that's great. I just wanted you to know why I was so delayed in getting back to you."

June couldn't speak. She looked as off-color and uneasy as I felt. I continued on like always when nerves got the best of me, completely unconscious of what came fumbling from my mouth:

"This looks insane I know. I think it is, too. Hell, I just spent the night with all those hippie-Jesuses over there and I'm pretty sure they think it's insane too. But I came here to tell you that I'm sorry and that this was not how I would've wanted things to go. Ya know? And wow. *Just wow.* Your voice! I was not expecting that. Like, at all. It was amazing. To be honest, part of me was praying you'd be bad so I wouldn't like you so damned much anymore." Her lips parted and a half-smile was shining through. "But look, you're good. You're really good and we spent one night together so this is crazy enough as is and yeah. I'll let this all be now. Okay? Nothing mental on this end, all right? Didn't mean to scare you...and when I saw you with your guy I wasn't even going to say anything..."

There was a much-needed beat, I took a breath and she finally broke in:

"I'm sorry. This is too much."

She re-read the note.

"No, I know. I'll go.."

"Let me talk for a second." She spluttered out.

"Okay."

She read more carefully.

"So wait. You just found this?"

I nodded.

"When?"

"Two days ago."

"And then you flew out here to see me?"

I nodded again.

She shook her head in disbelief.

"Just how crazy are you?"

"A little too crazy I'm afraid." I cleared my throat. "Runs in the family."

"I'll say."

"Well I tried to call, but your girlfriends told me you were unreachable while touring. I'm sure they think I'm crazy too. Paula and Chloe in particular."

"Paula...?" Her eyes searched for the face. "*Oh my god.* You went through Paula to find me?"

I nodded. "I won't show you the battle scars."

"She hit you?"

"Nah-nah." I laughed.

"Well, who knows. I wouldn't put it past her. She was crazy...But You! You are the craziest. This is the craziest! It's unbelievable, though," she smiled an old familiar smile at the note. "Really, it is."

My heart came back around.

"You really liked the show?" She asked, meekly.

"My god! You were on. You were so on. Seriously, just keep doing what you're doing. You'll get picked up. You *have* to get picked up. If not, the music world can go fuck itself."

She laughed. I saw a small flicker of light shine through a doorway. It impressed upon us the hope of finding a normal conversation. And just as I reached for the door handle, her man friend walked up from behind her and slammed the damn thing shut. He had swirling mousseline hair that looked animated and flammable and stood perpetually erect, completely defiant of gravity and style. He placed his arm around her and asked what was so funny. I saw the note crumple in her hand and with it, my chances with her.

"Oh nothing." She said. "Just catching up with an old friend from back east. Del, this is Frank. Frank, Del."

"Oh yeah?" Del said, eyeing me skeptically. "Well welcome to the best coast, brothah. Get laid yet?"

"Del." June wasn't amused.

"Ah, c'mon. He seems all right, eh? *EH?* What's that Frank?" He poked and prodded me a couple times, tickling me weirdly in the ribs. "You all right! Yeah?"

"Are you asking me if I want to have sex with you?" I asked. June spit out a frothy mist of beer. "I appreciate the offer, but I'm good right now."

Del did not understand sarcasm therefore Del was not a fan of sarcasm. Del was an LA native.

"Alright then." He brushed me off. "We goin' babe?" He tapped June lightly, playfully on the rump. I gritted my teeth. "The night's young and we've got *important* people who need to talk to you."

"Yeah, yeah. Just one second, I'll meet you outside." She said.

He left and threw shade my way until he got out the door. I guess that *important* comment was somehow directed at me. Sunny people throwing shade is a funny sight to behold.

"So. Del?" I asked. She batted both her eyes and pursed her lips. "Tell me, is he gonna come out with another *Songs About Jane* or did he peak back when we were in college?"

"Yeaaaah." She drank some more of her beer and chuckled lightly. "We've been seeing each other for a couple months now. He's kind of my manager and I – well, yeah, I thought you were nowhere to be found."

"That makes two of us."

"I like him though." She brought the glass to her lips and showed no signs of slowing its tilt.

"I know, I can tell. It's okay. We don't owe each other anything." The crowd was louder than usual so I leaned into her ear, her smell as subtle and as intoxicating as ever. "Whadd'ya say we don't go down roads already traveled?"

Her profuse drinking waned in relief, "Agreed."

"Besides, as far as I can figure it, relationships are like taxis."

"Oh yeah?"

"Yeap. They can only be hailed when both people have their lights on."

She looked pleased and comforted by that but I had to turn away. It could not have been more obvious how much I wished her light was still on. I felt desperate and knew it was my time to go. I did what I had come here to do and it was time to call a fold on a lousy hand. A rotten hand. Just then she cocked her head to the side and squinted at me.

"You look different?" She said, rhetorically.

"Well I'm much older now, ya know...refined some might say."

"That's not it. You look...ah, never mind."

"What's that?"

"Nah, it's okay."

"No. What?"

"I don't wanna say it."

"Just do it."

"Well, you look – your eyes look…sadder."

I felt that rod dig a little deeper into my throat, cutting off the last bit of oxygen reaching my brain. I was sadder. She'd gone right to the core of me in a mere matter of seconds. The wound needed to be covered up, and covered up quick.

"Of course, I am." I said, casually. "You're taken."

I wondered if my camouflage had had any effect.

She shook her head. "No. No. You're darker than you were before. It's not a bad thing. It just is."

"I don't know what to say."

There was silence.

And then more silence.

I drank a lot of my beer.

She was giving me time and space.

The only two things I wished she wouldn't give me.

"It's been a rough couple of months." I said.

I couldn't bring myself to talk about family shit – the envelope, the real reason I didn't make it out to her. I didn't want to put any of it on her but truthfully; I just didn't want to confront it again. I was a coward and she didn't deserve me. I looked downward, my eyes fixated on her shoes and nothing else. I couldn't believe it; even her feet were proportionately attractive. I grumbled and moaned inside. This was not how I wanted everything to go. The sympathy route was for suckers. I was a winner, goddammit. Then, amidst my sulking, I felt fingers glide slowly through my hair and find their way to the back of my neck. I looked up and she was smiling, reassuringly. It was her warmth again, in the end, that reminded me of why I had fallen so hard in the first place. She was comfort. She was solace. She was self- assurance. She was everything I ever wanted and everything I couldn't have.

"What ever it is," she said. "It's okay. Ya know? *It's okay.*"

"I know. I know."

"No, you don't. Listen to me. It's okay, all right? Nothing's great all of the time. It can't be. If it is then you're lying to yourself, *like most of the people out here.* Just remember there's nothing wrong with being down. It's just as natural and healthy as being up."

I gnawed on the inside of my cheek a little, "Never thought about it that way."

"Just find what makes you happy again...and try to enjoy the searching. To me the searching is the best part."

"Gosh you're an upbeat lady."

She laughed, and laughed hard. We had revealed our shared love of Bill Murray and *Groundhog's Day* the night we met, going so far as to say that if a future lover wasn't on board with him and that flick, we weren't on board with them.

"That'll be three hundred bucks," She joked. "You can make the check out to a Dr. Phyllis."

"Three hundred? That's a little steep there, doc."

We chuckled soft at our half-hearted banter.

"Hey...A doctor's gotta eat." She said, sticking to character. "Or was that overcharge?"

"Ha! Well played...I'm better now, really though, I am. I'm happy enough just to have seen you perform and talk to you and know you are just as awesome and alive as ever."

"Well if it makes you happy, I'm happy."

"It does. That's what it's all about, right?"

I was now fully speaking out of my ass. She nodded and downed the rest of her beer. I think she could tell I didn't mean half of what was coming out of my mouth. I couldn't even believe my own fluidity – the effortless false cheer that came with my own defeat. I felt like the sad, dumpy character in a sitcom – playing a role. I refused to let our conversation, our relationship end down that cheap, hunky-dory road.

"Listen, I know you gotta go." I said.

"I do."

"Well, two things before you do.."

"Shoot."

"Firstly, can I get a copy of the *Lickity-Split* LP?"

She laughed, broke out an album from her bag and handed it over.

"No charge."

"Thanks doc, I appreciate it."

"And the second thing?" She asked, her blue eyes brimming with hope.

"Yeah, right. Well, the thing is…" I gulped down my pride. "I just wanted you to know that I would've loved the shit out of you. Okay?"

She blushed heavily and fiddled with the zipper on her purse, "Okay."

"Good. Now get outta here."

"G'bye, Frank."

"G'bye.."

As she got up I felt a sudden urge to grab her tightly and kiss her like Bogart or Gable would've done, but ultimately held off.

"Just do me one more favor and don't forget what boils in your blood."

"And what's that?"

"Home."

She liked that. She liked that a lot. She reached her hand out and ran her fingers through the back of my hair again, locked on to it firmly and gave me her lips. They were salty and hot, still simmering with left over sweat from her performance. Then she was gone. Out the door and for all I knew, out of my life again, for the second time and forever. I hammered down the rest of my beer. The hops lingered on my tongue, bitter and sad, and I wondered if she knew that by home I meant me. Maybe she did. Maybe she didn't. Maybe I was a fool for hoping. I felt a bear paw on my left shoulder.

"That was good my friend," Hector said. "Real good."

"Was it?"

He nodded.

"Well, that's good," I said, as we made our way for the door. "'Cuz this is starting over."

Chapter 9

*A Not So
Gentle
Exploration*

A few days passed, not much of anything happened. Negative activity you might say. One of the futons at the Looney Bin was starting to form permanent indentations so I finally asked Hector if I could borrow his computer. I was down, way down and Jean Luc-Wharm was the only way out. And even through him, it wasn't looking good.

My E.D. Life,

There isn't too much to be said about that moment. That ghastly, unnatural moment when god shames you for all of your youthful deviances. It is His payback moment. Some say he works in mysterious ways, I say karma is when you can no longer get it up because you were a mischievous little shit and talented with a pair of binoculars. *Yeah. I'm talkin' to you younger self!* The youthful birdwatcher, the conniving little snoop in your friends' sister's underwear drawer, the dirty little perv who learned how to master the early age of Internet despite a dial-up connection all for the sake and betterment of the wang…yes you. You must now face the bone-collector. He has come to settle up but little did I know that it wasn't my hard-on he was after, but my potency in life.

When he came, he came with a hand out and little humor. Which, of course, I found ironic – why do you need money to cross a river? Why would money mean any thing in the afterlife? It all fit the bill to a T though, since what is Death's job if not humorous and ironic? Just ask Vonnegut if you don't believe me. Think about it, the man's job is to take life. What an absolute joke. I asked the apparition in black rags if he took bit coin, it was all I had on me. He just looked at me, blankly, blackly. Some sit-com sound engineer pushed a button and Death found his answer, it went: "Wah-wah-wah." It was the sound of everything leaving in life for this time around, Death did not want money. No, Death wanted something else and it was embodied in that sit-com sound engineer's button: It was the flop, the jiggle, the pickle with no tickle. He took all I had to offer in life – he reaped the man from my man parts and so I sat there windless, empty, the opposite of virile.

The woman of the hour looked at me and I at her. She was old enough to realize that it happens to every guy, now and then. Thank god. But this was not the usual for a young, healthy bull like myself. And yet, there I was, trying to pile-drive home a steamed string bean. It had happened so fast that the bull didn't even know his horns had been cut off until the girl would mention kindly that, "It's okay, we can try again in the morning." *NO! IT'S NOT OKAY!* The big-blue-headed Ox had been castrated! The Almighty Dethroned! The lady tried desperately to fix the situation, mouthing help and giving hand signs to the newly deaf, but nothing worked...

"What are you doing?" A voice came booming inside my brain.

"Huh?" I looked all around.

No one was there.

"So, this is it?" Again, the voice boomed with authority. "This life-long dream of yours is to write for Larry Flynt?"

"Who is that? What is this?"

"You know who I am."

The voice that had been moving all about the room now came and sat down beside me. I had never heard the voice before but he was right – I *did* know who it was.

"Who I am is not important." The voice went on, "Your future is what's important."

"Okay." I was timid. My story had been interrupted. These stories never get interrupted. Jean-Luc Wharm's stories were always the escape. Something had gone wrong. Very very wrong.

"So this is it then?" He asked again, Gently.

"My writing?"

"Yes, is this what you want for the rest of your life?"

"I don't know."

"Well you better think and you better think quick. Thirty-two is no time for doddling."

"*Doddling?* What kinda question is that? I'm not sure what I want for *the rest of my life.*"

"Why is that so hard? What is it that you want? What is it you expect from all this? Have you set any goals?"

"Goals? What is this? *Career and Life Coaching from the dead?*"

"That's exactly what this is."

I shrugged, "I want to entertain people. That's it. Okay? That's all I ever wanted. To help people get through their day-to-day bullshit, however I can. Is that so bad? I'm not gonna run for office and I'll never make millions running some business just to turn my house into a museum — that isn't me. I'd go crazy. And what is this bullshit, anyway? Did you know what you wanted for the rest of your life at thirty-two?"

"Yes. It was decided for me."

"Well, I never had that luxury."

"That is why I am here."

"Okay."

"Franklin, do not be so childish as to believe that having your life decided for you was a luxury. Freedom is the ultimate luxury and you know it."

"Yeah I do and my name is Frank."

"Okay. Well, that is why I am here. I am here because of how difficult freedom can be."

"Great! Glad you could make it!"

Flippancy with a ghost that is nothing more than a voice in your head has no payoff.

"There is a profound vastness and insecurity and fear that can come with such choice and opportunity. To live in a constant state of apprehension toward these natural emotions is to live forever unaccomplished."

"Jesus. We've gone Freudian."

"Ah yes. Sarcasm. That'll get you far."

"What on earth is your point?"

"You have been gifted with a talent, my boy."

"I didn't ask for this."

"No you didn't, *but you chose to use it.* I am here to make sure you are happy with the path you have chosen. That you use it to the best of your ability and of course — do what makes you feel most alive."

"Why should I listen to you? You are just a voice. And a voice that sounds like Ian Mckellen at that."

I'd always dreamt that my father would've spoken in the deep healing tones and all-encircling wisdom of Gandalf. The dream came true, except Ian Mckellen was speaking in tongues and sounded closer to Hamlet or Magneto than that of the great white wizard.

"Because I have seen all there is to see and I have been allowed one moment back."

Hold on. *Didn't Gandalf say that?*

Maybe.

I shook my head. Now, not only my life but my writing, my effing escape from the real world had been poisoned. I'd always wished I could've spoken with my father, but not like this. This is the conversation you never wanted to have with a father who was alive and kicking. This was the shit father and son avoided even if they loved each other unconditionally.

"You are my moment." He continued. "Unlike myself and your mother, you have been gifted with a second chance, a rare fortune to make every day as full or as empty, as different or repetitive, as spectacular or mundane, as honorable or corrupt as you see fit...Now listen: This day and everyday forward is yours to make of it what you wish."

"So what are you saying? I need to write a manuscript on life?"

"I am saying you need to do something that you feel is worthwhile."

I didn't like that he used my own words: *Worthwhile.*

Those were my words.

"I know what you are capable of," He said. "I have seen all the paths you can walk, the infinite amount of choices you can take and do take. They have all played out already...all you have to do now is choose which one you want to live out. There is such joy ahead of you, son."

"Are you talking about fate?"

"Yes."

"Well you got the wrong guy. I don't believe in it."

"It's not about believing in anything. It is about doing. It has always been about that and you know it. Leave the people to give it a name and screw it up with some silly behavior and ritual to worship. It's all about doing and you must do...now. *Get action!*"

"And what exactly do you want from me? Is what I am doing right now not good enough? What do you want, *Edward?*" I said his name and said it aloud. I had never said it before. I was fed up. "Another goddam *How To Live Happy and Complete — Your Soul's Guide to Prosperity* cheap-ass business venture for myself?! A lucrative mockery of all that I hold dear!? What shit. All of those books are fake and written by fake people; soulless lemmings that have sold themselves down a river of blown out ideologies, all for the love of money...not life. I refuse to write something that doesn't allow people to feel alive. And not tricked into feeling that way either! No. I will not be pulling some ridiculous curtain over their eyes...I am not here to ask people to walk on hot coals just to prove to themselves they are capable of anything. *NO SIR.* They're all born capable! I am here to offer one of those never-ending, undying emotions that trumps all others; one that is genuine and real and untarnished, I am here to offer everyone a smile."

"Be serious, Frank. Please, for once in your life be serious. Jokes will only take you so far. I ask only that if you are going to write, you write something worthy of remembrance."

"Jokes!? JOKES!? HA!" I may have gone completely over the edge in my own mind at this juncture. There is certainty in nothing when you're hanging off the edge, but I may be certain to have lost it. "I'm not talking about jokes! I'm talking about a smile, goddammit, a smile! That thing when your cheeks can't help but draw back tight in happiness. I'm talking about delight and hope and turning

the world upside down in an expression. And I'm not talking about a work of art when I say expression. No. I'm not
just creating another statement from an artist. I'm talking
about a turn of phrase. Yes, an expression that can be
warm and provocative and powerful and enchanting and
resonant, all the while short and sweet!" I saw his ghostly
face form in front of me and turn sour. I could tell, he
thought I was delusional, consumed by boyish notions. I
was forever the adolescent, dreaming that I could make a
difference. Lost to the childish belief that humor can
make the world a better place. He wanted me to be an
adult, to grow up. He wanted me to be serious. "No!
Nothing dark and serious. *Never.* The world is full of it.
Why should I be the one to remind them of how serious
life is? That's why they have CNN! No. No. No. The
staying power of a smile cannot be underestimated. It can
claim the brain and cleanse the heart — hell, it can reawak-
en the soul, man! (I was starting to sound like a westerner)
Are you worried I won't make it? Are you worried there is
no audience? Tell me, are you worried for the right reasons?"

"I did not come back from the afterlife to talk about
money."

"When is anything not about money? Everything is
about money."

"Sell the house!" His voice dropped an octave. "I
don't care. Do what you wish with the estate. You will
have more money than you could've ever dreamed. Nothing matters when you are dead except *who* you leave behind, not *what.* Do you understand? I made mistakes. I
got things wrong. But I wasn't given the choices that you
have today. I care about you. You and your happiness."

"Then let me write the book I set out to write."

"Then quit flopping about and do it."

"WHAT HAVE I BEEN DOING?"

"TO WHAT END, FRANK. ALWAYS ASK YOURSELF, TO WHAT END?"

"I am ending this conversation, there's your end."

"I did not come back from the dead to wallow in some childish squabble."

"Well I am not alive to deal with the bullshit that was handed to me."

"Yes. *That*."

"What?"

"The bullshit... you inherited. You need to free yourself of it."

"I am trying. *Hello?* I am out in this godforsaken land because of it."

"Let me tell you something, son: Victoria has a secret and it does not lie in skimpy women's underwear (see, your old man had humor, too – who do you think you got it from?) You talk to her and you'll find the truth, you'll find the freedom that you long for...and the voice your writing so eagerly thirsts for."

"Fuck this."

The laptop slammed shut.

Did my imaginary father literally just tell me that my writing sucks?

I was losing it.

Sure as hell.

I was lost.

＊

Hector came inside the room and peeked around the door with a worried look, "Were you just arguing with yourself in here?"

"No. No. Just mumbling, just mumbling. It's something we writers do to hear dialogue."

"That didn't sound like mumbling."

"What's it to you?"

"Hey man. Everyone talks to themselves in this house from time to time. Natural side effect of the shrooms."

He laughed at his own joke and asked me what my plans were. I shrugged. I had no clue.

"Now you're getting it, man." He was genuinely happy that I didn't know what I was going to do. "No plans! That's the way. Just fucking roll with it and ride that wave till she kicks."

"Hector, had I known you were going to say what you just said to me, I would've gladly told you I had plans."

"Gah," he shook his head rather appreciative of my stubbornness. "Still givin' those fucks, bro."

"I try, Heck. I try."

My mind slid off on a tangent and landed where my last Jean-Luc Wharm entry had ended: Victoria. The name still made my jaw stick out. I couldn't help it. It was now a Pavlovian response. Even if I heard the name Vic in passing, my chin would protrude violently outward, possessed with maternal rage.

"You like your parents, Hector?" I asked.

He was tinkering with a camera.

"What's that?"

"Do you still have a decent relationship with them, your rents?"

"Well, my foster parents, yes."

"You know your real parents, at all?"

"They *are* my real parents. They're the ones who raised me."

"Sorry — you know what I mean, though?"

"Yeah. I don't really think about it too much." He continued tinkering for a bit and I felt like I had overextended our friendship but then he went on, "Muh mom died before I can really remember. My cousins say it was from working around chemicals in some laundry factory. But shit, you can't believe them as far as you can throw 'em. They're all a pack-a-lowlifes, one worse than the next if you ask me."

"And your dad?"

"Meh. He might be alive. Who knows. When he wasn't workin' he was drunk, and when he was working he was probably drunk too. He left me alone for a long time when I was seven. A neighbor called social services and I was one of the lucky few who got placed in a decent foster house."

"Well that's good, I guess."

"Hells yes it is. A miracle. You know where I'd be right now if all that didn't happen? Right next to my old man, that's where. Guzzlin' down shitty tequila and catchin' a ride up the coast to scrounge a living off pickin' grapes."

"Was it that bad? Before you got picked up by Social Services?"

"I dunno, man. I was young. It's like, when you're young, even if you know something is fucked up, you think it's all there is. So you think it's fine."

"Hm."

"I still have trouble with dark rooms though, learned that in photography school."

"Jesus."

"Ah. C'mon man! Look at me now." He pointed at his gut. "Well fed, just like you! And check it: Me and the guys got to talkin' last night and we know you been through some shit and we want you to come up with us to Yosemite. We're gonna leave in a couple days. Jon and the guys were just cleared to climb El Capitan."

"You serious?"

"Oh hells yeah. Yous'ah stand up dude! You worry too much, but hay. We figured it might be good to have someone like you along for the ride, ya know? Have someone there who can worry enough for the rest of us. We already put in for the jalopy so all-a-the lights are green."

"The jalopy?"

"It's a *motor home*, bro." The two words came glittering out of his mouth with a sense of pride in his own creativity. "But it's better than a motor home because we don't call it a motor home. HA!" He threw his hands up to the ceiling like he'd just hit the big time. "It's just like the chair we got down stairs. We don't call it a *Lazy-Boy*. We call it a *Big-Daddy-War-Bucks*."

I just smiled at him.

He was a big bowl of positive energy, an iceberg of vast, unsinkable glee. Sure, it was uncalled for half the time, like an astronaut ecstatic to jump on a workout trampoline just to feel the G's, but because of him and the rest of the Affable Looneys, I was now going to Yosemite – The Land Before Time. The House that Muir Built. It was tough to believe the guys were actually going to scale the massive granite rock face that easily towers some three-thousand feet above the valley floor. And then the thought struck me that I might have to partake in some way. And thoughts like those could make a man crumble. At least, this man:

"Wait. You guys don't expect me to climb, do you?"

"Everybody climbs, bro. It's like *Fight Club*, but with climbing."

My eyes grew wide while my pupils shrunk to the size of pinpricks. My completely rational fear of heights blurred my vision and tunneled my focus to the most horrific of phobias.

"Ah. I think I better stay." I said.

"Bah! I fucks witch-you!"

I punched him hard, solidly on the shoulder.

"You think *I* could climb El Capitan!? Ha. HA-HA!" He was thoroughly entertained. "You're freakin' hilarious. That's choice, stuff, *choice*." He turned back to the hallway and yelled, "HAY. Dudes! We got a comedian up here!"

"Hector, we're gonna have to work on how you teach me to give zero fucks, 'cuz this – right here – this ain't workin."

"Bah! Stop it! Stop it. I'm crying."

I sloughed off the casual embarrassment that comes with being gullible.

"I need coffee." I stammered. "I'm going to Cafecita. Who the hell survives on tea alone?! You're all whackjobs round here!"

I walked downstairs and left Hector wheezing at his desk. Jon and Zev and Adé were all higher than kites in the living room. The fresh smell of diesel weed permeated the air. They were gathering and sorting gear for the ensuing climb. What must've been hundreds of ropes and cinches and carbineers were spread out on the floor and covered most of the couches and coffee table as well. They tried hard but were failing miserably to hide their twisted wry smiles that both the weed and my loud conversation with Hector procreated. They had heard me storm down the steps and even I knew I was joking around but I was still too pissed at life to laugh. The funny thing being, when that happens, when absolutely nothing is funny anymore, it is the most essential time to laugh. And yet, in my convoluted mind, I wasn't allowed to enjoy myself, at least not yet – everything was so fucked up right now, my life felt like a failure…how on earth could I enjoy anything? I could hear Hector's elephantine trunk tumbling down the steps after me.

"Dudes. Frank and I are going to scale El Capitan with you. That okay? We'll shoot it rogue documentary style. Call it mountain climbing for beginners! Make it a Youtube Channel. Bah!" Hector was beside himself with joy.

I fumed and walked outside. I could hear Hector's howl envelop the house along with the others as I made my way down the street. 'I should've known,' I thought. 'Non-coffee drinkers are maniacs. Freakin' hippies take cold showers, too. *Manson took cold showers!* How the hell did I wind up living with the dammed circus?'

"Fuckin' Whackjobs!"

<u>Chapter 10</u>

Loose Ends
Drawn Tight

Midway to Cafecito, I decided to take a roundabout course through the neighborhood to get everything I needed for Yosemite. I made my way up to the main intersection of Sunset and Santa Monica and popped into a little one-stop-shop. It was called the Mohawk General Store. Now, I hate to call the name misleading (or down right deceiving) for it was a general store and was loaded with all the proper accouterment one might expect, however something had gone terribly awry inside: ahem, your average general store's price tags don't normally cause cardiac arrest. After two or three quick price tag checks and the frightful gasps that followed, I quickly quipped to a pair of shoppers standing beside me that maybe they should've called it *Faux*-hawk General Store.

I was proud of myself for that.

A good find.

The young couple was neither impressed nor tickled. They had fedoras on — I wasn't impressed either, slightly tickled though. Both hats were tilted back and sat atop meticulously manicured hair that fluffed and frayed outward onto their foreheads, tickling the tops of their sunglasses they had seen fit to leave on while inside the shop. I wondered then if they played the local dive with ukuleles, or worse, had invented their own instruments. They seemed like the type who used bent forks and kitchen ladles on a Cello to capture the right *essence* of sound. You know the kind; they're the ones you pray you don't run into at a friend's backyard barbecue for fear they might offer to sing you one of their latest triumphs they'd written while out spelunking in Sri Lanka.

Naturally, I said nothing and continued shopping, half ashamed of the time I spent breaking down the couple's look. But that is what happens out here. That is what the face value of everything in LA does to you. It douses you in gallant cynicism; it makes you believe that there is no nobler thing in the world than to be a skeptic. To see everyone and everything for whatever they are not. I'm sure the couple had thrown the same internal monologue my way and would discuss my 'lack of style' when they left the store, or maybe I didn't even warrant the attention which, out west, was the ultimate sin. I have noticed it is something everyone does out here and we all seem happy to play the part, typecasting as we tumble along, making gods of ourselves at the expense of others. It doesn't need saying then that the aforementioned chivalry peeled away with the first burn of the western sun.

Keeping up with my knack for playing the fool, I figured that money was no longer an issue – what with the fresh idea of selling the Gently mansion tumbling around my head – and so I went ahead and got everything I needed at Mohawk. I won't tell you what the total damage came to, mostly out of mere shame but partly because I truly loved what I got. The mass sum on the receipt could've easily covered someone's monthly rent, I'm sure, but what's a man to do when he's down? Drink? Fuck? Read? Write? Tried 'em all and they all failed me horribly. So what else is there? If you take away travel (which was in progress), what is left? Buy something, of course. Yes, retail therapy, why not? It does make sense after all: when you accrue materialistic debts it takes your mind off of what is actually tormenting you. *Distraction, that's the ticket.* I'm just having a laugh now. I know this is, oh, how shall I put it, thick-headed. But, we all love nice shit, no arguing that. It makes us feel better. It's weird, right? Human Nature & Materialism. Just the diversity of it all. How some of us can have an outright perversion with jewelry while others seek the same hard-on in high-top sneaker-wear. It's astounding, really. Living on the edge of poverty most of my adult life, I never had the freedom to try out retail therapy but this seemed an opportune time to give it a whirl.

The good news, if you can call it that, was that everything I snagged for the trip was next-level-craft. All of it being the pride-riddled, family-owned, affectionately produced items that endure: I bought a big, rugged wax-leather bag, a pair of stiff stone-washed jeans, a wool sweater, two cotton flannels, a couple of short and long sleeve t-shirts, a multitude of briefs and socks – which I might add was the best investment ever – as well as sunglasses, a light inclement-weather jacket, fox-colored leather boots, water bottle, flask, four journals (which I vowed would be full come the end of travel), pens as well as all the hygienic wonders a boutique like Mohawk was made for.

Never again will I reek of B.O. singed with incense and Hawaiian Blue-Kush. Some people say you have to look good to feel good. I disagree. I think you only have to smell good. The proof exists in the botanical, olfactory orgasms that are in all of those high-end, man-products I purchased from

Faux-hawk: body scrubs, toothpastes, deodorants and hand salves. Ha. *Salves.* I bought something with the word *salves* in it. The boys back home would have a field day with that. I should've kept a better head about myself in that shop, I'm pretty sure those piney-scented douches ruined me. I mean, who can go back to Irish Spring after using stuff like that? I can't. Somehow someone figured out that you could put the smell of Yosemite in a bottle and you know what, nobody wants to smell like the Wal-Mart soap isle when a giant Sequoia will do. Or, let me put it this way, when your body has embraced a certain funk for an extended period of time, when you've become an overly-ripened piece of hot city garbage and your nose can no longer adjust, when you wake up every morning for almost an entire week on the wrong side of the pillow and that pillow has now become a pungent paper mill…smell is everything.

I asked the man behind the counter if I could wear some of the clothing out. He, in turn, gave me a once over, smiled with aching disapproval at my soiled attire and motioned back to the fitting rooms. I changed quickly, exuberantly like a youngster getting into a fresh new Adidas jumpsuit. I glanced in the mirror and was shocked – I *did* feel better. It was weird. It had been almost a week since I looked in the mirror and I was scruffier and almost ten pounds thinner than when I had left The Kill. My cheekbones had resurfaced and my gut wasn't so dammed offensive anymore. I guess kale and quinoa dinners without binging on Budweisers all night, every night, had had a better effect on my body. Still, I missed the Bud.

The rucksack, stuffed full of my new gear, fell heavy on my back and its bulky weight excited me. It felt as though my real adventure was finally beginning. The trip I was meant to take, the reason I was actually out west, *the journey.* One that would be free of every burden and hope that comes from home, that comes from your old sense of self. I stood there in front of that mirror changed. A new man unfettered by the shackles of expectation. I thought about Dean and what he had said just before I left and how there weren't any real adventures anymore. And as I gleamed from this shield of new clothing furnished by the prospect of Yosemite, I couldn't help but feel that he was wrong and my slow-churning, forward motion was a profound sign of it.

I called both him and Jack from inside the dressing room but both phones went to voicemail. I left them messages informing them about the loss of June. I kept it short. No sense in them knowing how bad I really felt. They would know, anyway. I shifted course quickly to the future of Yosemite. I told them both that the Garcon De Garrison was in their hands for a while and that I would be out of touch for a bit: *"shutting my phone off and checking out from the grid was something I desperately needed – more time to write and take in what I'm sure I'd been missing all along. I trusted them with the place and would be in touch soon."*

I shut my phone off and threw on my new shades. I would never tell Hector, but I think they put the burning man jams to shame. They had more than just a style and flair; through those thick-framed lenses was a new perspective, a completed metamorphosis. The physical giving way to the mental. My door of enthusiasm was finally reopened and I felt reborn, readied and ripe to hit the pavement and go on what was certainly going to be the first and probably, most interesting road trip of my life. It had been almost a week now out here in this bizarre town...was I now finally coming around to it? I guess so. It was odd, but it sure as hell wasn't rocket science: my old dingy, funkified outfit was now sitting in the street corner garbage can. My gut had receded along with the dependence upon June for a new life and I now considered myself to be somewhat attractive (in the most tepid sense). But beyond all that, my soft attitude toward LA could only be attributed to an even softer landing. I owed everything to the Affable Looneys. What tremendous luck I had struck amidst a pile of rotten shit. They were amazing people – strange and whacky as all hell – but still, kind enough to take me in and bring me along on one of their intense climbing trips.

Projected imagery of the famed National Park now floated in and out of my mind. I thought of the guys climbing El Capitan and it gave me vertigo. I could barely handle peering over the edge of a forty-foot cliff, let alone the negative-angled ascent of the world renowned, mammoth titan of rock-climbing feats. It was something I could never really understand, rock climbing. I put it up there with how most people relate to astro-physics in an inability to comprehend. Sure it took a certain physical genius and guts, but a lot of it remained unfathomable to me – to a point of madness. So much so I chose not to think about it and even when I would eventually sit there with Hector and watch those boys devour that godly sheath of granite, six inches at a time, I had to imagine I was looking at figurines, not real people. Otherwise I would turn an unhealthy shade of white and grow delirious with empathy to the point of needing a drink...*for them.*

*

I left the shop and walked past Sunset Junction, chock full of hipsters. The weather was outrageously nice and the hipsters were just outrageous. My new attire made me look like them in a way, but even in a flannel shirt and well-cut denim, I still didn't own what they owned: the belief that I was cool. Or, *weird*, since weird is the new cool or whatever the fuck. It was something I learned back east in the city; genuinely cool people get insulted if you call them cool. "What is cool!?" they'd ask, disgustedly. I have a feeling they, along with all of Austin, will be feeling the same way they do toward 'cool' about 'weird' in a few years time. "What the hell is weird!?" They'll say. I'll tell them it's the new normal and we'll all move on, happily pissed off. Whatever term you wish to use when you look at the whole crowd of Sunset Junction is irrelevant, all of it still manifests itself in the same manner. Swagger, some might call it. Pretension possibly to others. It all meant the same thing to me. It meant having enough money and interest and time to be absorbed in cultural trends. I suppose I had the time, I just didn't really have the effort nor the patience. And whether those oil-tasting, cheese-headed, music snobs are conscious of it or not, it takes a shit ton of effort to look and feel cool. Ahem, *weird*. Sorry.

I strolled through the back streets of Silver Lake (calling a back street of LA sundrenched would be almost as cliché as calling the main drag of London waterlogged. But, there was the sun, again, fighting hard and determined to make me use the word). Proudly supporting my new garb and admiring the fallen fruit on the sidewalks, I thought about the trip. I tried to picture just who, out of everyone in the house, could handle a motor home. Pardon me, *jalopy*. The answer was clear: nobody. Yes, there is no doubt they could all handle the ocean, the monstrous waves and the death defying perches of jagged mountainsides, but a diesel rig? No way. On second thought, maybe Hector could, but then again maybe I was just painting him the driver because his frame looked closest to what an eighteen-wheeler truck-driver's might look like: husky and Mexican. You know what they say about stereotypes, they exist because more often than not they're true. It might not surprise you then that Hector ended up handling the RV throughout the trip and handled'r swimmingly.

I finally found my way to Cito and the people who do god's work. I had been to all of the local coffee joints inside of five days and CafeCito was far and away the best: unpretentious with quality beans and stupidly curated brewing techniques, some kitschy Day of the Dead ambience, all of which came supported by one hell of a good vinyl soundtrack and a little backyard full of metal chairs and tables that all wobbled with indifference to who sat in them. My kind-a-place. It surely would've been where I wrote while living out west, should I not have had the ability to get out to the Pacific every day. (*Insert loud gratuitous sigh here. Mental note: need to get back to writing. ASAP.*) The only thing the cafe lacked, in fact, was anyone who resembled Adam Levine. This was by far its greatest feature. The Levines of LA all lived around the corner at Intelligentsia; the beautiful café of Sunset Junction filled with even more beautiful people who all lived their lives purposefully and adequately to let the name of that establishment down. Way down. As for Cito, it was my small little slice of caffeinated heaven. My daily escape from the oddities back at the house and a sliver of the perspective I had long dreamed was the whole of the West: *a place where every thing was easy.*

I ordered a cold-brew and took a seat in the courtyard and wrestled with the lone thing I needed to come to terms with before taking to the unknown promises a place like Yosemite had to offer.

*

"Is that a T-chart?" interrupted the young, bright-skinned girl sitting to my starboard. She was shamelessly peering over my shoulder and continued the intrusion, reading aloud from my journal without a whiff of wrongdoing. "Victoria, My Cunt Mother."

"Excuse me," I said, pulling up the notebook from the table and turning slightly away from her. "This is a little private if you don't mind."

"You shouldn't call your mother that, you know."

"I know."

"You shouldn't really call anyone that, ya know."

"I know."

"*Prick* is much more widely accepted." She waited for me to catch up to her supercilious tone and continued, "unless your from Great Britain. Then it's okay."

I laughed. "Oh yeah? That makes it okay?"

"Yeah sure."

"Well what if your mother is British. Can you call her a cunt then?"

"Is your mother British? *And don't say that word!*"

"Well, no. But hypothetical: If she were British, can you call her uh-uh...a C-word?"

"Hmm." The girl was very cute, surprisingly talkative and quick. A pistol. She was animated and spoke as much with her hands and her eyebrows as she did her wily mouth. Must've been a transplant or something. "No. If she is British, *she* can call *you* a cunt. Not the other way around."

"You draw a fine line there. *And you just said cunt.*"

"Ah Fuck!" She laughed at herself. She was foul mouthed and a happy sailor to boot. "And what's a fine line if not drawn correctly?"

"A doodle." I said, peering over her cartoonish artwork, returning the same intrusive favor. "Is that...holy shit, *is that The Animaniacs?*"

My voice had been cut dry by a twinge of youthful disbelief. It was *The Animaniacs* all right. Yakko, Wakko and Dot – my favorite characters from my favorite childhood cartoon show. Pinky and the Brain were there, too. The drawings were spot on, fluid and textured and showed no signs that she ever used an eraser. The little kooks were the zany, crackling creatures I had always known them to be. It was great, just great. The girl had a real talent, let me tell you. I had unknowingly walked into a visual time-machine and the driver – this gal's gifted pencil – had delivered a haymaker of pure nostalgia to my gut; boyhood joy bubbled up through my bones and I felt young again.

"Hay! That's mine." She said, lifting the notebook from the table.

"Now you know how it feels."

"I'm not the one calling my mother, a – ya know. *Cunt.*" She laughed at herself again. She was awfully endearing.

"I have my reasons. Believe me, I do." I said. She raised her shoulders and her eyebrows at the same time, as if to say she was all ears, but I wasn't there just yet. "So, do you draw professionally?"

"Mph." Her lips pursed a moment and then relaxed again. "No, it's just a hobby of mine."

"That duhdn't look like a hobby. What the hell do you do for a living?"

"I pour beers."

"You serious? With that talent?"

She was flattered. I meant it.

"Well, I have been trying to get my book in front of someone for a while now." She sighed, a champion of dis- enchantment. She was almost off-putting in her tone and from the look of her dejected face as she spoke, one might discern that she had been out here quite a while now and despite what could've been hundreds of well thought out e- mails and tiresome applications and passionate pitches, noth- ing had come to fruition. "I just don't know anybody in LA," she sighed again, this time resignedly.

"I'm sure that's everything out here."

"It's everything, *everywhere*. But here, you can forget it...I might as well hold my breath for rain." The sun beat down on us hard and she withdrew even deeper into the back of her chair. "Don't really know why I came out here in the first place."

"Because you have a gift. *Obviously*." I cleared my throat and took my sunglasses off. "Can I see it again, please? I shit you not, it reminded me of sleepovers at my friends' house and Saturday mornings and toaster strudels and sucking the vanilla icing out of the packets before the strudel was done...oddly enough. It made me *feel* something. I want more."

Though my smile remained, the sentence itself made my jaw stick out and my mouth grow arid with contempt – my mother had raised me without a TV. Like everything else in modern society, she thought it "toxic and corruptive." She failed to notice what was actually poisoning my brain, and what would linger long after the toxins had claimed my nerves as their victim: dysfunction. To retain some sense of normalcy in my youth, I was forced to binge watch the boob-tube at friends' houses. Staying up late into the night while others slept to watch Nickelodeon and TBS and USA, which eventually shifted to HBO and Showtime, hungry, starved to absorb any ounce of Americana I could. Watching movies like *Hook, The Goonies, Die Hard* and *Jurassic Park, The Terminator* and *Bad Boys* and *Con Air.* Oh, *Con Air.* If you don't understand America, just watch *Con Air.* Then you *really* won't get it. The raft of pop-culture absorbed late into my Friday nights and Saturday mornings somehow made the passage of time more enjoyable, more graspable, more relatable, and gave me the ability to weather the house-held shit-storms of one Victoria Gently until I could be out and on my own. Away from the controlled and souring environment that was Victoria, my cunt mother. It wouldn't be until college that I would come to discover cult-classics and the importance of loving older films and all celluloid in general. I snapped back from my begrudging walk down memory lane when the girl angled her drawing book back toward me.

"Wow." I said, remembering all the lost icons of my youth. "This...this is really something else."

"Thank you."

"No seriously, *The Animaniacs* is one of my favorite shows of all time."

"Me too."

We caught eyes. Hers were milk chocolate, big and wide and soft. I hadn't noticed but she had taken her sunglasses off while I sat transfixed in adolescence. She had a round face and short, stringy blonde hair that was cut a few inches above the shoulder. It bounced when she spoke. She was wearing a sheer, see-through shawl that revealed a white burlesque top underneath. She didn't have a lot to work with but the vintage, tight-laced corset forced what god gave her to the top with a hefty amount of authority. My peripherals paid close attention. I hadn't felt attracted to anyone, couldn't think of anyone else in a certain way since June. But I'll be damned if that white burlesque top didn't make me think differently. Hell, I almost forgot to introduce myself.

"I'm Frank. Frank Gently."

"It's Katherine." We shook hands. "But you can call me Kat."

It was a cute name for a cute girl. Let's face it, it wasn't Juniper but it certainly was miles above my ex's name – Carla. I always had problems with marrying a girl whose name was only one letter away from Marla. If that sounds shallow or childish, I can only ask what you are doing here in the kiddie pool? Faulker and Fitzgerald were a letter back.

"You from here?" I asked.

She shook her head as if it were obvious.

"Kansas City, actually. I can tell you're not." She said.

"I'm that dead of a give away, huh?"

"Yes."

"The way I talk?"

"Well, of course the-way-you-talk, but more so your boots. Nobody wears boots out here. At least not right now."

"Ah. Maybe I'm just some eccentric local?" She gave me a smirk as if to say – *not at this coffee shop you're not.* I sipped some more of Cito's delightful cold brew and proceeded to climb deeper into her untapped cave of Warner Bros. memories. "Do you mind?" I asked, leaning toward her. She slowly capitulated, lowering the book ever so slightly as I spoke. "I hate to use the word, but this is awesome. That is exactly what this is. Just awesome."

"That's very nice of you."

She leaned in toward me.

"I don't know. I'm sure this city is full of people who *think* they are gifted and really aren't. But this, this is like, a sure-fire stairway to heaven. If you think I'm being ridiculous right now, my buddy Dean from back home would set you straight. He had *a problem* with cartoons. Okay? Hell he'd-a-probably already gone to the bathroom with this to – uhh.."

"Rub one out?" She cut in, blurting into abundant laughter.

"Yes. That exactly."

"To a cartoon?" Her voice was high-pitched, expectant of a punch line.

"Some people are sick."

She laughed some more, "Well thank you. Most people around here don't care for it."

"Well that's just sad. But remember most people are dumb and have forgotten what it's like to be a kid…to dream and be happy."

The thought depressed her.

"You remember what Picasso said, right?" I continued, hopeful to persuade her from the gloom growing in her eyes. "'*Everyone is born an artist – the trouble is to remain that way as you grow up.*' This could be your way to help with that and keep all of those teetering on the edge of adulthood from completely going asunder." She feigned a look of happiness. "Look, you're not allowed to become disenchanted, okay? I will not have it. This is too good. People need this. *Kids need this.* Just keep doing what you're doing, all right? And *Hoah My Gawd, is that Slappy Squirrel?*" I had turned to the next page when another one of her ACME lot characters, this one being the incorrigible curmudgeon squirrel with the infamous New Yorker accent, leapt right up from the page and slapped me in the face with her purse. "This. Is. Ah-mazing."

She giggled at my gawking, my impish attempt at inspiration, my borderline embarrassing jaunt through childhood.

"That's her alright. Here, have at it." She handed me the entire sketchbook.

It was unreal. All of the Saturday Morning Cartoon characters were in there. *The X-men. Life with Louis.* "I'm Louis Anderson!" I cackled aloud, mimicking the rotund and nasal comedian rather well. "That's uncanny," Kat echoed. "And a little scary." I flipped feverishly through the entire body of work and found that she had invented characters of her own: wild, troll like figures with flaming hair and dumpy frames. "Those are The Weeklings." She said. "Each troll is a different day of the week. Look," She pointed toward each one as she went along, "Saturday is the care-free beautiful one, she smells of jasmine and bohemia. Monday is a detestable prick, Friday is the party-hard lush while Wednesday, as you can imagine, has a hunch on his back – a nasty hump that nobody likes dealing with. And then there is Sunday," she turned the page to her latest masterpiece; his eyes aloof, his demeanor randomly wild and disheveled while both elderly and sullen. "He just looks confused." I said. "Exactly." She reverberated. "He doesn't know who or what he is supposed to be...pious with the church or rambunctious and leisurely with Football. A day of rest or a day of zest? He is lost. Sunday loves Saturday but she has grown bored of him and his insecurities and muddled sense of self." Kat stopped and paused thoughtfully to get her words right, and then went on. "Sunday is my tragic hero and represents the confused society we live in and how we are constantly pulled in different and silly and counterintuitive and hypocritical directions…and often times, all at once."

I tell her that is wild. I tell her I'm kind of blown away by what she just said. I tell her how most people who speak that way out west don't make any sense, but she did. And I'll have to think about that a little more, because if it's true, it will completely blow my mind for it means there is still one human being in LA who can speak English. She laughs at that and tells me she can sympathize.

Something is happening between us.

I am liking this girl.

But how?

I don't even know.

Maybe the fact that I hadn't been laid in six months had something to do with it, but I think it is much more than that. I think I am forgetting what the past six months of my life were like and I believe much of it is coming from this conversation. And then out of nowhere, Kat cuts back to my T-chart. Of course! Just when things were getting good, only Victoria Gently can ruin a conversation from three thousand miles away.

"So what's the T-chart for?"

"If I should call my mom or not."

"Why wouldn't you want to call your mother?"

"I hold her personally responsible for ruining my life."

"Well isn't that a bit dramatic."

"If you knew the situation, I think you might take that back."

She gave me the same inviting gesture she had shot me before — her shoulders jabbing upward, her eyebrows raising gradually, her torso twisting and easing backward as if to encourage open space — *the floor is all yours, and once again,*

I'm all ears. Despite her natural ease of conversation, I didn't want to go into it with her. Who would? Who wants to tell someone you just met your most deep and unsolvable problems? I looked down at the chart, which had sat there empty for almost half an hour before Kat had chimed in. Then, like a lightning bolt came the sudden decision that it might actually help my cause if I went through the process with someone else by my side. She was still kind of a stranger after all and I think that made it easier.

I unloaded the baggage.

Kat was an amazing sport and listened to every little detail, nodding along encouragingly throughout most of it, smiling at the times when I relied on self-deprecation or humor to break the seriousness of the situation. All were obvious coping mechanisms, and yet, she stayed right there with me. When we finished I couldn't have been gladder that she was the one by my side through it all. She had a Midwestern tact, what must've been some cold German-Polish descent that helped cut right through the emotional bullshit. After the entire story unfolded we got down to the actual pros and cons of me calling Vic. She joked that we were doing something Benjamin Franklin would've done and then I thoroughly indulged in my nerdery by telling her that he was the reason I had made the T-chart it in the first place. She shook her head, laughed at me purposefully, and then took the pen and started the "Pros" section that had formulated from our back and forth conversation. We traded off for each point and I'd take the pen and write whatever the hell I wanted for the "Cons" section. The results were as follows:

Victoria, My Cunt Mother

Pro: She's my mother.

Con: She's the absolute worst.

Pro: Very much of who I am today is because of her.

Con: I'm a mess.

Pro: She meant well and believed what she was doing was right.

Con: That is the singular excuse used by all tyrants and dictators throughout history.

Pro: She was a do-gooder to society.

Con: A seven year old shouldn't have to help out at the soup kitchen line half the year and be forced to participate in every sit-in protest for the union just because his mother felt guilt from her waspy upbringing.

Pro: You only have one mother.

Con: One was enough.

Pro: She raised me with a sense of humor.

Con: Dark humor.

Pro: I still got a pretty good deal in the end. She did love me after all. How many kids can't say that?

Con: Shit.

Pro: She's my mother.

Con: But she's a c-word. She kept my father from me. She kept half of my life away from me. She lied. She is a liar! She had no right. She shouldn't get the satisfaction of me forgiving her.

Pro: She's still my mother.

Con: I have to forgive her.

Pro: Forgiving her will probably help me get over a lot of shit.

Con: She will be forgiven.

Pro: I will learn more about my father.

Con: The thought scares the shit out of me.

Pro: I need to know everything about him — how else will
I know myself?
Con: My mother is the only one who can tell that story.
Pro: I'll have closure.
Con: Closure doesn't mean a happy ending.

"You ever feel like you could just pour your whole heart
out to a stranger?" I asked as I put down the pen.

"Of course, isn't that what therapy is all about?"

"I suppose. But it's different. With therapy you pay that
stranger to listen to you. And then everything shifts to how
long the appointment lasts, what labels you fall under, which
prescription will make it better, how many sessions it will
take...it all kind of gets lost to money. But with a genuine
stranger, like you — there is no guarantee of anything. Just an
ear. Ya know? Sometimes I think that is all people really
need. Someone to listen. Not to offer a way out or a pill to
depend on or a false sense of hope. Just someone to listen.
Like you did...thanks for that."

She grabbed the pen and added another Pro:

Pro: How about a happy ending right now?

Without hesitation, I grabbed the pen and filled in a con.

Con: There's a creepy guy in the corner looking at us.

"Not here!" She yelped, her cheeks embracing a grapevine
red. "My place?"

I nodded but couldn't quite grasp exactly what I was
nodding along too. She was just messing with me, right?
Apparently not, but were we really about to go hook up?
Does it happen like that out here?

"Okay, except one thing. " She said. "You can't fall in love with me. I'm serious. Don't do it. Don't even think about it."

"Okay." I couldn't tell if she were joking or not but I didn't care, I was up and walking and on my way to getting laid.

I was astounded.

*

Her body was chiseled yet elongated and her skin as smooth and as fragile as porcelain. She was sporty yet elegant and everything about her seemed drawn tight with what looked liked years of intense Pilates training. She reminded me of the gal in Hector's book with her leg up, except Kat had darker skin – it was the color of a café au lait. She had everything off except her white burlesque top and was sitting on her bed with her legs crossed, waiting patiently for me to get my boots off. I fumbled nervously with the new laces but eventually the bastards kicked off. She stood up and walked over and turned around. "I'll need a little help with this," she said, arms raised behind her head and pointing down to the corseted back. She bent over as I loosened the bust and thrust her ass up against me. I went full throttle before I could even get my pants off. It is not an enjoyable experience, being suffocated by stonewash denim. It makes a man bend over awkwardly at the waist to release the life-threating amount of pressure put on his main-vein. If a man doesn't do this, it feels like his holy tendon might tear off. I found the buttons and ripped downward. They came off along with my briefs in one fell swoop and I was finally out there. Swaying Free. Kat smiled at my naked body. I couldn't tell you if it was a smile of "Oh fuck yes, this is happening," or "Oh lord, what have I gotten myself into," but, either way, it was still going to happen so I smiled back.

We got to dancing the horizontal tango and there was no talking. Just the rough, pulling, sloppy, slapping, leg-locking, sweat-beading, hard-driving fornication that only the cheap excitement of strange love can produce. We were at it for a while, bumping pelvises for fifteen minutes plus and by then I had grown exhausted and was now lying on the bed with her on top, riding in reverse. She had an arch of her back that allowed her short hair to dangle in my face as she slowly pumped up and down.

I had a thing for flexible women.

Who doesn't?

We kept plugging, turning, thrusting — she ever in control of the rhythm. I grabbed her hair and locked my hand around her neck. Fuck me, it was hot. I felt proud of myself for my stamina but the second I thought about how long we'd been at it was the second I knew it was about to be over. She asked me intuitively if I were about to go. I must've been making horrific noises that clued her in and then I growled, "yes" all too loudly. She yelled "wait!" and jumped off of me, throwing her lady lapels back down on my face while she brought her mouth down to my sex to finish the job. We were now in a position I hadn't done since high school and I was euphoric. I could only lick her twice before she cleaned my heavy load whole. My body winced at the sight of paradise and I made a face like my balls were set on an electric fence. And then it was over. I fell asleep and woke to her reading beside me. I apologized for dozing off afterward. I told her sex either energizes me or makes it seem as though the life had just been sucked out of me. She shot me a face that said 'that was exactly what happened' and I felt corny and unoriginal.

Note to self: try not to speak after sex.

"So what is it you do, Frank?"

I thought it odd that we hadn't covered the question before the humping commenced. We had covered the thick of my backstory, my most daunting problems and setbacks – my mother and father – but how had we not touched on my aspirations? Back east "what do you do?" is pretty much a given inside of the first two minutes. Usually, the question ruins everything, at least for me. Actually, now that I think about it, I'm pretty sure it ruins the majority of people's conversations who aren't proud of what they do (ahem, which is a majority of the people). And what was it that I did again? Ah, yes, I'm a writer that hasn't written more than a page in six months. So what does that make me? A nothing? A loser? A do-over? I sat up and started to get dressed. It would only be a matter of minutes before she put two and two together and sees me for what I am and asks me to leave.

"I'm a novelist." I sighed while sliding on my briefs. "Well, aspiring novelist. I want to write Romance Novels for men."

"That's interesting."

"Oh no…" I felt hopelessly glum over her word choice. "You said it."

"Said what?"

"*Interesting.*"

"Yeah, so what?"

"It's a telltale sign of failure."

"Not following you?"

"Interesting is something people say today when they are really not that interested at all. It's one step away from *awe-*

some. It's become a placeholder in conversation. Dead air. A new ruin."

"You're a weird guy, ya know that?"

"Unfortunately." I say, nodding and buttoning up my flannel. "It's okay, interesting is still a rung up from boring... I guess."

"Frank. I said it because I thought it was genuinely interesting. Not because it's boring or because you're a pedantic paranoid. I've never heard anybody else say what you just said. It's original...in a quirky sort of way."

I sat back down on the bed and slowly continued to tie my boots.

"Well I was kind-a-going for quirky. I mean, men don't want a Romance Novel. They want honesty and humor and if somehow those two can deliver it – a little bit of hope. My aim is to give them that and poke some fun at a genre in the meantime."

"Why don't you just give them that and say fuck the genre?"

My posture struck upward and I felt suddenly changed. Her words were so obvious and true that it was as if someone had just severed a few of the fibers between the left and right hemispheres of my brain. I must've sat there dazed for a little too long because she ended up asking me if I were okay. I tell her yes and she apologizes and then tells me she didn't mean to intrude. I tell her that she wasn't and she might've helped me in the long run. Then she asks me about my name and I don't understand where she's going with it.

"Frank Gently. It's kind of an oxymoron, ya know?"

"How so?" I was genuinely perplexed. Pointing out oddities in wordplay was my forte.

"Well if someone is being frank they are rarely gentle about it. Right? Harsh, if anything, but gentle? Never. So, your name is kind of beautiful in a way. On the one hand it means to come forward and speak your mind, be truthful, be frank, and on the other, it is a reminder to be soft and mindful, to tread gently into the waters of others…to be Frank Gently is to be thoughtful yet forthcoming at the same time. It's rather remarkable, actually."

Water found my eyes. It didn't seem natural for me to well up over a compliment, but no words had ever hit me with such force before. What was casual had turned touching and what was touching had turned liberating. I felt my feet plant firmly on the ground. My shoulders relaxed and my breathing steadied. I had been baptized, rearranged and unveiled in such a way that I was now vulnerable again. I guess I hadn't let myself be vulnerable in a long, long while. Kat's words had unfurled my chest to the world and all that went along with it: pain and happiness, sadness and joy. Her words were all of those things together – a new beginning.

"That's one of the nicest things anyone has ever said to me." I turned back to her smiling cappuccino-tinted face. "And to think, I've hated everything about my name for the past half year."

"Why?"

"Because my parents gave it to me."

"Well, it's a great gift. All the more reason to call your mother and tell her thank you." She winked at me and I got up and gathered the rest of my things.

"*This* was a great gift." I said, bending over to kiss her swollen lips one last time. I whispered "thank you" in her ear and made my way to the door. I turned the knob and glanced back at her once more to drink in the scene. She was a still image, naked and composite, lying coolly and poised on the bed. A vision. I didn't want to leave her but something about our conversation and the way we were speaking said it was right. It was as if our sand glass had just run out and we were both thankful and readied to turn it back over again.

"How do you do it?" I said. "Your light, it fills the room."

Her artistic demeanor turned girlish, losing its aloofness straight away. She bit her lip in an attempt to keep it from curling upward.

"I'll keep my eye out for The Weeklings." I said.

"I'll keep my eye out for Frank Gently." She said.

We glinted eyes once more, nodded to one another gracefully and then I shut the door.

Chapter 11

The Call

I dialed the number.

She didn't pick up, so I hung up.

She was not going to get some pithy little voice mail from me that said all was forgiven (for in truth, it could never be forgotten).

No. That wasn't going to happen.

The Affable Looneys and I were set to leave bright and early the following morning for Yosemite. I needed this to be resolved by then. Was I to sit and wait for her to call me? Linger on in some perpetual state of unrest? No, I was tired of the shit of my past looming overhead. It was time for resolution.

I called again.

This time she picked up.

"Bud?"

"Hi Mom."

"*Oh my god*, Bud!" She had called me Bud since before I could remember. "Did you just call a second ago? I saw your name but I didn't think it was you. I thought I was seeing things – hearing things. I have been really low lately and my mind has been playing tricks on me and when I saw your name I thought the phone company was purposefully messing with me. It had to have been? I thought you never wanted to speak to me again.."

"Mom." I interrupted her, she would have gone on for minutes, possibly hours, recounting every detail of the last time we had spoke at the funeral: how what I'd said almost killed her and how she never gave up hope that I would one day come back around to her and then, segue into some lofty tangent, talking rotten of the government tapping her phone-lines, *everybody's phone-lines*, and how the Patriot Act is the end of the world as we know it and "the death of habeas corpus" and then ask if I had seen that-one-documentary-on-it, it was an amazing documentary and everyone should see it, and then, somehow clamor on about her new passion surrounding Tibet or the liberation of the child slaves outside of Mumbai or even the latest union-lead victory in Beacon, NY that, all of which, had her vociferous backing...it was just her way. Even now, on the phone, I quickly realized I could no longer hold it against her. We are all built with certain defects in the system, certain bugs in the beta software, hers just happened to come with no filter and absolutely zero awareness of the importance of the situation at hand.

To Victoria Gently all situations were important, all causes eminent, all people essential and though that may sound lovely or what you might even call saintly, if left unchecked, had the ability to topple the pillars of love that are so essential to family life. Now, I'm not saying she was ever on the wrong side of an important topic – her entire being has been dedicated to living on the right side of history – I am just saying that by design, she was unaware of the fact that when you get wrapped up in too many topics, your attention spreads thin and the one issue that was never supposed to be a topic of importance to begin with, for it was inherently important – family life – would always suffer. Perhaps that is why most saints don't have kids. Or maybe that is because the church is still backwards on celibacy. And those two things might be completely irrelevant, but either way, I could no longer blame Victoria Gently for who she was.

"If we can," I continued. "I'd like for this to be as painless as possible. Which I don't think is possible. But I think we should try."

"Okay. What would you have me do?"

"If it is alright with you, I'd just like to ask some questions. I know I said some pretty horrible things to you at Edward's funeral."

There was dead space between our phone lines. I *had* said horrible things. I also couldn't stand calling the man by his first name – Edward. How formal and grotesque. But, I couldn't call him dad either. It had something to do with the difference between father and dad. He would always be my father, of course, but he wasn't and never would be my dad. Your father was your reason for being. But your dad, on the other hand, made you mac and cheese with Frank's hot sauce on it; he poured milk over your Lucky Charms and told you to wait to drink the milk until after the marshmallows had changed the milk's color; he tucked you in at night while reading to you the wild stories of Jack London and woke you up early in the morning to go fly-fishing and he taught you how to work the grill or check the oil or how to tie a fly on; he showed you how to be a Great Dad yourself, should you

one day decide to join the ranks of explorer in the last grand
adventure there is – parenthood. It wasn't Edward's fault, but
nevertheless he could never be my dad. It would never feel
right.

"I – um." I stumbled slightly and then found my footing.
"I said some things I'm not proud of, and I want to start off
by taking them back." She started to cry a little through the
speaker. "I just need some understanding, though, and I don't
have much time. So I want to get down to the bones of
things, all right? I'm tired of this skeleton hanging in the
closet."

"Oh Bud! I'm just so happy to hear your voice! To know
you are doing well. You sound so good and healthy and I'm
just.."

"Yes, I'm okay." Another interruption. "*I am okay.* Honestly, I am. But I need to know some things..."

"What do you want to know?"

"My father."

"Yes, yes, of course."

"At the funeral when I walked away from you, you said
that you kept him from me to keep me from getting hurt. I
know there is much more to it than that: Your problems with
money and inheritance and that he wouldn't run away with
you and a whole bunch of other things that make little sense
to me, but...*why?* Why did you take me away from him?
What was the one thing that did it? And I want the truth or I
hang up, okay? What was it you were hiding from me?"

"*Gently Gentry & Co.*" She said.

"What about it?"

"So you know it?"

"Of course. It was his publishing firm. Failing now. But it
had its heyday back in the '80s, right? I Googled it and

skimmed over it at face value when I realized I might have a new way to publish a book."

"Oh dear."

"What?"

"*Gently Gentry & Co.* isn't just a publishing firm, it was originally *The Company of Gentlemen*." She'd said it in such an ominous way that I felt my stomach rise into my throat. I muscled through it. "Have you heard of it, Bud?"

"I think so."

I had heard of it. *The Company of Gentlemen* was an underground coalition of powerful businessmen in the publishing world that started back around the time of Hearst. Think Freemasons meets Big Oil but with absolute control in the realm of paper – and therefore, at the time, information. By creating an unspoken monopoly, (I would later learn that my great-grandfather along with some of the other powerful robber barons had been instrumental in its creation) they controlled the materials behind both paper and presses and in turn, had both journalism and literature in the palms of their hands. Their power over raw materials and labor was supreme and was only surpassed by their disregard for the human race – sacrificing herds of Irishman, Italians and Chinese by the boatload all for the sake of progress. Granted, it was a different time back then; one of Manifest Destiny and 'Capitalism At Any Cost' but to hear that the Gently family might've had a hand in it almost seemed unsurprising. Sickening, yes. Horrible, of course, but to me – and this is probably a testament to the maddening teachings of the lady on the other end of line – no land throughout history was ever aquired by just means, it was taken. And more often than not, taken at the cost of human life. I guess that is why the d'if could never be mine, would never be mine. There was no way in the world one man deserves that much. It was a museum for chrissake, and museums are meant for the public. But what was I supposed to do? Give it away? Donate it to a charity and let the Gently name float on air for the rest of history? No. That just won't do. Unlike Frick and Getty and the rest of the white-haired usurpers whose private islands of opulence and art were all built to chisel their family name into stone, and in giving it back to the public, they saw to it that their stone would live on polished and perfect, forever cast in a positive light – a giving light – the people ever forgetful of the actual history and ruthless actions they took to build their fortunes in the first place...I for one would not add the Gently name to house-held emblems of hypocritical philanthropy. No, I wasn't going to play a role in refracting some bullshit trick of the light...exactly as all those vain men had done before me.

"Well if you looked it up," she continued. "You wouldn't find any part of it attached to *Gently Gentry & Co.* and for good reason. Hundreds of millions of dollars were spent to keep the ties between the two companies undiscoverable by the public."

"And this is where you tell me why they spent all that money."

"Yes. But it is not that easy. Nothing in life ever is."

"I'm listening."

"I loved your father. We were in love for many years all through our youth and all of boarding school. He traveled from Taft to visit me at Miss Porter's every other weekend. Our lives were filled with romance, bereft of problems. We had no worries, no wants, no needs – we only had each other and the endless floating clouds of a promising future... together. *We were so young...*" She had a wistful tone about her, one that was so far away and foreign it was as if she was speaking about a life she'd read in a book, not one that she herself had actually lived.

"It looked like we could make it and be happy and we were talking about running away and eloping. But then came the eighties and the floundering civil rights movement and the failure of Vietnam and Reagan and everything changed between us. His family thought me unfit for him and my family threatened me with an asylum if I wouldn't follow the path they had laid out for me: I was to go to Barnard University and if they would've had their way, gone abroad to study law. But this was when I started to get 'involved,' as everyone said back then, with the wrong crowd. After I graduated I went to rallies, spoke to union officials, I became active... awakened. I became conscious of what side of the struggle I was on and I realized I was on the wrong side. It not only felt wrong, but abusive and corrupt, caring only for status and keeping it. *It just felt bad, Bud.* More than that, self-serving. You could feel it in your bones that this wasn't the way things were supposed to be if other people were hurting. Your father and I would still see each other that summer, even though he would jibe at the feminist movement, putting me down and calling me and 'my childish aspirations' an 'outcry for attention' in front of his family. You should have seen their faces, Bud. They called me a socialist behind my back. A Marxist. I had never even read Marx! I'll never forget them and the pitiful looks they gave me."

"So it was just a political difference?" I asked.

"At first. And then came the end of our summer and the pressures of prep for University. I was set to go to Barnard and he, Princeton. My mother took me shopping...for a BMW. A graduation gift. *You hear me, Bud?* A BMW for graduating high school! I wanted nothing of it. She said it was the first step in a long list of steps for becoming Barnard Ready. She did nothing but talk of all the past influential women who came from there and how important this next step was for me and how I can't screw it up by entertaining these embarrassing pinko beliefs any longer. I hated her for that. Treating me like a child when I was no longer a child. I could never go to Barnard – I had been institutionalized my entire life! It got so bad that when they threatened me with putting me in a hospital I'd yell back that it would probably be no worse than living at their compound."

"I understand Ma, I do. But how does any of this relate to you taking me away from him?"

"Listen and I'll tell you. I would ask your father over and over again, how were we to live freely when our entire lives had been laid out for us? Pre-decided down to the make and model of the car we drove? Where was the choice? Where was anything that we could call *our own*? He said it was the sacrifice we had to make for being who we were. I disagreed. I said there was still a choice and it was the money. I told him that this money, our family inheritance was our prison. I told him we were shackled by tradition; we were bound to it like the chains that were placed on all of the people who made our families unbelievably wealthy. Except all of those unfortunate families didn't have a choice – they *had* to work. We had a choice though, we could leave. Leave it all behind and start anew, together. I felt as though he couldn't see that. That he couldn't connect the dots, or didn't want to. He couldn't see that all of our wealth came delivered on the backs of others. I asked him to research his family name and he grew deeply offended and irrational over the matter, screaming and ranting that he would hear nothing more of it.

The truth is, Bud, he didn't *want* to know. Or maybe he already knew and was playing me for a fool. Either way, he said his job was to do the best with what was given to him and that was that. And when Edward Gently's mind was made up, there was no going against it. He was eighteen and narrow, and I'm sure the same could've been said about me at that age. You might actually still think that about me, Bud..." Deep breaths came through. "But I have changed a lot. Really, I have.

"Okay."

"We made love the night I ran away and it was the last time I would see him for almost thirty years. I would find out a couple of months later that you were conceived that night. And I couldn't go back. I had left everything behind. I didn't want that life anymore, for me, for Edward, for you. But Edward stayed, and I don't blame him for it. It was what he felt was right and I did the same. And listen to me, Bud. You have to believe me...I didn't want you to be raised by a nanny and some boarding school faculty. I didn't want you to inherit the money and the control and the guilt that surrounded it. I wanted you to have a free life. And look, you still inherited all of the shit that came with the Gently name in spite of everything. I'm a fool for believing it could've been different. I realize that now and I am sorry. So so sorry."

Her voice was breaking; regret came seeping out of the phone. I started to feel poorly myself. She had been living up the river in Beacon for almost ten years now and we never saw each other once besides Edward's funeral.

"Is that why you took his name?" I asked, seeking justification. "Our last name?"

"Yes, you were still *his* in a way and I figured it was a clever step to hide my own tracks."

"So that was it then? That was the major reason why you kept me from him?"

"No. That was what started it...what finished it was the cover up."

"The cover up?"

"Yes, when I saw the man for who he was, when I saw Edward Gently for who he'd turned into."

"Okay?"

"Listen, I thought about taking you back to him, I really did. When you were four and I felt guilty about you not having a father. I was struggling. It was probably the worst time in my entire life. He would've raised you and loved you and I felt miserable over keeping you from him. But then I learned about the cover up. I had sent a letter to one of my closest friends from school. Her name was Julie and you and I both owe her a lot to this very day. In the letter I described my harrowing four years by myself and how they'd now come to a frightening head with you having the flu, a hundred and four fever and with me having no money to get you into a hospital. I had just been laid off from my cashier job at the supermarket which left only the babysitting and that only made enough to cover the rent or the food – not both. I wrote Julie to come meet me but only if she would not tell a soul and that if our ten years of friendship had meant as much as it had to me then she would come alone. I left her specific directions and she came, the angel! She came by herself and wanting for nothing but to help. The first thing we did was take you to the clinic and they put you on antibiotics. It probably saved your life, you had contracted strep as well. Everything about our situation was horrid and it was terrifying for Julie to see us that way but I knew who she was, who she really was. She was help, goodness incarnate. She left us that night and said she'd be back tomorrow and she came back the following day with five thousand dollars in cash. She'd gone down to the city and pawned her pearls. I started crying and told her I couldn't take it. It would kill me if I took it. I told her I had been thinking of going back to your father anyway. He had graduated by now and was probably going to start working soon and could easily take us in. And then Julie told me about the Gently cover up. Gossip spreads faster than wildfire in high society, you know, that *is* all they have to do – talk about one another. Apparently UNICEF had taken the Gently family to court two years earlier involving the use of child slaves in multiple countries in Asia and Indonesia. This was exactly the same time when the firm switched names to *Gently Gentry & Co.* A new moniker, free of all its past lies and dirty dealings and blood money. Julie told me that your father had taken over the reins of the new company and was not only on board with the whole cover-up, but had helped engineer the entire plan from inside out. Julie had been out for drinks and had even heard Edward bragging to his cronies, gloating about 'plausible deniability' and how it meant he and the company of amoral gentlemen would go on, untouched and beautiful. 'A well-oiled money making machine,' were his words. This was before computers and the Internet and eventually the entire print world would suffer and the company, by divine providence, would go under, as you very well know. But, as far as you are concerned, why I never let you – let us – go back to him was easy. To learn that he was the brain behind all of the swindling, that the innocent and warmhearted boy I once knew had now turned into his father – cold and corrupt and purely focused on money – well, I could never bring you back to him for fear of the cycle continuing. To my eternal embarrassment, I took the money from Julie and it gave us a buffer. Enough to survive and enough for us to create a somewhat normal life until I found stable work and could support you."

I imagined myself to be smiling at this moment but forgot that she couldn't see me and still had no way of knowing what my face was really doing. If a smile were there, it would've been the first time I smiled in the presence of my mother in over a decade.

"I wouldn't call it normal, Mom." I said, half-joking.

"I know, Bud. I am sorry. I have done a lot of thinking and…"

"It's okay." I interrupted again. I had heard what I needed to hear. "Listen, let's not go down roads already traveled." There it was again. The same line I had fed to June not a week ago. I still didn't know what it meant. Was I growing up or was I faking it? A bit of both?

I told her that it had helped to speak to her and hearing her out was something I wish I had done in the first place. I told her I would be in touch with her again soon and that I needed to figure some things out on my own but, she should know she had helped. The other end of line felt fragile and I could hear a shakiness in her voice, a worrisome tremble that this still might be the last time we'd speak to one another. I reassured her that I would be in touch soon and to prove it true, I told her I was thankful for her in doing what she thought was right for me. I told her it fucked me up something fierce the past six months, but it also made me cherish the life I had lived just up until that envelope arrived. As small and unaccomplished a life it was, it was still a life full of everything worthwhile:

People and the words that bond us.

And now I wanted that life back.

I was going to have it back.

And that was that.

It appears that despite Victoria's best efforts, I inherited one of Edward's traits after all: When my mind was made up about something, there was no going against it.

Chapter 12

Movers and Shakers
Monumental

"Yes. This is the place. This is perfect. This is where it will all go down." The voice felt extremely far away. "This is where we will forget ourselves, my friend. Can you hand me that wide-lens...?"

The words slowly drifted out of range. I could hear them but they weren't there. Something had happened and I was shut off. A wall had formed and I stood there engulfed in a muffled silence of solitude, a translucent haze of awe that hung bold in the air with nothing but the light chirping of birds and a balmy spring breeze to keep me grounded. The wind rattled the branches of stoic cedars and pines together and reminded me that the valley floor was not the end...it was the beginning. There were some deer in the foreground as well but they made no noise. They seemed tame. *They were tame.* Two fawns and two mothers, all playing gleefully amongst each other, dancing hoof to hoof, tails flipping white amongst a golden painted field of hay. Disney could not have captured their unbridled joy. Nope, old Walt would've been lost to their exotic innocence as they frolicked about, completely indifferent to their surroundings – a land that was older than time itself.

The holy land.

"*Frank.*"

Just above the deer was a thin green line, a fringe of what was actually a large bunch of evergreens in the distance that had become small and figurine-like, dwarfed by the grand vision that lay looming above, fatherly and commanding with its warm absorbent yellows and polished greys and time-worn face. El Capitan had come out of the earth. It was carved out by slow moving ice over millions of years ago, so smooth and pristine in its architecture that it spoke a silent language of immeasurable honesty. One whose loud truths were heard internally. What it says cannot be forgotten. It says the water was and always has been the hand of the creator, and we had now come to pay that creation homage. I had not come properly prepared. I had not known that when you look into the face of the mountain, the mountain looks back – and brings its enormity with it. It is too big for us to offer any dialogue. We try and we try and we fail. Again and again, we fail. Our silence is the only thing worthy of its time. There is nothing like shutting up and just being, looking...attempting to *see* in Yosemite. Time passed and I looked and looked but still could not see. I had gotten lost in its immensity and drifted in and out of mind. Looking into the face of El Capitan was like gazing into a hypnotist's charm, listening to a siren's call, every sense was drawn in and then out again, like a slow moving tidal wave that recedes and pulls every ounce of you out to sea at first only to come barreling back through you, leaving everything rearranged and washed anew, not damaged but certainly not the same either – better. I was still out to sea when Hector came calling again.

"Frank! There will be plenty of time for that. We're gonna be here a couple weeks, bro." Hector had removed the lens-viewer, a two-foot technological wonder that looked like a futuristic sea-man's telescope, from his face and noticed I had wandered down into the high grass and unknowingly moved almost fifty feet away from our setup. "*Punta!* Hey! I need that wide-lens box!"

My gaze finally broke, "Sorry. This is just too much."

"Happens to everyone." He continued, "Only gets better. We got the best seat in the house."

He had a knowing smile about the place that could only come from a regular. It was of someone who had been here many, many times. He brought the telescope back to his right eye with the casual authority of a man who knew what he was doing. His entire body posed, left foot slightly in front of the right, his shoulders back and belly sticking out just enough to help produce the presence of an explorer on the brink of discovering the fountain of youth. A modern day Juan Ponce a De Lee-Hector.

"Right. Did you say weeks?" I said, swinging my gaze back toward the illuminated monolith.

"Yeap. The best guys in the world free-climb it in twenty days. Our guys'll probably do it in twenty-five or so."

No one had mentioned to me how long the entire trip was going to be. Again, everything was vague – the goddamn Affable Looney way of life – details didn't matter. It was the trip that mattered: the climb and the capture. I stood staring once again at the wall, dumbfounded. At that moment, I didn't care about details either. Then something salty melted on my lips. I couldn't believe it. I was crying. The tears had now streamlined their way down my cheeks and only their salty brine reminded me to bring my sleeve to my face. It was a confusing cry for it wasn't sadness that brought out this reaction, it was the mountain. It had filled me with every emotion at once. As unsettling as it was, I imagined it to be exactly how a baby feels when brought to light, when every single thing is new and frightening and entertaining and alive, that you yourself are a part of it all and all of it is an adventure. *Every single thing is new.* 'No wonder we're gifted with a latency period,' I thought, starry-eyed and woozy, 'to be constantly overwhelmed like you are in infancy had to be a dream that constantly turned nightmare.' There was that in its entirety here, at the base of El Capitan. It was not so much nightmarish as it was just all-around frightening. Through and through, the thing shook you. To stand before the wall was to submit yourself as nothing more than a child, an infant who knew nothing but a toddler capable of everything. That was what Yosemite gave you and that was why so many people flocked back to its hallowed ground, year after year. It gave you your childhood back, the feeling that the world was still yours.

"...gonna need that lens sometime today, cabrone."

"Okay! Okay!"

I wiped my face again and walked over to the big pile of heavy black boxes that we'd set up under a small tent. I scoured labels and finally found the box whose duct-taped label read WIDE-14mm. Before the trip got officially underway, I volunteered to be Hector's assistant cameraman. He mentioned it'd be nice to have an extra hand on deck while the boys did their thang. He had said it just like that too, *did their thang.* Casual, like they were going to power-wash a deck or gamble on some horses. What he was really talking about was *free climbing;* scaling hand-by-freaking-hand the vast grey shale of white that sat there menacingly before us, blotting out the sky. Sure, the massive rock was an inspiration from where we stood, but just the mere thought of hanging off that monument by two hands and a couple of ropes made me think otherwise. Made me sick. Jon and the rest of the guys were already at the base of El Capitan now making last minute preparations – re-checking the formulated path, testing rigs, saying Hail Marys, sacrificing a small goat to the rock gods – doing whatever it was rock climbers did. I would've been drinking heavily and talking fellow climbers out of the job, but that's just me.

"Ah, yes. Perfect." Hector swapped out the thousand dollar lenses like he was handling two cheap rolls of aluminum foil. *Shlap. Crink. Snap!* He had it back up to his eye again in seconds scanning the rock-face, back and forth devouring every inch of the scene. "Say Frank. I never did get to ask you."

"Yeah?"

"How'd the call go with Vic?"

"Meh. It served its purpose, I guess."

"Like all motherly convo's, eh?"

"I wouldn't say that."

"I meant to ask earlier but didn't know how you would've felt with every one hangin' around the jalopy."

"It's fine."

"Yeah? So it was a good call?"

"Meh."

"What does that mean? You on better terms now or what?"

"Well better, I guess. But not necessarily good terms."

"Then why call her if not to make up with her?"

"Well Hector, it wasn't really a make-up-type call. It was more an informational interview if you know what I mean."

"I don't really know what you mean." He removed the scope from his eye. "It's your mom. You only get one."

"I know. I know. Things are just still a little gray."

"Hm."

"Listen. You wouldn't know about it. You have good parents now."

"Yeah. *Now.*"

"Shit." I was embarrassed. How easily we shove our foot in our mouths when upset. "I'm sorry, that was really insensitive of me."

"It's okay."

"My mom and I are fine. It just is what it is, man."

Ahem. Did I just say *man*?

"And what *is...it?*" Hector said, not without a flicker of chiding.

I felt like he was challenging me. I had nothing left to say. I had just found out that almost all of my father's wealth came from covering up its ties to child slavery and other, probably much worse things – things I didn't even want to know about. My mother was finally straight forward about everything but does that mean I should up and forgive her for everything? Was she courageous? Or was my life just one big Molotov cocktail and she one of its main concoctors?

"I don't know what it is, Hector, that's why it is that way."

He laughed. "I'm fucking with you man! I never liked that saying. *It is what it is.*" I held back from telling him that I loathed almost every other saying that came out of his mouth. "It just never moved anything forward, ya know?"

"I guess. I think it is just an easy way to let things be for the moment."

"Right, but philosophically speaking. What is the point of *it?*"

"*It* is a misnomer, Hector," I was now fully annoyed and wanted to be back out in the field and enjoying the feeling of transportation. "*It* is whatever you want it to be. And please, this is our first day, let's maybe save the *deep* jawing for the second week when my ass is itchy and my back is sore and I have now regretted ever coming to this heavenly place."

"I doubt that'll happen." He smirked and we both looked back at the giant slab of stone that seemed to shake hands with the sky. "*Misnomer*, eh? I like that word. That would make sense then 'cuz I think *it* is a cherry."

"As in…the fruit?"

"Yeap." He switched back to the telephoto lens and brought it up to his eye, racking focus with grace and practiced ease. "The *it* has always been a cherry. And life, well, life is just a big bowl-a-cherries."

"Yeah?"

"Yeap. *The sweet, sweet pits.*"

"I like that. Who was that, Dear Abby?"

"Ann Landers."

We chuckled a bit. "This another test about me giving fucks?"

"Nah. This is about us being in Yosemite right now. To be here is to give no fucks."

"And the cherries?"

"They're pitted here."

He put away the gear and snapped the cases shut. I lit up a Toscono and offered him one. We smoked in a cheerful silence and our clouds of gray plumed and danced along the backdrop of El Capitan, saluting the old general on his long-time active duty as Awakener.

"I think we're pitted here, too, Heck."

Chapter 13

*The Climb
and
The Capture*

The climb started early the next morning, as did the capture. Hector and I had set up three different rigs: The first
was a wide-angle shot that wouldn't be touched through out
the duration of the trip save to change batteries, and even that
had to be a fragile, gingerly done exchange. Its legs were dug
a foot into the ground and then covered up with sand and
dirt to minimize the chance of the frame being jostled. It was
primed to take a photo every two hours of the crew's entire
climb — a massive time-lapse is what it was. Completely
unprecedented in the climbing world, it was the camera to
etch the climbers' names into the stone of Yosemite as much
as it was Hector's. The other two rigs were more for "glam
than glory," as Hector put it. The massive telephoto lens was
almost a foot and a half in length itself, would be moved and
shot merely for close-ups (as would be the Go-Pros mounted
on each climber) and to put a face to the difficulties that
arose throughout the climb. It was the magazine rig, the
photo-op tripod; the pretty-picture-taker, in laymen's terms.
It was the camera that financed the whole trip; Hector had

pitched a short doc to Red Bull about the struggles climbers must face with such a feat and, of course, the X-games reps gobbled it up whole without batting an eye. Boy would I love to've been there for that pitch:

"See fellas, there's like, a whole bunch-a-hard shit you have to overcome when doing something truly badass. It's like mental *and* physical. It's not just balls, but brains too. And that's Red Bull, yo: Brains, Balls And Broken Bones. *Bravery in a can.* And that's what we'll call the doc: *The Brave.* Boom."

I forgot to ask him if he dropped his mic on the way out. Or if he meant *the brave* as a euphemism for those who have the fortitude to put the contents of what lie inside that can inside their body.

…Shit, I don't know what I'm laughin' about – I'm in Yosemite because of it.

The last set-up was something I, being the noob that I am, didn't really understand. It was some special camera that would shoot in the wee hours of the morning/evening and the photos would come out looking like a singed daguerreotype of the early 1900's, except painted in Technicolor. Hector said it all had to do with the magic hour of lighting, a time when the sun's rays weren't so harsh. He said that the exposure could be left open longer when the sun wasn't so hot on the film and capturing the boys at sunup and sunset was the real reason he was so excited to be here. It would "make the most ghostly and beautiful and pastel-tinted imagery we had ever seen." He said, "It would be sumptuous, so good in fact it should be illegal." Hector then drawled on for too long, romance sadly giving way to science, and talked about the temperature of sunlight and how celluloid burns and all the minutia of film. The shit only nerds care to hear

about. I stopped him halfway through his spiel. I told him I
was down with being his sidekick and all but I knew, just as
he did, that this wasn't going to be a lifetime career change –
so the chemistry lessons could be kept to a minimum.

✳

Jon, Zev and Adé took to the wall and so began the nervous wreck that was me and my fear of heights…for others.
Eventually the vertigo would wear off, but for the first week
or so I felt like losing my lunch every time I saw one of the
boys fall from a lost grip and rely on a rope for support.

"They've been climbing things since before they could
speak." Hector would say, in a paternal attempt at comfort.
"They're happier up there than they are in the house, drinking around the fire pit or safe and sound in bed. So let it go,
bro."

I nodded and chose not to look into the telephoto lens
anymore. Every grip was too frightening, every fall sure to be
the last. Instead, I would follow the small figurines with my
eyes and if they got too tired, binoculars would do the trick.
It was easy during strong daylight to see them. They looked
like small little dots of highlighter blue and green and orange
from their climbing jackets. They moved so slowly it seemed
like they never moved at all, like watching caterpillars move
across a deck, all the while praying that a bird doesn't come
down and swoop up the little-soon-to-be-butterflies before
they got their deserved chance to bloom. It was a reminder of
Muir's famous lines about the National Parks, "Everybody
needs beauty as well as bread." If you cannot tell, I am with
him. We should all get to see the butterfly before the birds

have their fill. I'm sure Darwin would have a thing or two to say about that, but he's not here right now, so fuck 'em.

I realize now that I am just regurgitating what has already been said more thoroughly in the journal I kept while camping in the Yosemite Valley. Of the four notebooks purchased back in LA, one was dedicated to the climb and the three remaining 7x11's to the continuation of my book. I had ample time to write and it was the best place for it. I've notched out almost all of the boring gripe, the usual and expected complaints, the my-ass-is-itchy-from-haven't-having-a-shower-in-a-week type stuff, which was rampant throughout the entries. If I left some of that in, forgive me. It was Yosemite after all and the things we gripe about in Yosemite aren't your usual nine-to-five whine. What follows here is the journal – the book comes later.

THREE DOTS ON A WALL
A JOURNAL OF YOSEMITE

WEEK ONE:

Cold morning to start climb. Our thermometer read below freezing at sunup. Hector said it was good luck to climb in the cold. Something about the grip and cold rocks being sticky. It sounded mad to me but Hector seemed to know what he was talking about. He sounded more and more like a Native American the longer we stayed in Yosemite. Abundantly wise, compulsively superstitious...tan. We started recording and Jon, Zev and Adé crested the fringe of green pines late in the evening. Their journey was 3,000 feet straight up. I can barely sustain myself while writing it. They were to ascend a vertical labyrinth of razor sharp rock edges, handholds smaller than golf balls and a cliff face as smooth as a kitchen wall. No one asked me but if they did, I would've told them that this is the place where Insanity & Impossibility screw each other and make a baby called Stupidity. It was to take them three weeks at best. They would sleep in a tent that was suspended off the wall by chained-in supports. They would poop into compost bags and pee off the side of the wall. They would get food delivered by the support team they had climbed with before who would rappel down from the top. It all sounded like some bad dream, that the sport of it had been lost long ago and the competitive sickness was all that remained. Forget rock climbing for the love of rock climbing, the need to be legendary was all that mattered anymore. I once again told Hector that it made me ill to think about. He said worrying the whole time didn't do anyone any good and I might as well make my peace with it on the first day or go find another cameraman to be an assistant to. I got my shit together. Hector and I cooked on a little Coleman stove and on our first night he made the best fajitas this side of the Rio Grande, or at least Chili's. He said I should enjoy it because we won't be eating this well again until they are at the top (he kept to his word). We drank two bottles of strong wine and then I got loopy. I hadn't really been drinking all that much and christ if I didn't hear a loud buzz through the grapevine that night.

Later, I was sent back to Ronda Verula, our hostess with the mostess — the jalopy that also just happens to share the same initials as an R.V. — Ronda Verula. *Ronda, she is something else.* I think Hector found her in a junkyard somewhere. With her anti-yuppie exterior and her pro-patchouli interior, hippies and surfers have been using her up and down Route 1 for the past thirty years. She smelled of must but was charming, in her own way, and had felt-pull-curtains and carpeted walls of rust-ugly-orange. (Interior decorators from the '70's should be shot.) She was our charging station for batteries and was parked a couple miles away in a tourist nightmare of a parking lot. I was glad we didn't sleep there, though the pull down double bed in Ronda's rump might've been nice, but still. You were packed in that parking lot like sardines: Loud people and noxious cars one on top of the other, fire pits five yards away from your neighbor, communal bathrooms, picnic tables full of hotdogs and beer. It was society vs. paradise and society won out. Garbage cans and loud chatter and litterers along with the overall ugly ignorance of people came included in the package. I made the trek there every day to change out batteries unless Hector said he wanted to, which was rare. He saw movement as a declaration of war on his body. Every morning Hector and I would wake up at 4:30am to set up shop and make sure the boys were where they had projected to be. They climbed mostly in the early & late hours because it would get too hot during the day and the sweat on their hands would halt their progress, sometimes stopping them dead in their tracks until they had completely cooled off.

By the fifth day the camp had taken on a life of its own, as did the heart-stopping ascent. Hector and I, though now sore from little sleep and uneven grassy beds and a tad smellier than when we first arrived, had found our groove and none of it could ever qualify as work. When you are looking up at that massive tribute to nature, I doubt even cold-calling tax lawyers for new business would seem like work. At the end of the sixth day, the boys were ahead of schedule and almost three hundred feet higher than where they had expected to be. It gave me hope. And when people you know are literally hanging off the side of a cliff, hope can be intoxicating. Jon had turned on his phone and called Hector on the seventh night and said Adé had dislocated a finger joint and that they would all rest the next day and see how it heals. It was bad news. If he couldn't continue the climb, they all must come down. It was a very long day. Hector let me drink more wine to calm my nerves. I drank too much and 4:30 came way too early. The hurt wore off quickly though, as I imagine any injury would in this place: The sunrises and sunsets of Yosemite are therapeutic and its restorative wonders cannot be captured on canvas with oil nor watercolor. Nor can they truly be captured by our expensive, high-powered cameras. They could only be felt. You think your eyes are the only things doing the work but this is untrue. It literally wraps itself around your head, your entire body and gets inside you, slowly seeping into your skin. The magic hour...with its vast array of pastels splashing and dancing on the wall, evolving as they mix; exotic spices of cinnamon and paprika turned pale yellow, embarrassing vermillion giving way to fair and light-headed pinks that dive quickly into deep purple and end, ultimate and undulate, by way of an unforgiving indigo...it is something I will never tire of; I hope it never tires of me. I stay quiet as to not disturb the slow illustrious work at hand.

To let The Painter paint.

The brush strokes on with a rolling hush into night, an unlabored breath into twilight. A Boom. Thunderclap! Lightning and then stars.

WEEK TWO:

Adé continues to climb despite a ring finger that has now swollen to the size of a small link-sausage. They are all warriors and I am not made of the same blood. Wearing the same clothes day in day out makes me realize this. These men are pooping into bags while I bitch to Hector about putting on the same pair of socks I wore last Tuesday and Thursday. Hector enjoys my ranting. He has labeled me the man "incapable of not giving fucks." It fittingly sounds like a Native American name and I tell him that I will return the favor soon. It will be a name 'worthy of the great valley,' I say. We then fell into talking about the name Yosemite itself and how it was derived. Apparently, it was given by the first rangers who rode into the park back in the 1800's. Hector spoke of how the first time the rangers met the tribe that had lived in the valley for thousands of years and how they had mistaken the word Yosemite for what the tribe had labeled the valley. The tribe's label was actually describing the white men they were talking to. Yosemite, in the native tongue, means, "they are not to be trusted, they are killers."

A truck hums off in the distance and our jokes trail off and we sit somber and reflective the rest of the day. I ponder past mistakes the country has made and they slowly meander into the personal mistakes I have made and I then dwell for too long on the hope that forgiveness has meaning...the small herd of deer continue to play and feed before us despite our gloomy atmosphere. Mercy is a word that comes to mind often now when I think of Native American reservations...where was our mercy? Where is it now? Will it ever show its face in the nation's follies to come, both private and public? When will we become soft to one another? Learn and grow from history instead of repeating it? These questions go on and on, circling round and round, spiraling ever downward into loathing and contempt for the black-hearted.

Finally, the sun wanes late in the afternoon and the boys are back on the wall climbing arduously, albeit slowly, and I am reminded of better things to come. I am reminded of the future and the sweet smell of the hayfield around me, its permanence and the history it has born witness to, reminds me that I myself am not permanent. I am okay with the thought and walk back to Ronda in the dark feeling painless and unafraid. A wolf howls in the distance on my walk back to camp and I feel wild. I am alive and grateful to feel that way. Most people live their lives without ever feeling alive. I breathe out steam in the cold and pass my hand through it and am delighted as it disappears like magic.

> I am alive!
> Goddammit!
> *You hear me!?*

> I AM ALIVE.

This is our twelfth night in the land before time and all things, big and small, are just the way they ought to be: *Flirtatious and strange.*

THE THIRTEENTH DAY:

A huge problem. There is a call from Jon at 2:30am. I was awake — couldn't sleep from the heavy conversation I had with Hector the night before. Jon told us that, with his hand as weak as it is, Adé is incapable of making the last large jump to a small hold on his own. He has been trying for the past four hours and his right hand just won't hold up. Jon whispers into the phone that Adé is beaten, broken down by the mountain. He knows the look, he's seen it before. It's traumatizing to a climb. They are now in deliberation over what should happen. If he can't make the jump they must either help him across with ropes and jeopardize the integrity of the climb, or the whole expedition must end and go back down – tails tucked. They are 1900 feet up. Just shy of two-thirds done. A calamitous situation. "It doesn't get worse than this," Hector says, after he hangs up. I asked him what we should do. He shrugs his shoulders. He said it was beyond him, beyond us. "The wall will let them know," he says, again, ever more sounding like a man who just left the reservation. Jon calls back and says that Adé wants one day of sound rest and then another hour of fresh attempts with taped hands and super-glued fingers. Jon abides and informs us nothing will be happening tomorrow on the mountain, "the tents will stay up." Hector says this is good because now it is my turn to climb. He tells me I will take the Mist Trail and walk the same steps as Muir in the morning. He tells me he would go with me but the equipment mustn't be left unattended to. I crack wise about the real reason of his not wanting to move and it having to do with moving itself. He snarls and then reminds me that he has walked the entire two-hundred and twenty miles of the Muir Trail and what I will be doing tomorrow, though difficult for a day hike, is a fraction of it. Still, he says, my eyes need to open more and that is why I am going. "The valley floor is for tourists," he says, "the trail...the trail is for the naturalist."

The Mist Trail:

Would never ever have believed to find myself agreeing with Hector, but the man was right. The trail was the portal – the way into the heart of Yosemite and the way out of society. The way to believe adventure was still real. The drive into and the camping around Yosemite were things everyone did. A glossed over lens of reflection.

Even at our campsite you could hear the bustling of trucks and tour buses careening down the main artery in and out of the Valley. It wasn't all the time, but it was still there, a reminder that you weren't *out there* – *in it all*. Wild. Not everyone actually got out and put their legs to use, their senses to overdrive, their mind to solitude. And as I would soon find out, there are moments on the Mist Trail that make you question your sanity. Tiny moments that make you wonder if you should turn back and mutter "Muir was a lunatic," over and over and over again all the way back down to safety. But no. You keep going. You tell yourself you must do what others have done, and what others will continue to do and you try to figure out why? And then it hits you: with each step you are working your way closer to a freer state. Liberation of the mind and soul.

And sometimes, it takes confronting your greatest fears to do it.

There are narrow steps cut out of the rock face along the Mist Trail with nothing between you and a nine hundred foot plunge to the end. It is here at the top of the Nevada and Vernal Falls where I am soaked from head to toe with thunderous, rushing glacier melt that I confront my petrifying fear of heights. It started with the water, the sound of water falling. It bounces, crashes and clamors off the side of the granite rock faces and proves that The Mist Trail takes its name seriously. A little too seriously if you ask me, it soaks you to the bone. If you're like me and didn't wear the proper attire, you stand there like a jackass, swishing in socks and clingy clothing while other vets of the trail pass by trying admirably to cover up rookie-mistake-smirks. You pay them no mind for your eyes and ears are too tied up, feverishly working to make sense of the waterfall's noisy and monstrous plunge over the side. The rushing violence and endless fall of the water jump-starts your heart while your throat clamps shut. This was a rational fear, mind you. Like any other sane being, I didn't want to go tumbling over the edge and have my last scene be of me, flailing arms and legs, screaming something like 'I should've tried sushi once!' before splattering my entrails on the rocks below.

But up there, as other more adept hikers and veteran trailsmen so effortlessly showed me, these falls were merely a pit stop en route to a longer and much higher trail above. It was all onward and upward to them. Forward motion is what kept them going, and in the end, what kept me going. Every time I looked down I wanted to stop. So, I no longer looked down. I continued hiking, up past the falls and the Mist Trail and on to the legendary Muir Trail. My shirt dried quickly from the steep elevation gain only to be replaced by sweat. My knees started to throb. I took a break and sat on one of the large stones and had a granola bar and some water.

Now, safe from the precipice edge of the steps and winding paths, I caught eyes with mighty Half-Dome, El Capitan's monumental counterpart in this grand world of power and allure. It was there across the way, perched magnanimously at my exact height on the opposite side of the valley floor. Its unique viewpoint and presence allowed me to see the park through the eyes of a man of the forest. A natural man. I had hiked almost four miles and four thousand feet higher than the Mist Trail and now found myself at a confluence of trails. Hikers passed, said hello, all properly dressed and decked out in actual hiking gear. I felt novice but enjoyed looking like an amateur. I was one after all. Everyone was nice and chatty and full of awesome and expected comments like, "Jesus. There it is." And "Wow. Look at that." All of them taken aback by Half Dome. My most favorite and most heard phrase being, "And just when you thought it couldn't get any better." I heard that one three times in fifteen minutes. It made me wonder how many times you heard those little gems on the trail. Probably not a whole lot for I don't expect you spend that much time with people on the trail. Maybe a few, here and there, in passing. I do, however, expect you'd hear those phrases riddled throughout your own inner monologue. And if you are as boyish and as nerdy as I am most of the time, you'd hear that inner monologue come fumbling out loud even when you're purposefully tight-lipped and in the company of others.

Bzz. BZZZ. BZzZZZT!

Three bees came and were humming about me while I tried to not say things out loud to Half-Dome. I played the whole just-lie-still-game figuring they'd soon move on to greener pastures and sweeter smelling flowers. That didn't happen. That didn't happen because those bees weren't bees; they were yellow jackets, or *man-eaters* as they are referred to in Yosemite. They are rumored to have killed many horses back in the day when horses were used on the trail. Just two or three stings in the neck and it would be all over. And then, the little bastard stung the shit out of me! It felt like being whipped on the shoulder. I hadn't even moved, the little son-of-a-bitch! Fucker pissed me off! It stung me for no reason other than being human, which I suppose is reason enough. I swatted at the little shit and then more were upon me (I didn't know this till later but yellow jackets are pure evil. If swatted at, they will send out a pheromone that brings the whole effing nest and its deadly wrath upon the swatter). They will sting you for no reason and most of them don't die from stinging like other bees do. They are now up there on my list right next to the Mosquito as Nature's Worst Mistake. My shoulder swelled to the size of a softball and knowing how funeral parlors are always looking for new clientele, new shoes to shine, I took off running. That wasn't going to be my end, no sir-ee, certainly not from a bunch of goddammed mutant bees. I slowed a good hundred yards later and the adrenaline wore off. I realized it might be a good time to turn around and head back to camp, especially if my reaction to the sting got worse. My shoulder was now one big mushy grapefruit. It was a good seven miles back to the camp, the total trip being a sixteen-mile hike round-trip with over eight thousand feet elevation gain. When you do all that, and when you do it in the Holy Granite Temple of Yosemite, with its baptizing waters and fear-confronting lookouts and hell-born insects, something comes out of you: a song and dance. It is something like an Irish rural jig mixed with an African stomp, clap and yell to the heavens.

When I got back to camp, I paraded around the campfire, illuminated bright with grandeur, singing and jumping all around Hector and kissing him on the forehead gratuitously for pointing the way. My clothes were now hung up to dry and I was in nothing but my boxers, prancing around gleeful and fairy-like. He threw me off of him and laughed as I continued to dance and clap and beat my chest like a gorilla that just escaped the zoo.

The steps to this dance, as unique and changing to each person as they are, once learned, cannot be unlearned. So fair warning, walk and hike the trails of Yosemite at your own risk of self-liberation.

WEEK THREE:

ADÉ MAKES THE JUMP!

Hector and I drank a case of beer together in celebratory splendor and botched some of the camera work the following morning. Thankfully, we didn't mess up the wide-angle time-lapse camera which, if jostled only slightly, would've effed up the whole damn shoot. Something happens in the days following and Hector talks of a big gathering in Yosemite's highlands to celebrate the climb. He speaks in a different, almost rigid tone about it and I can tell he is hiding something. Obviously, Hector is one of the most laid back people I've ever met and now he's acting like he is hiding an eight-ball of cocaine up his rectum every time I even mention The Gathering. You think he'd just be his whole ridiculous self but he's not. It makes me feel unsettled and makes me think I shouldn't go to the celebration afterward. Foolishly, I wrote it off as the same nervous feeling someone might have before going to Burning Man for the first time. You know, the whole uneasiness of going to a place where drugs and weird shit will be forced on you. Considering the last three weeks of my life, I figured I was now ready for all that was weird and bizarre, and so I decided I would remain open to it.

I was wrong. I was not ready.

The three climbers hug euphorically on the top of El Capitan and the Telephoto Lens image reveals three men who have changed physically just as much as I have changed emotionally. It is sensational and dramatic. They are hairier and more sinewy than I could have ever imagined. They look oddly older, stressed and beaten down, but wiser and glowing bright tan with contentment. *They have now found legendary.* There is a congratulatory phone call and then we are packing up equipment. Hector and I hurriedly scurry back to Ronda and we are off to the golden Tuolumne Meadows.

If this last entry seems short, you will have to excuse me — Hector was now fully beside himself, quiet and cool...all things not Hector...and glorifying the accomplishments of Jon & Company had lost all its whimsical luster, especially after one rehashes all that went down in Tuolumne...

Chapter 14

*Flirty Fishing
And The Tumult
Of Tuolumne*

It started off great.
Yeah. I mean, great.
Just great…
It went downhill quickly.

The girls were amorous and anonymous. They left the tent just as quickly as they had arrived. At first it was just one, but five minutes later another showed up, and then finally the third. It was a harem. What sounds like every man's wet dream – being wanted by beautiful women who want nothing to do with you post orgasm – was very much the opposite. Awkward hushes, eerily practiced groping and quiet whispers of *"relax"* danced around a mildly hard, seriously nervous penis. It was dark but I could tell the girls had been shooting each other looks of confusion as to what to do with the over-ripened squash that lay there, sad and desperate, below my unkempt shrubbery. The shrooms had now worn off, as had the alcohol from the previous days' raging so there was no substance to blame on this poor performance. Just nerves. All that was left now was a means to an end. A quick end, hopefully, because it was now beyond embarrassment. It was pathetic.

"Use your mouth," I whispered.

My hands were shaking.

This was not my scene.

It didn't feel like the girls' scene either.

They tried to calm me down, but it didn't work.

Why'd they choose my tent, anyway?

What the hell's going on here?

✶

This was now a "time of *Reflection and Peace* in the community," as Jon put it just a few hours ago at the closing ceremonial jamboree. It had been three full days now of what I affectionately referred to as The Hot Air Festival of Whackjobs and Wieners (there was some nudity going on and none of it was easy on the eyes). But to all of the spiritual loons who paid Jon and the boys homage, this traveling menagerie's meet-up was called The Odyssey or The Gathering. It was something all right; a carnival side-show with plenty of indulgences for the spiritually inclined: drugs, neon colors, feathers and body painting, meditative portals, pristine yogi experiences, loud desensitizing EDM, as well as teas and herbs and goji berries and also a bunch of jag-off storytellers boasting positive, life-affirming LSD trips and Molly wags who never stopped smiling for seventy-two hours straight; and of course, finally, *the love of nature*. Never did there exist a better excuse nor more blatant lie to go and get fucked up than to use the backdrop of a beautiful landscape. Oh wait, they did find a better excuse, *conquering* a beautiful landscape. The chalices were continually held on high to Jon and company, that's for sure. They had done the impossible – conquered El Capitain – and therefore, gone meta.

It was a term I heard constantly throughout the circus: *going meta*. But what was, in the modern tongue, usually used as a term to make fun of the mental conundrums that come with technology, here, at The Odyssey, it was used for short to mean…well, *transcendence*. Tapping into that next place. That *meta* place. What a trip. The Affable Looneys had certainly found their people all right, and the people had certainly found their Leader.

Hm. Wait.

We're not there yet, that comes later.

I'm still on about this last bit. This bit about reflecting and being at peace with each other and the environment within. This shit was the icing on the cake! What Jon really meant was that during this last night of The Gathering, nobody could speak to one another and no one could make eye contact with one another outside of their tents. If they were outside, they were to be in some deep transitive and meditative state, taking in the beauty of Tuolumne…floating. 'Suspend yourself children!' I remember the one yogi saying a day or two ago. She had on a fully feathered, chieftain head-dress with a dot dead center of her forehead. We're talkin' full Indian here. The rub? She was chubby and white. I was waiting for all of the mystics to come out of the woodwork wearing antlered crowns and get to freaking in the name of Satan but that never happened. 'Be free. Be meta,' she'd bellow to the group from deep within her rotund belly. All those breathing exercises had created a tuba. It was all I could do to keep from laughing as she played her notes.

But right now, there was to be no laughing. There was to be nothing but silence and letting the beauty of Tuolumne inside our hearts. Or, if we were inside the tents, we were to be listening, harmonizing with the souls of those around us. I was harmonizing to these girls' souls all right. The one had her boobs in my face and there was some serious thumping going on – I tried to keep the beat.

"Beat-bat-beat-bat!" Her boobs went against my cheekbones. Alas, I remained woodless. She did it again, "beat-bat-beat-bat." Nothing. Nada. Not even a courtesy flop. I couldn't believe it. She switched up the tempo and added some rubbing. She knew how to work those things, "beat-bat-bat-fzzzt-beat-bat-bat-fzzzt." There was finally some movement downstairs, but still no twenty-one-gun salute.

I hadn't been keen enough to pick up on it at first, but now, looking back on that moment when Jon had made the closing ceremony announcement, I can specifically remember the strong majority of guys' faces being ecstatic, damn near euphoric over the news. And then there was Hector. He was even more despondent and glum than before, downright upset over the announcement. He had been in a funk for some time now but he wouldn't talk to me about it. I guess this was the part he wasn't looking forward to. I felt like shaking him and telling him to wake up and enjoy the great outdoors, *brah*. Give him a taste of his own medicine, ya know. But something was different this go around. He was seriously upset, quiet to a point of worry. I couldn't pinpoint its genesis and this was because I had no idea what was really going on in Tuolumne.

Admittedly, I was blinded by a general distaste for the whole get-together and it camouflaged the scent I should have picked up on since jump-street: bad juju. Even now, looking back, it is hard to know if I could've seen what was coming for the whole thing sounded like some huge spiritual

bore to me, some snoozefest of an exercise that was all bull-
ocks and would end, no doubt, in some New Age circle jerk.
Little did I know how accurate that last turn of phrase would
be, and as I lay there with these three naked, nameless women
circling my body – chanting at my penis, dancing to the dick
gods in hopes of awakening the boneless piece of meat that
lay squishy on my person, encouraging him to hop on the
ferry to Happyland – I was well aware we'd missed that boat
a long time ago.

"I'm shy." I said to the girls, virgin in tone.

They all kept after it anyway and finally forced me to lie.
I told them I was too tired and that it was okay, they could
go. I had had a wonderful time. An obvious lie, I just
couldn't handle that much flesh in my face at once. It had
sent me reeling, that vast pile of soft skin around. Nerves are
a goddammed hard-on killer. I guess I'm not a ménage man
in the end. Or maybe I was, just not in the way this particular
episode went down…when there was no work done to earn
the gratification, no banter or game played to win the right
and pleasures that come from social triumph, the entire thing
ended up feeling off…worse than that, forced and unnatural.
Wrong. Not a word had been exchanged between these
women and myself. Hell, I had only seen one of them – the
last girl to enter the tent – the day before sitting around one
of the fires, high as a Georgia pine. She had had her eyes
closed and her arms out, smiling with her hand swimming
against the wind, loose as a goose. Rolling with the homies.
Mental function: zip-zero.

The girls were still severely tilted in my tent and in my
book, hooking up with women who were too fucked up for
their own good was the opposite of an accomplishment. It
was cowardice. I was glad my backbone had finally decided to

show up. I guess it was a decent trade then, in the end, one bone for another.

✻

There were well over two hundred people at The Gathering to celebrate the climb and it doesn't need to be said that everyone was wasted. Gonzo. Kaput. Completely jacked out of their minds. The entire blob of hazy-brained people were bingeing with the same disregard for life that is shared by Big Ten schools. Except here, in the picturesque setting of Tuolumne, their right to partying was based around the religion of the spirit and the beauty of the wild, instead of the religion of the game and the beauty of an eighteen year old with double-Ds. I'm not sure that this was what Muir had in mind for celebrating the gift of nature, then again, I'm not sure any of the founders of today's universities would appreciate the severe amount of vomit and urine that is dropped on their common ground year after year all for the love of the game. Still, the partying was different out here. There seemed to be a purpose, albeit a nutty one, but every single drink that was drank or drug that was dropped was done under the pretense of liberating the mind, freeing the soul. It was all, of course, a big crock. A leftover dream of the seventies that had now gone stale. Every single feather sporting, tie-died, toga-dressed-clown there knew none of the substance was needed for us to truly feel free, but no one talked about it. Everyone was having too good of a time. Even I was starting to let my hair down despite all the madness. Shrooms'll do that to you.

Shrooms taste like shit by the way. Actual shit.

There were a stray few who I spoke with who had now gone clean. These were the ones who had now attained a permanent sense of connection with their surroundings and no longer needed the *help* (drugs) to be one with nature. They were permanently-meta, *perma-meta,* which meant they were more jacked and bonkers than the ones popping multiple sheets of acid. They called these corkers *gurus* and every single one of them gave me the creeps; all of their incoherent rhetoric touched on repetitive themes of vibration and light:

"It can be both, Finn, it can be both." I heard the long-haired, sinewy man say to the younger, leaner, high-knotted grasshopper. "Sound and Light. One Wavelength. That is us: People. A wavelength fighting itself, at war with itself. Oscillating in uneven paths that have been taking place for millennia. We are just ape-men fighting over the same banana bush, prehistoric flies after the same turd..."

I'm pretty sure I made up the turd line but you catch my drift.

I can't remember which day it was but I remember I was stretched out on the grass behind one of these gurus projecting a monologue that would've made Shakespeare proud of its length, horny over its cryptic text and weep over its contents. The shrooms were in full effect then so I laughed a lot, but I had to lie to the intent crowd of listeners and tell them that my laughing wasn't because of the man's words, but because the clouds were dancing on repeat and looked just like Steamboat Willie. They bought it and I continued my eavesdropping and giggled along to the Tolkien wannabe. The supernatural soothsayer with bad breath, bad teeth, and bad language.

✢

It was hard not to notice Jon's presence in the community throughout the entire three days in Tuolumne. I have to admit, he was quite the charismatic leader. He had won me over and done it in such a way that it never felt forced. Nothing about him was forced and it reminded me of why people succumb to one another in the first place, and that natural leaders take two forms: the vocal and the physical. Jon was the latter and he led by the calm, cool, laid-back action that all of these people couldn't get enough of. They were all surfing the wave of a man who could literally inflict his physical prowess over nature — riding monster waves and toppling the untoppable. The result was a scary, damn near obsessive following. I was waiting for the rose petals to be thrown at his feet and one of his apostles to claim him the next prophet.

What might sound like a weak joke on paper was very much the opposite in person. He was the poster child for all of the nature-lovers and extreme outdoorsmen and spiritual-acid-heads that made up The Gathering, and I soon noticed that these groups had gotten wrapped up in some New Age movement, co-opted by some faux-transcendentalism nonsense that was all the rage. It consumed every conversation at The Gathering. Every goddamn thing was *meta*. I couldn't stand it anymore so I zoned it out. It was freaking everywhere, I tell you. In every conversation, in everything they did — even dancing — it was all a way to get to *that next place*. I quickly became numb to it and was readied for the "time of peace and reflection" by the end of the third day. Granted, I was somewhat prepared for all the crazy jabber for I had heard some of it before back at the house. The Affable Looneys had fleetingly talked about the same shit, and over the course of that short time in Tuolumne the curtain was being pulled back on the group and its wacko theologies. I thought Jon's silence on the topic was because he didn't care for any of the conversations and rhetoric that were so pervasive in his followers but, to my ultimate sadness, I would soon find out that he cared and cared very much.

✼

The girls, as beautiful and as unexpected and as naked as they were, never gave off any weird vibes. At first, it made me think that this was just something that happened here, like a hippie-swingers' colony or something of the like. But that was not what this was, not at all. The smoke and mirrors were blown away when the brunette, the last gal to leave my tent, became overwhelmed with worry over my failed sexual performance and asked if I would tell Jon that I was unsatisfied.

"Tell Jon?" I asked, quizzically. "Why the hell would I do that?"

"It's nothing, nevermind," She said. "I'm sorry I asked."

"Can you explain it a little?"

She shook her head, "I shouldn't have said anything, I just wanted to make sure you were happy before I left." She reached out and took hold of my forearm, "*You can be happy here, with us.*"

It was something about the way she said the last line combined with her worry over upsetting Jon that opened my eyes to something larger and darker looming in the distance. I told the girl she had nothing to worry about and that I *was* happy here. She smiled, kissed me on the cheek innocently and left. That is when I decided to sit in my tent and, instead of suspending myself or discovering the art of being meta, go ahead and shame my penis for making everything weird after sex. I had to hand it to him; whether he was successful in his efforts or not, the little man had a remarkable gift for making everything sublimely awkward.

The effect of the shrooms completely wore off and I now found myself with an upset stomach, drowning from the experience with these three women. The sobriety and its hangover of frustration forced me out of the tent and into the early morning night sky. Out there, I tried to digest what the hell just happened...why it happened.

Thankfully, Tuolumne Meadows are just as beguiling as the Valley Floor, if not more so, and their serene soundscapes produce the most beautiful music. The tunes this early morning were cathartic and mended much of my scorned, limp-dicked pride. After winding my way through the tents that littered the field, I was out and into the wild again. The majority of tourists rarely stopped at the meadows so beside the groupies of The Gathering, there wasn't another soul to be seen outside of the campsite. Just silence and wind and clouds clearing...then stars and a thumbnail-moon. With its high-elevation plateau full of barren granite lookouts, Tuolumne makes for some of the darkest, and therefore brightest, night skies you could ever imagine. To lie down on one of those granite surfaces at midnight is to float in space, suspended in a constellation-filled dream. And drifting there, you will notice long out-of-use satellites whizzing around the planet from the time of the great space race, slowly, desperately, terminally falling back to earth. You will see galaxies; one star that is a billion stars. Yes, what Hubble saw through his telescope, is what the naked eye sees in Tuolumne and it changes you the way the world was changed when it saw Hubble's photographs.

I wandered out a little further with a flashlight, still downtrodden and confused, and came upon a good spot to lie down and take in the stars. The view helped but a little for the constellations reminded me of June. Reminded me of our first conversation, of our antics with astrology, of the Grand Central Terminal ceiling, of my unsaid wishes that she was around to experience all this with me. I always had a thing for looking up; it always made me feel young. But now, I was questioning if I was plagued to be a damned sentimentalist for the rest of my life, or worse a hopeful romantic. A downright lost cause. It was a sickening thought; I can only imagine how nauseous you must be reading it. I closed my eyes and thought of other, more relevant problems. When it came down to it, I was upset with myself for coming to The Gathering. It just wasn't me. It reminded me of the conversation I had had with Hector just before everything got underway:

"Relax, man. *Relax.*" He said, "It's gonna be a good time, bro."

"You realize that is what everyone says when they know it isn't going to be a good time."

Hector grimaced at the remark and bit his lip to gain the proper focus needed to back Ronda into a parking space in Tuolumne.

"Look at this." Hector said, taking the keys out of the ignition and throwing his hand out to the open wilderness and sun-splashed meadows. The sight set me at ease. It looked like Monet had taken his brush out of retirement and painted the view just for us. "The fellas will be here in a couple hours...take a moment and enjoy this, will you? You worry too damn much." He stopped a moment and looked at me again. "Your face looks like you need to poop."

I laughed and told him I needed to go. I had been holding it in the last couple of days in hopes of finding a real bathroom. As I walked away from Ronda I yelled back to Hector that Yosemite had changed him. He had been acting differently the last couple days and I should've known something was off, but I was still too busy playing nubile nature boy, too wrapped up in the gift that was Yosemite to take in what was standing right in front of me — a warning sign. Beyond the park itself, it was our little inside jokes that kept me going amidst the strangeness of the Affable Looneys. It was more than that. I liked Hector and he liked me. I could tell. It was a sure thing, like when you embrace a new beer and can depend on it to give you the same buzz a few years down the road. He would never change and it was reassuring to have a good friend again. I yelled to him that he had a profound sixth-sense for shit and that that would be his nickname in the park from now on. He was confused so I clarified the message:

"If I am to be 'Incapable of Not-Giving-Fucks,'" I was pretty much yelling now, "then you sir, are to be deemed, Hector, 'Man with Shitty Sixth-Sense. Or, The Shit Detector, for short!'"

He bellowed out a good laugh and pointed toward a communal bathroom that was off in the opposite direction of the way I was walking. I hopped in the air, turning on a dime with excitement at the thought of not having to squat for once in three weeks. Ronda was a gem, there was no doubt about it, but the one thing she lacked, aside from modern devices like air-conditioning, was a bathroom. If I were shameless enough with my money, I'd buy the over-sized out of date, boat-on-wheels, have a bathroom installed and drive the thing cross-country back home.

✻

I awoke to a scream. It was the kind of scream that demanded action and I found myself running toward one of the tents. I had dosed off while stargazing and my drowsy legs were pumping faster now with the advent of adrenaline. The tent was close by and I was there in seconds. To my astonishment, the blood curdling sound was coming from one of the girls who had visited me. She was now naked in a tent with Adé and pulling at him, begging for him to breathe, yanking at his arm telling him frantically, forcefully to move, to react to her words, her noise. It was an awful sight. Adé was foaming at the mouth, rigidly shaking, the whites of his eyes showing and then, went completely still. It was a stillness that sent the girl into an even worse frenzy. I motioned to another guy who had stumbled into the room, drunken with sleep, to grab her and cover her up. Adé was not breathing at all now and his lips were slowly turning blue. More people gathered in the tent and no one knew what to do. The majority just stood there and watched. Horrified. Helpless. High. I hated them for just looking and doing nothing. The lot of them had nothing to offer but their thumbs up their asses. I wished they would just leave, they were so worthless. I questioned aloud who knew mouth to mouth and asked if anyone knew if Adé were diabetic. No one knew anything. I got down beside him and tried to listen.

Nothing.

Death whispering, that was it.

I instinctively started pumping on his chest with my hands and asked the girl what drugs they were doing. She wouldn't say anything.

"Jesus Christ woman!" I screamed, fuming over the help-lessness of the situation. "He is going to die! What were you doing!?"

She meekly uttered out, "molly."

I felt his head. It felt hot. He was OD'ing. He was dying. Christ, are you kidding me! The man who just free-climbed El Capitan and had what was probably the most euphoric moment of his life, was now going to die from a fucking drug that induces euphoria. Un-fucking-believable. I quickly real-ized I had no idea how to perform proper CPR and not wanting to make things worse asked again, this time flat-out-desperate:

"Does anyone know *actual* CPR!?"

A man jumped in and I told him to focus on heartbeats. I didn't know what the hell I was talking about but everyone else was too fucked up to help. Somehow Adé's life had fallen into my hands.

"Okay-okay-okay." I said, scrambling thoughts and op-tions aloud. "This is going to sound crazy but does anyone have food allergies?"

The collective faces went blank.

"What?"

"Huh?"

"What are you on?"

"He's fucked up himself."

"How will that help anything!?" The final, panic-driven mongoloid shouted.

"Oh God! His face! It's turning blue!" Screamed a girl from the back.

"He needs a shot of adrenaline." I commanded. "Does anyone have an epipen? For allergies?! It could save him for fucksake!"

One of the men bolted out of the tent and brought back a small leather pouch. It had been almost three minutes now of Adé without oxygen and we all agreed that it was his only hope. The nervous man steadied his hands, pulled out the syringe and applied the injection.

Long breaths held with hope.

Time slowed and blood flowed backward.

We were all one.

A collective.

Willing the life back into him.

And...

The body reacted!

It was a goddamned miracle!

Horrific gasping sounds for air never sounded so sweet.

In seconds Adé was breathing and woozily regaining consciousness. His eyes came rolling around from the back of his head and his pupils dilated with oxygen and then shrunk and refocused on familiar faces. He breathed deeply for a couple of minutes and almost immediately, his skin color resumed its natural and healthy pinkish hue. Soon he became hysterical; his shock giving way to tears and outbursts of joy and thanks. I looked around and a lot of the people in the tent were crying too. A girl had hugged me and had been holding on to me for a while before I recognized her smell. It was the brunette who first visited me only an hour or two beforehand – the same one who was worried over me telling Jon about my performance. There was a thunderous roar of ambient conversation and everyone quacked like parrots reciting who was doing what while Adé lay lifeless on the ground. I felt like reminding them that they were all worthless pieces of shit, but I didn't. I was too happy myself. Adé was up and walking around. It was unreal how strong yet fragile we all are. Eventually the group's incoherent ramblings got back around to me, and how resourceful and clear-minded I had been in the time of great distress. Adé walked up to me, threw his blistered and broken hands from three-weeks worth of climbing around me, and refused to let go.

His strength was back and his arms tightened around my shoulders and I too became overwhelmed with emotion, "You were sent here to save me." He said, eyes ablaze.

It was at that exact moment, when I saw how dilated his pupils were, that I realized Adé was still high. I didn't understand it; I figured the shot would've knocked it out of him. Neutralized the chemical reaction somehow and canceled out his high. But it didn't, he was smiling and touchy-feely and dancing sans music in no time. The molly was back on track. How utterly bizarre...

Of course, we would all soon learn that it wasn't a drug overdose – it couldn't have been. An epipen doesn't work in the same way an OD kit does. He had simply had an allergic response to something he ate. We were just extremely lucky that of all the things I could've yelled, the one random suggestion ended up being the correct course of action. I tell you now it was a million to one shot that that happened. Any other night we would've been waiting for a coroner. Now, the severely stoned and smiling man is telling me how he had never, not once eaten almonds before in his life. Twenty-four years and no almonds. Can you believe that? Said he had always hated nuts so he never even tried trailmix. Absolutely absurd – an outdoorsman who had never tried trailmix! Either way, even after everyone realized that it was no doubt the almonds that did him in, he and the group of onlookers still held me personally responsible for saving his life. I suppose I kind of was...in a way.

Amidst all of the commotion and pat on the backs, I didn't bother to see the massive elephant still standing in the room, staring me down and begging me to remember what was truly fucked about the situation. And then I saw her again, the gal who had been screaming naked next to Adé…

….my bones went cold.

She was…young. Too young. *Horribly young.* I remembered how she was in my tent not but two hours ago and my heart sank at the thought of her barely being sixteen. Now, I was the one losing air, feeling the color of life leave my skin.

"You okay, man?" A random shmuck asked.

I could only slightly nod my head. I broke into a nervous, confused sweat. The three girls who had visited me had gone on to make rounds in other tents. I felt weak and spread-thin, disgusted with myself and The Gathering at large. Just what the hell was going on around here? Was this swinging? No. No way in hell. It couldn't be. Not that I knew what went on between swingers, but this. This was like women trafficking. I looked at the girl again. *She was so young!* My god! I couldn't look at her anymore. She was *that* young. *'Fuck me.'* My eyes dropped to the floor in self-loathing. I felt less than human. *'I'm horrible. A gross human being.'* I thought. *'Fucking scum.'* I got queasy and stumbled out of the tent, preparing to empty my stomach but my selfish, personal discomfort quickly bounced back to the women and just how fucked up the situation was…*for them.* Everything was getting too heavy, too real, and I could not escape the falling feeling of a relationship going horrifyingly south – that the Affable Looneys were not who I had originally cooked them up to be. I had to find out what was going on and I had to find out now.

There was only one man who held the answer.

❋

"Brother." He said it with such repose and dignity that at any other time in our journey I would've been flattered. But now, the sunburnt Jesus hair and see-through-blue eyes had taken a nasty turn in my mind and the word felt methodical; practiced – a malicious attempt at friendship and subordination.

"Don't call me that, Jon. Not till you tell me just what the fuck is goin' on around here."

"I'll tell you what is going on around here. You saved the life of my friend of ten years, that's what is going on around here." I shook my head, sour and incensed. He was pandering. "You're a legend, bro." He continued, blatantly ignoring the scowl on my face. "Everyone adores you. As do I. We are forever grateful here. I am in your debt."

He was talking like a zen-master. This was the most he had spoken the entire trip and I wasn't having it.

"Right....and who exactly is *we*? And what is *here*? I don't wanna be rude but shit. *Is this a cult?*"

The word's edgy tone came out hard-boiled along with the steam that was pouring from my ears. I couldn't believe I said it but was happy I did. I would've surely fumbled around and fucked it up had I not acted on instinct.

"Whoa man. Easy...*easy*. We don't say that around here. Cults are messed up. That is not what we are."

"Okay. Then what are you?" His face lost its jovial laziness with my challenge and grew into unappreciative angst. "I had three women come visit me tonight to sleep with me for no reason and then I find out that one of them hasn't even graduated high school yet...OH. *And* they were going around and doing it with other tents, too. How can you explain that?! *There is no explanation.* I know what flirty fishing is and you know what.."

"You're just talkin' rot now, man. That's just rotten. Calm down. *Calm. Down.*" He was authoritative, his voice booming a bone rattling bass I had not thought possible to come from such a skinny man. "Let me be clear. We are not putting women out to get guys to be a part of this. The girls...they are doing what they do by their own will. They are happy here and want you to be happy here too."

His words, "happy here too." The same words the girl had used in the tent.

"Are you like a professional liar or something?" I said, sarcasm nowhere in sight. "I hear it comes with the territory of being a cult leader. You are either lying to yourself or lying to me. Either way shit is fucked up."

"You should watch your mouth." He said, squaring up his shoulders. "You are not yourself right now."

"You took me in, man." I felt like crumbling inside, but I was too pissed to give way. "I loved you guys for that. Tell me, why did you do it? Was it really out of the *goodness* of your heart?"

"I don't think you want to go down this road, Frank."

"And what road is that? The truth?!"

There was no sound.

Even the trees stopped moving on account of the heated exchange.

"You forget you are a guest here and that can change."

All of the sudden the wind picked back up and the tree branches started knocking violently against one another and I felt the hairs on the back of my neck rise. I remembered that I was all alone out here and that I could easily be dumped in the ocean by everyone on board with this man if he saw fit. I had to choose my words more carefully. I wanted to find out what was going on and offending the man wasn't helping. I guess I was just hurt, too. I wanted to believe he and the Affable Looneys were just a do-gooding troop of space cadets. I wanted it so badly that I had sold that lie to myself.

"You're right," I said. His eyes relaxed and glinted a bit. "I am sorry. I didn't mean to insult you. I'm just caught off guard by what is happening here."

"That's okay. It's only natural." He put his hand on my shoulder and shook it lightly. "We are freethinkers here and strong minds take time to adjust."

I couldn't believe what he just said. I mean, he had to be shitting me, right? If he was in control of what was said here – how on earth was that freethinking? I could only muster out a grunt of acceptance.

"Listen, we all head back tomorrow, why don't you spend some more time with us at the house, we all love your company. I can tell that Hector relies deeply on your friendship."

"I don't think I can do that." I nudged my shoulder free from his hand. "Something is wrong here and I think that is why you want me to spend more time with you; to woo me over. I think you have sensed it and I don't think things can go back to the way it was...I'm thankful for you all taking me in, I am. I just can't.."

"*Thankful?*" He cut in sharply. "This is not what I would call thankful. This childish blathering. You think you know what is going on here? You have no idea. You haven't seen anything. You don't know anything. So do not come after me like some journo hot off some paperboy tip! WE GAVE YOU EVERYTHING AND NOW YOU OFFER US NOTHING."

I was scared. His vocal chords rattled like Orson Welles but I still found my voice, "I didn't realize it was a two way street, Jon." My tone was smug and confident but my insides were shaking and I felt my teeth start to grind. Fists could be thrown at any second. "I thought you were helping me because you just wanted to help."

"You arrogant little shit." All of the sudden Jon's surfer-bro tact vanished and what came out was a North Atlantic accent, void of all other influences. It was what you heard on television. The man had been faking it! All along, he was a fraud. It was a frightening revelation though, for it wasn't an — aha, I caught you, you have been lying to everyone the whole time, moment — it was much more of an *hoah my fucking gawd*, you are a true blue sociopath, a magnificently talented maniac — Hannibal Lecter, Charles Manson revelation. "I should've known you'd be a thankless little faggot."

"Who the fuck are you?" I said, squinting my eyes, clenching my jaw and fists, prepared for hell.

"Who I am doesn't matter, it is the mission. That is all that matters. Liberating the soul. That is what you cannot see. I should've known. You are too small for this place. We should've never brought you here. You had a gift to give to these people and you are squandering it. We are done with you.."

"You're insane."

"Am I?"

It was a challenge.

Again, silence fell upon us and again I thought he was going to let me have it. I thought twice about telling him off and then the image of that youthful girls face flashed across my mind. She was innocent and unknowing and sad. I remembered the nervousness we shared in my tent together. It was jet fuel to my fire and I bore full steam ahead:

"Yes. You are fucking crazy!" I yelled. He puffed out his chest at me as I spoke, "And you're right, I don't even know what the fuck really goes on here, but I can tell you one thing, this conversation makes me happy as hell that I'm never going to be apart of it. *Any of it.*"

"That's for sure. You will never know, never can know, what it means to handle vibrations and light."

"YOU SOUND LIKE A SCIENTOLOGIST." I yelled.

"Tread lightly, Frank. Tread. Lightly. The only reason you will be allowed to walk out of here is because you saved Adé."

"*Was that a threat?*" I was incredulous.

I can't really remember it, I was borderline blacked-out from the adrenaline coursing through my veins, but I'm pretty sure my entire trunk was shaking like a dog shitting razor blades.

"I will say it again. You saved him. So if I were you, I'd get my things and hit the road. You are no longer one of us. *Never were.*"

"I hope you realize what you're doing to these people."

"And I hope you realize," he shifted mid-sentence back into the now truly terrifying, surfer dialect, "that if you don't go and get your things right now, I *might* change my mind."

He cocked his head to the side, and smiled an eerily psychotic smile. 'Go ahead, try me,' he was saying. I shook my head in a half-fearful-half-sad look of disgust and turned back on the path to Ronda. On the brisk walk back, the adrenaline that was pumping throughout the conversation left my bloodstream and my rational brain was all that remained. I realized I needed to get the fuck out of Yosemite as fast as humanly possible before Jon changed his mind. My jog soon gave way to a sprint, and mid-stride I came to the conclusion that my best bet was probably hitch-hiking my way out. But it was seven in the morning and even that was a crapshoot. Hell was raining fire and brimstone down upon me, and there wasn't a goddammed angel in sight.

And then there was Hector.

✼

"You are leaving us aren't you?" Hector asked, despairingly. He was sitting in the driver's seat of Ronda with his chin on the wheel, peering out over the many tents of Tuolumne. The sun was rising and through the lens of the windshield was a magnified beauty, absolute. We both had no time for it.

"How'd you know?" I asked.

"Well. You're packing your bag, aren't you?" He sighed a long sigh. "I knew this day would come. I guess part of me was just hoping you'd stay."

I had already gathered all of my things from the tent and was now hurriedly finishing up the last little tidbits of leftovers I might have forgotten in the RV.

"What exactly is going on here, Heck?" There was a beat. He bit his lip a little harder. "Is it *that* bad that you can't even tell me? Should I be worried for my life?"

"It's not that bad, Frank. I promise you, it is not that bad. The people are just wrapped up in something here. It isn't ugly. It isn't Jonestown Beach or anything like that. I promise you, I wouldn't be here if it was…they just like what they have here 'cuz it's different, because they can call it their own…and they feel free. It's not that bad."

"Hector. That's exactly how all those communities started out. All of 'em were happy at their different way of life,
their so-called freedom, but all of 'em and I mean every single
one got messed up the longer they went on and the more
their leader got wrapped up in his own megalomania."

I quickly glanced over my shoulder, prepared for Jon to
be rearing a massive nine-inch blade directed at my back.

No one was there.

"That won't happen here." Hector said, clearing his
throat. "There is a pact."

"Oh Christ. I never thought you'd be so naïve, man. It's
already happening!"

"I don't expect you to understand it, Frank. You are
strong minded, and sometimes the strong minded are too
closed off."

He had used the same language Jon had used, the same
exact words, *strong minded.* Was Hector's brain already
more tainted than I originally thought?

"Well fuck me." I said. "That's the second time today
I've been called close-minded for not being open to insanity."

"The people are happy here. What do you say to that?"

"Blinded by wonder and charm."

Hector shook his head in disagreement.

"It's called faith, Hector. Everyone here is chock full of it.
Except you." He looked me square in the eye. "Yeah, I saw
you when Jon made the announcement for the time of *Peace
and Reflection,* I also saw how much you changed leading up
to The Gathering. You don't like this part of it. I can tell.
Why couldn't you just tell me this – *the women* – was what
happened up here?"

Hector's eyes caught mine, "Why would I tell my new
best friend I belong to something I wasn't proud of?"

"Because that is how you keep your new best friend."

His tear ducts gave way, his head falling tragically into his hands.

"I'm only here for the capture, man. I'm not here for everything else!"

"But *everything else* is the fucking scary serious shit!" I waited a second for Hector to gather himself and continued, "You laugh at me for giving fucks, but this is why I do it." I buckled up my bag and stood up, assuredly. "'Cuz shit is royally fucked sometimes."

"Nothing bad will happen. I promise you, Frank. I fuckin' promise, bro."

He was hopeless, a tape-recorder stuck on repeat, a product of a poisoned well. I had to leave and didn't have the time to withdraw the muddled ideas that now clouded his judgment and convince him, he too, should leave. I had a feeling it wouldn't have got to him, anyway.

"Listen, I know that." I said. "You've been great to me. But I've gotta go and I've gotta go now. Jon made that all too clear and though I'd love to sit here and make you believe that I'm grateful for everything you did for me despite all this shit going on, I don't have time – I've gotta get the fuck outta Dodge and fast…It's just I got no idea how to get the hell outta Yosemite."

"I'll drive you," Hector said.

"You will?"

"Yes. It's the least I can do…I let you come up here after all. I mean, I *wanted* you to come up here and I'm still happy you did…despite all this." He let out soured air from his gut and steadied himself. "That was my best time spent in Yosemite…with you." He tried to smile fully but his lips failed him. "I'll take you to the major exit heading east. You can thumb it to Bishop and from there you'll be fine."

"What about Jon? Won't he be pissed at you for helping me?"

"Jon needs me as much as I need him."

I then finally saw Hector for who he was in the group and why he was there. He was a business partner to the Affable Looneys. Not a true believer, but still the man who could bring their vision to life through photography and film. It was a bizarre venture to be a part of but I then remembered he had been doing it with them for years now and he was in it for himself too. Some part of me wanted to believe that it was all going to be okay for him, for the Affable Looneys as well. It was another lie I sold myself to feel better at the time and only when I hugged Hector goodbye, warning him again about Jon being a "horrible and deceptive fuck," combined with Hector's following ignorance of the matter, did the romantic seal between us fracture into its proper form of one part truth, one part fantasy and all parts tragedy. I would never – could never – forget Hector and the Affable Looneys, but couldn't tell just yet if I would ever forgive them. I was once again confronted by the same unsettling reality that had been plaguing me since the news of my father's death:

Why is it that the ones who save us are always the ones who want to control us, and therefore, hurt us, in the end?

Chapter 15

Running It Hard

"You heard me."

"But Frank."

"I want it on the market...*today.*"

"Don't you think we should talk this over?"

"Gerry. I've been thinking it over since I got it. I don't want it. None of it. Okay?"

"Okay."

Mr. Goldstein really was a good man. He had looked out for me and the d'if ever since he dropped the bomb of its existence on me. He had been my father's lawyer, an honest man and transparent advisor, who ended up swallowing much more than he bargained for with the inheritance passing on to me – the illegitimate, unappreciative son.

"What about the art, the furniture, *the Rodins?*" He said, helplessly through the other side of the phone.

"E-Bay." I snorted.

"Fra—"

"No wait." Divine sight fell upon me. "Donate the art to whatever museum deserves it – a museum that has ties to children, helping children or allowing all kids free admittance. Or no, something better. Something that promotes the arts for youth. Maybe it's not a museum then? An organization? I don't know. I trust your judgment in that regard. Just make sure it is an *anonymous* donation. You hear me?"

"This is crazy. Absolutely crazy." He was frazzled. He was the kind of man who said absolutely too much, so when the time actually called for it, everything fell way short of absolute.

"I respect your personal opinion on the matter," I said, playfully. "But I'd rather act crazy on my own accord than be driven crazy by external circumstances."

"Listen, I get it. You're going through a lot right now and your father made it crystal clear that I was to respect whatever your wishes were with the estate, even if it came to something like this. But I never thought it would happen. I might not be the right man for the job...I was hired by your father two years ago because I am the best at keeping things the way they are – in fine working order...I don't know if I can do this for you, Frank."

"You can and you will. It'll work itself out. You just find a trustworthy agent and let them handle the rest."

A gruff yes could faintly be made out over feedback.

"Oh, and Jesus, I almost forgot." I coughed up some left-over cigar smoke. "A few of my friends have been squatting in there the past couple months. Please have them arrested."

"What?"

"For squatting. Have them hauled away, please."

"Your friends?"

"A joke, Mr. Goldstein, a joke. I'm sure the place looks like a damn dorm room right now. If you will, can you go on over there with some cleaners and let the boys know that I'll be back soon and it's time to hit the road. Tell them the party is over, back to reality. And if they whine or complain or say they are too hung-over to move, just have them call me."

"This is absolutely the craziest thing I have ever heard."

*

Of course, there was nothing crazy about it to me. Not after the year I just had. Not after the last three weeks I just had. Not after the past seventy-two hours I just had. And for damn sure, not after the last forty-five minutes I just had:

A thumb out in the wind gave way to a white cargo van screeching to a halt. The thing looked sketchy as all hell, dinged up and old, and gave off a harsh heebie-jeebies factor in its piercing breaks that sounded more ring-wraith than friction-inducer. But I was in no position to judge. Shit, it could've had blacked-out windows and guys with ski masks opening up the side door and I would've most definitely hopped in and asked who was up for Scrabble.

"You can't live your whole life in some damned rubber box." The man's voice raddled as I climbed inside.

I nodded to him. He told me his name was Bob and I told him mine was Frank. He then went on to call us the odd couple of joe-job names. He smiled at himself for that. Boy was I glad that it was this joe-job Bob who pulled over. He ended up being more than just a ride to Bishop; he was a way to understand the shitty situation I was in. He was help personified. Forward motion. Progress in human form. *He was your everyday average shmo, and therefore, a source of sanity.*

Bob had pulled-over, though he mentioned openly that he "wuhddn't plannin' on it, but seein' how you reminded me of muh younger brother – he was about your age when he hitch-hiked from Florida to Alaska to work a job on a fishin' boat – well, I figured this dadgom fear-mongerin' society has to be told to *shove it* every now and then."

"Well I'm sure glad you did, Bob."

"Yeap. He ran it hard, too."

Bob was full of racing/motor jargon that didn't make too much sense to me at the time. He was passing through Yosemite on his way to Vegas for the Las Vegas Motor Speedway and was fixing to crash in Bishop for the night. Finally, my luck was lookin' up.

"Shoot. Maybe I'll even get my fly-line wet." He said. I paused and pondered if the man meant the line as a metaphor for his noodle…nope. "Bishop is one-a-them unknown places with the best fly-fishin' in the lower forty-eight." He added, "Like Jackson Hole without all 'em goddam yuppies."

He chucked a heaping pile of sunflower seeds into his mouth.

The van smelt of ranch. They were ranch flavored sunflower seeds.

I asked for a couple and he tossed the crumpled-up bag my way.

My mouth watered with artificial flavoring.

I told him, "For a second there I thought you were talkin' about your pecker."

"Ha! Hail no." He spit a shell out the window. "The fish I like chasin' don't give ya heart-attacks."

We laughed and Bob carried the conversation with an effortlessness that suggested ancestors who parleyed and saved thousands of lives on the battlefield merely from the gift of their words. He had on a black Nascar baseball-cap that had seen too many summers and was bespectacled with the kind of non-pretentious, thin-framed bifocal sunglasses that lost their tint when we hit shady patches of highway. He had on what you might consider the Midwest, blue-collar uniform. 577 Levi's that were originally dark but became work pants over the years and reflected the treatment. A light grey t-shirt of no particular importance and crosstrainers. Jeans and cross-trainers – that's how you know if someone's legit blue-collar or not. He sported a southern accent that wasn't quite palpable. Foreign and damn near Yankee, his Fort Lauderdale upbringings had smashed together with his current residency in Charlotte, North Carolina and produced a sound that neared a slow-drawled Bostononian. All of the elements wove together seamlessly when he told me he traveled the states to build engines for Nascar Stock Cars.

"Yup. Me and muh older brother built one when we was about thirteen and fourteen and pretty much haven't stopped since. Muh dad wouldn't let us race it. He felt the same way toward motorcycles and everything else that had any little bit-a-danger to it. He was a Orthopedic Surgeon so I'm supposin' he had his reasons....and I know they was just."

'Our fathers and their reasons.' I thought. Bob went full-steam ahead without even taking a breath. He was a true-born chatty-kathy. I mean, he wouldn't stop. If he broke off for a second, all I had to do was hum "mmhm" or the more in-quisitive "hmm?" and he'd roll right on past me. Eyes always on the road, left elbow out the window, right hand on the wheel. He spat sunflower-seed shells out from time to time but for those forty minutes, he was an artesian well of per-sonal history and life lessons. I needed it all and needed it bad; something, anything to get me out of my own head and my own past. I was, for that short time, a silent sponge of sorts.

"I owned muh own team for a bit." Bob continued, "from the early seventies on into the late nineties. But shoot, I was young then. Days on end with no sleep, hardly a weekend at home, flyin' all over the country just to come back home just to wake up a day or two later to do it all over again the next weekend. Hell, you can't do that at my age. We was turnin' over at eight or nine (rpms) with no time to switch out. You can run that hard when your young, like you are right now, but eventually the weather catches up to you."

"So now you're just building engines?" I asked, enthralled. He was such a natural and unlabored storyteller I had temporarily forgotten about the tumult of Tuolomne. "You miss ownin' a team?"

"Well sure, you miss the competition. But I had to face some facts. I could compete with other teams usin' my hands, building engines and trainin' the right people, but not in the boardroom. I'm no bull-shitter, and that's the whole damn sport today — the only thing that'll getchya the money to win is sellin' your soul by runnin' your flap and well, I'd rather run a car into the wall before going down that road."

I swallowed hard. Something in me said that I was one of those bull-shitters he was referring to and I kept quiet the rest of the ride. He jabbered on and I found myself in one of those Emersonian, self-reflective states — happy to be thumbing it and free from Jon and the rest of the loons, but another part of me was intensely saddened by the loss, that they were now officially out of my life. As Bob spoke I realized I was oddly comfortable around strangers and was shocked at the way this whole thing worked; hitch-hiking. You'd think that hopping rides from strangers would churn out some agreeable, whatever-they-say-goes disposition from whomever hitches the ride, but more and more I was finding the opposite to be true. I wasn't presenting myself as being agreeable, maybe affable, but in truth the pretenders, the phonies and the snakes wouldn't make it in such a world. What was actually churned out of the process was an open, unsaid acknowledgement that we, the helper and the helped, stumbled upon perfectly aligned, chance-mirrored reflections of one another. The generosity and warmth that he exuded in the driver seat is what spawns a whole new generation of people like me to stop and help out someone on the side of the road. It is the same feeling that drove the Beats to feel invincible – feel real. For those forty minutes, a daguerreotype of joined personalities was captured. It was only meant to be then that the exposure was left on for too long and burned in ghosts and overlapping impressions of one another that all at once became art turned affection and appreciation turned admiration. Hitch-hiking embodied the undeniable beauty of a stranger. Not sharp and poignant, as one might've expected had we known each other for years, but faded and forever; that place in one's memory somewhere between boyhood, where running it hard was the only way to be and adulthood, where cutting her back and easing your foot off the pedal meant helping someone else find their ignition.

There was an intuitive understanding in thumbing it, a heightened state of empathy for I never told Bob why I needed the ride, *he just knew I needed it* and that was enough. It was everything I longed for at that moment in my life. Sure, it was strange to find it in the passenger side of a cargo van, but it was there at the main intersection of Bishop when Bob dropped me off that he told me the real reason he had stopped wasn't because I reminded him of his brother, but because, for a flash moment, he *thought* I actually was his brother.

"Yeah...he passed on a motorcycle 'bout thirty some years ago. Apparently, fathers tend to know more'n we give 'em credit for." He paused, I didn't say anything – couldn't say anything. "Anyway, I pretty much thought you was him, on his way to Alaska again, until you opened up the door and sat down...but for all I know from the time we spent, you might still be him."

I got out of the van and threw my bag over my shoulder. "Well, I'm runnin' it hard if that's what you mean."

"Sure is."

I nodded.

He nodded.

The door clapped shut.

And as the roaring noise of the cargo van's engine faded, succumbing to the growing distance between us, so did my troubled thoughts on the Affable Looneys and the far-off idea of one day calling the Garcon de Garrison home.

It was just another big rubber box, after all.

I pulled my phone from my pocket and called Gerry.

Chapter 16

Two Love Birds

> *On a bench in Bishop,*
> *Old man,*
> *Toucan*
> *Nose.*
> *Young Writer.*
> *Frightful prose.*
> *Young Writer - Aspiring Writer - Failing Writer.*
> *Since failing and aspiring are same thing,*
> *One just sounds better.*
> *Toucan Sam told the pen to "cheer up."*
> *Said, "Even a sparrow gets something*
> *Besides the crust eventually."*
> *He chuckled at himself.*
> *He was throwing the crust of his*
> *Sandwich to the birds.*
> *What he was really saying was this,*
> *"Don't rhyme.*
> *Rhyming was something the Victorians did,*
> *and you are not a Victorian."*

His face tough and overdone,
Like a broiled porterhouse
served up extra crispy.
Pungent pastrami hung from purple lips,
Shoes orthopedic.
Pants high-watered, high-waisted,
A low-brow brown.
The birds paid him no mind.
They had better things to do,
Like each other.
Courting. Dancing. Romping. Rutting.
And then
A scrap, a tussle,
a flap, a flourish...
Avanti!
"How 'bout that," said Old Toucan.
"A flying-fuck."

✳

The old man with the large beak had now sauntered off down the road, wheezing one painfully loud, gout riddled step at a time. His hands had been swollen, his skin a freckled mess that burned underneath the surface with an unhealthy diabetic red; the likes of which could've only been brought on by early-onset Irish alcoholism. He had been sipping from a flask while laboriously downing his sandwich. He was the embodiment of the route I did not wish to take on my way out. It was a path of hurt and struggle and unease. His life was now all things uphill. I imagined small tasks like rolling over in bed brought egregious amounts of pain. Chewing gum, putting on a watch, velcroing his non-existent shoelaces down . . . all now an arduous feat. It is undeniably unfair that we grow old. It, more than anything else, is the crock of being born. More so even than the absurdity of death was the plague-infused circus act of old age. I mean, at least death was certain. Grotesque and unfair but still, inevitable. You can find acceptance there. Growing old, on the other hand, took time, and with it uncertainty. The only thing you did know for sure was that it would all pass – the birth, the youth, the ego and the id. All the trivial shit that consumes us in our early years will fade and all that will be left will be figuring out how to do things without feeling enormous amounts of pain. When you really sit down and let it marinate – all those years – I think you'll quickly find that Old Age is a literal pseudonym for a path of least resistance. This all said, should my eighties deliver the same outcome as that pallid and ele-phantine gentleman, I can only hope to possess half of his sense of humor and outlook come the twilight:

The birds had moved on by now but as the aged-alchy gingerly maneuvered from the bench we shared, he wished me a good-but-not-too-eventful-evening and said, "sure hope things worked out between those two (he was looking off into the distance where we'd last seen the birds). I've never done it in mid-air muh-self but I imagine it to be pah-ritt-ee darn tricky."

I chuckled with him, "Not a member of the mile-high-club I take it?"

"Hoah-hoa. Lord no. Don't think the old ticker could-a-handled it."

"I hear ya."

He took off his ten-gallon hat, combed his snow-white hair aside before placing the monstrous, tan-felt-bucket back on his head and dusted off his pants in such a way that no dust fell off.

"Ya know. It's none of my business..." He glinted warmly and waited for me to pull my head up from the furious scribbling of notes taking place. "Old age teaches you this stuff. But, it looks to me like you're havin' a hard go-a-things."

"Relatively," I said, rather saddened that that was the impression I gave off.

"No shame in that, son. The heck's-a-mountain with out a valley? But if you don't mind," He waited again for me to nod off his non-imposition, "the other thing being older-n-dirt teaches you is that it all works out. Even the worst of it. If you keep your head down and keep pilin' away at it...it all pans out. And if a vet's tellin' ya that, you know it's got to have some truth to it."

"I'll try to remember that."

"Don't try, young man. Do."

I nodded, taking off my sunglasses. "Well, alright then."

I noticed the Vietnam pin on his light-blue denim shirt and thanked him for his service. He waved it off in the same nonchalant manner all vets do who made it through the worst life has to offer and can still afford a smile.

"Now I best be gettin' on." He said. "Don't want to keep the woman waiting."

"How long you been married for?"

"Oh no, not my wife. She passed a couple years ago."

"I'm sorry."

"Ah, I appreciate the gesture but don't be sorry. It was her time...Alzheimer's." His exhale labored and noisy, there was a hard struggle there. "Son-of-a-bitchin' way to go if ya ask me."

"Mm." I tried to offer sympathy but didn't know what exactly that was at a time like this.

"It's muh daughter though," he continued. "Little pain in the ass, she is! The girl's like a hawk after me now to get healthy. But what she don't know don't hurt her."

He knocked on the empty flask hidden in his breast pocket and then tapped his own head. I think he knew he wasn't fooling anybody, especially his daughter – as if Jameson wasn't his favorite cologne – but we both laughed the good laugh anyway.

"Now remember." He said, "don't try, do...and you'll be just fine."

I told him I would and he was finally on his way.

The bench was now a lonely place and I longed for home. I had chosen to sit there of all places because the old man had smiled at me in passing and well, he looked like decent company while I wrote. He was an open-book, the sort whose cover didn't say too much, but when he did speak it would certainly be worth listening to. His flying-fuck comment made it more than worth it – it made it unforgettable. And I'll be damned if when he left he didn't take all my words with him. I drew a festering blank in his absence and ended up retiring the notebook and pen for the rest of the day. I had been writing non-stop since landing in Bishop – scrawling notes and doodling ditties about birds humping, compelled to get everything I could down on paper since landing out west. At least the main scope of things. I think it's fair to say I laid it all down as squarely and as unevenly as I saw it...all things considered.

I now stood at a crossroads in Bishop. Watching that elderly fire-cracker peter off into the distance, slow and steady, made me question if home could in fact be anywhere, for he too was like every other old man I'd ever seen trudging down the streets of The Kill. *Gah, Peekskill.* I never thought I'd long for that town, but I was suddenly overcome with a need to return. A flash of the kitschy wooden signs that are posted at the town's entrances with big white, wide-brushed words tickled my memory. They all read "WELCOME TO PEEKSKILL, A FRIENDLY TOWN." A silly sign, of course. A sign that said, don't worry, no drug dealers and child molesters here! Which, to any level-minded twit, normally meant the exact opposite. But this time the sign held true to its promise; the little one-horse town was incredibly friendly and I was ready to head back. I was ready to see the buds, soak in local suds and say goodbye to the d'if. I was ready to say goodbye to the rubber box and the ever-lurking shadows of inheritance. I was ready to write the new book – the better book – the one that everyone deserved. The one that I deserved. I was finally ready to…I am finally ready to…well, what I was going to say was 'move past June.' But that doesn't seem true at the moment.

Dammit.

I wondered then, about her happiness and how her tour was going and if she was getting the acclaim she deserved and if she broke up with that gelatinous cube of a boyfriend yet…and of course, I wondered if she wondered about me too.

Chapter 17

A New Moon
Come June

(Five months later)

As it were, he couldn't fathom the idea of living life without her. Her skin, her smell, her smile, her soundless promise of everything. To him it seemed sure to be a life without color, tasteless and hollowed out and sad, but again, he had to remind himself it was not meant to be. He cursed Fate as he looked up at the night sky one last time with the romance-filled dream that she too would be looking up and thinking of him. 'Star-gazing is for astrologists,' he thought. 'And I am not an astrologist.' He knew this was ludicrous but he knew no other way to get over her than to stop looking up for a while.

Or, at least for tonight.

You see, it was a new moon and the midnight sky was without its luminescent celestial body. It was a dark night, a new night. His gaze landed back down on his feet, kicking rocks, and he thought long and hard about his infatuations and previous adventures and the lady who brought it all about – the one deserved of the chase – and he came to the happy conclusion that she was the moon. He felt her absence deeply tonight. For she had ignited in him the much needed spark of wonder to see the world and it is a bug he would never be rid of, but, he also knew that he had built her up to be something she was not. He had spent very little time with her and yet he had created her in his own mind to be the very savior of his heart and soul. The light. The way. *The only way.* Perhaps it was because they met at such a rocky and vulnerable time in his life, or perhaps, she was in his eyes, the very definition of perfection: Being perfectly imperfect. She had meant everything to him, the wellspring of perseverance, to go on and keep doing despite hardships and aimlessness along the way…meanwhile, in all actuality; he had to wrestle with the hard truth that she was very little to him. And by putting his pride aside, he could more easily admit that should the tables be turned, she most likely would not be thinking of him right now. She would not have been so moved by his candor and jest. So touched by his tenderness and warmth. So open to impression and desperate for attention as he was when they first met.

He had to admit that she was his muse, not the love of his life.

Though easily confusable and a tough raw-hided, damn near unchewable reality, it took him almost a year of twisting and turning about inside to snoop out the truth; that the moon, new or old, will turn about every month and enjoy its cycle once again. She was a woman who more than needed the cycle, but was of the cycle; a woman in a constant state of change – in love and all aspects of life – and he was just a very small blip in her worldly, interstellar travels. Still, as heartbroken as he was over the sobriety that came from waking from such a good dream, he found a comforting happiness for the time and affection she had so generously laid upon him.

It was gravity.
She was gravity.
A majestic magnetism.
She grounded him and yet,
Set him adrift at the same exact time.
It was magic.
Real magic...
He was in orbit.

He looked up again. But this time it was not only upward, this time he looked beyond the moon and saw the stars shining incandescent, glittering white gold down upon him. And, in her absence, he felt for that short moment true bliss, the notion that the night only grows brighter after a new moon.

Some call it acceptance, but to a romantic that was not, and never could be what this was; this was a way to discover that her love, though invisible to the eye, was still there, and more importantly, pointing out what should've been seen all along: Love and Inspiration are the same thing and they are not. Like water in its different states of being, they are the very workings of what drives us to be great and can reveal themselves to us in different ways at different times in our journey. And in his long-breathed strive for greatness, he knew she had made him a better man.

Which, if for nothing at all besides a way to move on, was love eternal.

And he was eternally grateful for it.

For her.

"Are you fucking done yet, Hemmingway?"

Dean was good and warmed up off the sauce already. He was fixing to tie one on and I would soon join him, but not yet. I was re-reading the above final passage to my book a couple more times and would do so a couple dozen more times before acknowledging his existence. He had been sitting there beside me for a while now at the picnic table, outback of the Peekskill Birdsall House, elbowing me anytime a pretty dime walked by.

"Frank." He nudged me again. "Look Frank. *Blonde.* Shew. *Legs. Frank. Legs!*"

I didn't look up.

"You've been castrated." He said, stomping his feet like a third grader. The gal turned her back to us and he jumped up a couple of grades, re-entering puberty with a plastered on school-boy-smile. "Hoah. *Sheezus.* Would you look at that ass? That thing could cure cancer."

"Can you just give me twenty more minutes you one-minded fiend."

"Hay! Somebody's gotta pay tribute 'round here since you've gone all eunuch on me." He was gnawing on his knuckle, anxious to start the night. "I ain't that bad, man. I just love a great ass...guess that makes me a crack-addict."

I laughed on the inside.

"Oh c'mon! You haven't even typed a letter in twenty minutes. Close the fuckin' thing already!"

He was right. Any more changes would ruin everything I worked so hard for these past few months.

"I guess it's time to walk away." I said.

"Yeah, but not from that." Dean said.

He motioned to the shivering blonde in a halter-top.

"Dean it's the middle of October. Can you not tell she's desperate?"

"And I'm not?"

We chuckled together.

"Oh, look. She's on her phone." He said. "I'm-a-see if she's on Tinder."

I shook my head at him.

"I can feel your disdain." He said, as he flipped through photos of local women without blinking an eye. "Just keep your self-righteous trap shut."

"Why don't you man up and do it the old fashioned way?"

"'Cuz this is easier."

I shook my head again. We were the new lost youth. Floundering twenty and thirty somethings, caught between an app and a hard place, desperate to settle down but completely clueless as to how to go about doing it. All I knew was that Tinder wasn't the answer…this is where you tell me that womanizing most likely isn't the right course of action either. And this is also where I agree with you, but fuck. We're men. Where's the line in the sand there?

"Shit." Dean said. "She's not on."

"Isn't that a good thing?" I asked.

"Well, yeah. Suppose so." He held up his glass and swirled around the little bit that was left. "I'm gonna *need* an Old Fashioned if this is gonna go down in person."

I lit up a Toscano and enjoyed the view while Dean went inside and got two more tall boys. Filament lights strewn across the back patio of Birdsall swung in the cool night air and showered warmth on all of the seedy characters swaying about. The local variety of social alcoholics were in their usual rare form; smoking, laughing, playing baci-ball and generally forgetting their troubles one sip at a time. It felt good to be back. I had been writing and working so much since landing back east that I hadn't really taken the time to enjoy it. And Birdsall was the place for enjoyment, let me tell you. It offered everything the Brewery didn't, and aside from being planted in the epicenter of Peekskill's downtown, grimy

art district and being one of the few places I never worked
(essential) – it felt like a bar. Like a bar's bar: shades of a dive
clashed with a Cheers-y, stylish attitude. Old western films
were projected on the wall while gritty rock n roll held the
vibe and let's not forget, the females: there was a plentiful
amount of pretty inked women with anemic skin clad all in
black circling about. There were others, of course, like the gal
Dean had been eyeing up, overly tanned and most likely
working in health insurance but that wasn't the end goal, the
end goal was to find someone who drove you wild. And these
women drove us wild! Naturally, they had no time for Dean
and me. We were some weird mutant hybrid of bro and
hipster and well, they saw right through our bullshit. To be
honest, we liked them all the more for it. What was it The
Fonz said? *"AY! You always want what you can't have."*
When it comes to women, never were truer words uttered in
a sitcom.

"You catch any action?" Dean asked.

Two pint glasses slammed down on the table and hoppy
liquid spilled out.

"Dean," I said, rather confidently upon his return. "It's
done."

"What's done?"

"The fucking book, you shmuck."

"Well hall-ay-fuckin'-loo-yah." He hollered, gulping
down glory. "It's only taken you what, five months!"

Jesus. Had it already been five months since the trip out
west?

"It took Twain seven years to write Huck Finn." I said.

"Twain's overrated."

I looked at him the same way a religious person looks at
you when you tell them God is overrated. And normally,

you're thankful they're religious because otherwise, they'd probably cut you. I wasn't religious so Dean ought to've been thankful there weren't any sharp objects around.

"So, how long is it?" He asked.

I shrugged, "Does that even matter?"

"Yes, yes it does." Dean put on some airs. "According to one of the latest pieces in *The New Yorker*, volume is everything. I heard a first book doesn't even get looked at – let alone published – if it's not over five hundred pages."

His words, though completely off the cuff and more full of shit than your local politician, had a wisp of truth about them. Again, I shrugged him off.

"Its one-fifty, Dean."

"Christ, what have you been doing all this time?"

"Smoking and drinking. What else?"

He smiled. It was a true statement.

"You finally land on a title?"

"Yeah." I winced a little.

"Well?"

I held back a moment, "*A New Moon, Come June.*"

"Always fingered you a pussy."

"Blow me."

"HA! That's some soft-ass-shit right there but hey, if it feels right, just right – like a pussy ought to – who'm I to say anything?"

"Thanks, Dean."

"No problem." He smiled at his own wit, the ass. "So I know you don't want to talk about it, what with your whole," he brought his index finger to the tip of his nose, pushed upwards and then continued haughtily, "'*writers write so readers can read and to talk about it is to ruin the whole affair*' bunch-a-asinine-self-preservation bullshit, but you're just gonna have to bite the bullet here and tell me what it's about."

"Now? Can't it fuckin' wait. Wouldn't you rather focus on those legs?"

We both looked up and the conversation skipped a track.

Dean grabbed the needle and brought it back down to vinyl, "She ain't going nowhere. Besides, it's not every day your best friend writes a book. Now spill it, Beans...what's it about?"

"Life, I guess."

"Don't gimmie that. Everyone fuckin' says that."

"Well it's a bit of a love story...but it's more about living life on your own terms."

"And...?" He waited a good while but I didn't want to talk about it. It was horrible to talk about your writing. Especially the flowery bullshit I wrote. His girl wandered inside for a refill and he finally cut back in, "Hundred and fifty pages and that's all there is? Don't make me break out the pliers."

"Okay, okay." I walked the plank, "it's about how hard it is to define those terms until you've seen all that is out there. It's about taking the blinders off and just being *out there*... and the struggle of finding your way back. It's about discovering that place between where you once were and where you now are, the protagonist describes it as a Happy Medium."

"Now we're talkin'," said Dean. "I love it when you get all poetic, Frank. Gives me a half-chub."

"Anything to help with your E.D."

"Ha! Nice. Seriously though, gettin' a little meaty over here." He readjusted his crotch to make it seem as though he was in discomfort. Light chuckles echoed into pint glasses and Dean continued to eye up the senorita across the way while he spoke. "Kinda reminds me-a-that quote...ah, shit. What was it again? *'The more you see the less you know for sure?'*"

"That's it exactly." I said. "Losing Certainty. That's what it's all about."

"Hm." He thought for a second and decided if he liked it or not. He did. "Good shit my man, congrats! Hot damn, shall we drink to your health?"

He slapped me on the back and raised his glass. He knew that always got me – the irony of drinking to good health.

"Yes, Dean. To our health...and halter tops."

Dean's attention floated back to the lassie now coquettishly throwing glances our way.

"If you won't talk to her I will," he said.

"She's all yours buttercup."

Dean downed the rest of his drink and got up.

"The old fashioned way, eh?" He said, smiling a little at his own courage.

"Yeah buddy."

"Well she do look hungry. Ten bones says I whet her appetite."

"Not in a million years brother."

He moseyed on over, in spirit, too big to fail, but in body, to small to succeed. Just then Jack rolled into the bar with a couple others. They piled in at the picnic table and rounds ensued. We soon tumbled into yet another small discussion about my losing the d'if over a minor legality. The conversation could not be avoided the past couple of months and gave me good reason to stay inside and write. I was tired of hearing about it: everyone offered a plethora of condolences and annoying anecdotes. "I don't know what's worse," they'd say, "never being rich, or tasting it for a little and then losing it all." I was ready for everyone to be over it, the whole ordeal: How my father had not followed procedure correctly with an amendment to his will and therefore, the Garcon de Garrison was to be repossessed and given to its rightful inheritor, some long lost surviving cousin across the pond. There were talks of Goldstein, the lawyer, doing a dirty deal or some other backhanded pay off that made it all go south. People would constantly ask if I was going to sue, as if that would be the answer to finally putting problems with my father behind me. I would just shrug and wait for the convo to veer off as it always did, and end with an even more ridiculous anecdote about how I was lucky in the end because people who hit the jackpot normally end up more miserable and worse off than they were before they won. There was some truth to that, I guess.

Jack looked at me wryly, as he always did, while we spoke of the matter. It was an unbelievable story – it was unbelievable because it was completely contrived. My regards to fiction. Only he and Dean knew the truth, that I hadn't lost the d'if, but had sold it and given it away. *All of it.* My regards to Goldstein. UNICEF received a mighty check from Anonymous almost two months ago now and I have never felt better in my life. If you're asking yourself why I did it or have turned this thing over to reread blurbs and are now wondering who you can call to get your money back, I apologize – I mustn't have done my job with the damn book. And even if I pulled off a miracle and knitted a half-decent yarn out of everything, let me break it down for you one last time:

It was more than just the goodness that came by doing good; by making sure the art went to the proper museums to inspire youth, and that the money from that castle of misery went to serve against what produced its vast wealth in the first place – a history…a family history of cold and deceitful acts toward humanity…toward children – but, because it wasn't even mine to give away to begin with. It was about my life on my terms. And had I stayed there and lived that life, it would've been on someone else's terms. Their decisions, their debts. Sure, I was almost five grand in debt myself now from the trip out west, but my new clothes were still serving me well and the earned tread on my boots had worn in quite comfortably since that red-eyed flight out of Bishop Airport. And not for nothing, but words have never been easier to come by…or well, shall we just say, they've been slightly less painful to come by.

Dean came back and sat down, sour and unsuccessful. Jack patted him on the back and told him "maybe next time, Champ. Or maybe the next *fiftieth* time." Dean blew him off and sent everyone into a cock-eyed frenzy when he mentioned that I had finished the book. I just looked at him. He knew I didn't want to talk about it, but he was embittered by his poor performance with the flirty feline and sought out entertainment on my behalf. *The SOB.* If only that man had game, I expect I'd be a lot happier in my day to day.

"So now what?" Jack asked, anxious and interested. "You're not going to self-publish again are you?"

"Fuck no. We all know how that worked out."

"I still think *The Unbearable Whiteness of Being* should be published somewhere."

"Meh." I muffed. "Perhaps someday. But not today."

"So you got a plan, then?" One of the guys chimed in.

"Hell no. I just did the hardest part. All I want to do now is drink and smoke and fuck for a whole year…and it doesn't have to be in that exact order."

There were some laughs.

"To Frank!" Boasted Jack, holding up a shot of Four Roses. "May it read on your epitaph, 'Hey. At least he wasn't boring.'"

"Frank!"

"Beeeeans."

What a bunch-a-assholes.

Though quaint and loving orifices, they were, I reveled in their inability to take me seriously. It was a gift; I had to give it to them. If anything, it kept my lofty ego grounded that's for damn sure. It also made me want to inspire in them a seriousness about me. And I know they were well aware of it, but their prying, their relentless prodding forced me to do and be better. It made me want to be the goddammed best there was around. It made me want to instill in them a pride in Frank Gently so deeply rooted it couldn't even be talked about without fear of turning red. I knew it was there already – their support or whatever you want to call it – but I wanted it to burn in them as it did in me, the belief that I was not only meant to be read, but privileged with the gift to entertain.

That I was worthwhile and all that.

Either way, it certainly kept the words-a-flowing, and provided me with the downright gut-wrenching drive it took to see to it that this one, this time around, got fucking laid to print.

Chapter 18

Beginning Softly

"When the hell are you gonna get over pretty women?" Sean asked, huffing away on his sunglasses and polishing them with the bottom of his high-end flannel.

"When they stop being pretty." I said.

He shook his head, "Seriously, pretty women are just the worst. When are you gonna get that?"

Jay was sitting beside him, nodding along in full consent while allowing his salt and pepper hair to whip around in the cool autumn breeze. Behind him lay the beautiful tree-lined Havemeyer and my ADD took hold for a moment…fall in Brooklyn comes second to none.

"Well?" Sean pushed a little more.

I dropped my head to the right and gave them both a confused look.

"All you guys do is mingle with pretty women." I said. "What on earth are you talking about?"

"Yeah." Sean said, rather deadpan. "*We're gay.* It's what we do."

"And that makes it okay for you and not me?"

"No," Jay interrupted. "It makes it the opposite of attraction. We are not attracted to pretty women, we just like them because they're beautiful."

"Me too."

"It's different. We like *everything* that's beautiful. You think you actually have a chance with them."

"Of course I do."

"Hopeless," Sean said, looking around for the waitress. He glanced down at his watch. It had been too long since she checked in with us and he had grown irritated. The Lodge was overflowing with people so he couldn't be as pissed as he wanted to be. He swirled his straw around desperate for the last little bit of Bloody Mary juice to slurp up. He brought the rim of the glass to his mouth but the ice remained in the way and ended up poking himself in the eye with his straw. The episode ended in an effeminate flurry of emotion as he slammed the mason jar down, rattling silverware in the process. He looked at his watch again and said, "Where *is* this bitch?" Poor service to Sean and Jay might as well have been a direct affront on their manhood. "See, *this* is why I hate Brooklyn."

"Relax your life," I said. "She'll be around. It's one o'clock on a Sunday, whaddya expect?"

"I'm so over brunch." He said, placing his shades back on. "Why'd we choose *this* place again?"

Jay shot him a quick look that said 'you know why.'

I was the reason why: I loved The Lodge. And once again, in the presence of men who demanded perfection, I felt the need to defend why I liked the place. But of course, that would've been dreadfully boring and besides, these men had taught me one of life's most invaluable of lessons: a good defense is never as fun nor entertaining as an offensive offense: "This coming from the man who made me wait an hour to brunch at some all-you-can-drink-mimosa nightmare of a sorority house in meat-packing."

"At least they served you there."

"They also molest you there."

"You enjoyed it."

"I remember nothing of the sort."

"Of course you don't, you had champagne-brain."

Ahem. A draw.

The alt-waitress whose every appendage was covered in colorful tattoos finally made her way over. She looked frazzled; it might have been her first day.

"Everything okay?" Sean asked her, not without a hint of impatience.

"Sorry. We're down a server right now." She said.

"Oh it's alright. Please, we just need our alcohol." He threw his arm around Jay and changed his tone to a more understanding, sarcastic note, "talking to *this* one is all but impossible without the mother's milk."

She nodded a forced smile, grabbed our empties and made off for more spirit.

"So what are you two saying," I pushed back. "I need to lower my standards?"

"Yes. That is exactly what we're saying, Frank. *Lower the bar.* I'm surprised anything gets into that thick skull of yours."

"Well what then?"

"It's about changing your perceptions on what is beautiful." I rolled my eyes but Jay went on, unperturbed, "Seeing what isn't necessarily beautiful by today's standards in a different light doesn't mean lowering your standards. In fact, it means raising them. You, of all people, should know that."

"Christ." I was frowning now. "You're talking about *inner beauty*. Had I known this was on the docket for today, I wouldn't have come down."

"*Please.*" said Sean, pissed off. "We're just trying to help you out."

"Whatever. Am I delusional for thinking I can't find both? Outward and inward beauty?"

"Yes," said Jay. "Pretty women are ruined. Damaged goods. And you guys are the ones to blame for it. You hetero-Neanderthals."

"How the hell is it my fault?"

"If you let me talk I'll tell you." Sean's earlier comment about needing alcohol was spot-on; strong drink was the only antidote to the severe amount of sass being thrown around the table. Jay went on, "pretty women have been totally loved by men without reason, poisoned by come-ons and empty promises, over and over and over again since they turned fifteen...all because of their looks. How on earth can you expect them to have any semblance of what love is from a lifetime of that? How can you even expect them to be normal? Let alone well adjusted? It's fallacy."

I pushed my eyebrows together and wrestled with the idea.

"And it's not their fault either," Sean added. "Obviously. It's your fucked up, cream-filled testicles doing all the damage."

"Hey. You guys got lil-cream-puffs danglin' down there too."

"It's different. A man's ego needs to be cut to pieces. A woman's very much needs the opposite."

"Well I think you're wrong. I'm sure there's still a bunch of good lookin' women out there who've remained grounded despite all the assholes. I mean, look at us. We made it through the shit and we're all pretty decent looking."

"Well, two of us are." Sean smirked. They pecked at each other and I made a face like I would blow chunks if they didn't stop.

"You're missing the point." Jay said. "Pretty Women and Pretty Men are a false equivalency. *You know that.* You're just being an idiot because you want to be with someone who looks like a ballerina."

"We want what we want."

Loud sighs answered the snark that echoed off the floor-to-ceiling windows of The Lodge.

"Fine." Jay said. "We'll drop it. But don't you think there's a reason why you haven't been able to settle down yet?"

"Aside from now living with a gay couple?"

"Bah. We all know that helps your chances ten-fold."

"I don't know. I'm just not ready yet, I guess."

"OH THAT'S IT." Sean volleyed.

"SURE. RIGHT." Jay returned.

The two of them weren't having it. They had a point, I suppose.

"So what do you want from me then?" I asked. "To tell you that I still think about her? That I'm not really over her? That I just tell myself I am and it's beyond sad now?"

"You don't have to tell us that. We *know* that." Sean said.

"Okay then."

"Which brings us to why we had you come down here to meet us for brunch."

Jay pulled out a torn and weathered flyer that had *Lickity-Split* front-lining a show at Glasslands Gallery in

Brooklyn that very night. Maybe ten or twelve blocks from where we were perched. I looked at the shitty piece of advertising with an odd sense of pride and foreignness. I didn't know what to say or do. It had been a while now, a long while. I had become a real admirer of the band over the past year and June had now drifted from a lost love that I wrote about to get over, to a musician whom I only knew through her art. I felt faint and saddened by it, both whimsical and wistful at the same time, but the harsh truth was that I had now become that most distant and bizarre of things – I had now become a fan.

"It's not sold out yet, ya know…and it's your birthday next week," Sean said. "That makes it a full year. Jay and I chatted about it a bit and we agree, either you go to this and tell her you still love her – tell her she inspired you to write a book for fuck-sake – or you don't, and you move the hell on."

"Is this where you tell me I'd be better off moving on? Since June is just another 'pretty woman' in your view?"

"No. That's not it at all." Sean said.

"You're in love with the idea of this woman, not the woman herself." Jay pre-concluded, coming uncomfortably close to the heart of it. "The pretty woman thing was just about you getting over your idiotic obsession with ballerinas. But all that has got nothing on your mental delusions of June. She might as well be a Greek goddess in your book. Kinda fitting, I must say, *since mythology isn't real…and more often than not, tragic.*"

"Seriously," Sean added. "What do you know about June except for what you read in an interview or devoured on *Lickity-Split's* Wikipedia page?"

I shrugged my shoulders. Again, they were right. I didn't know jack shit about her, but that couldn't fully explain away why I shouldn't like her.

God.

Listen to me.

Pathetic.

Rationalizing irrational behavior again.

It seemed writing the book about her, spending all that time crafting a tale to get over her and fictionalizing our lives together only emboldened the illusion. Beyond bizarre, it was now an affliction; a medical condition and these men were having an intervention. The jig was up, and rightfully so.

"Here you go, gentlemen." The waitress dropped off the goods.

"Ah, the life source." Sean said. "Thank you so very much."

"No problem." She smiled. "Again, sorry for the delay."

"Say?" Jay asked. "Maybe you could help us out for a second. We know you're busy but it'll just take a sec? We're in need of a woman's point of view."

"Of course. What's up?"

"Just a hypothetical: Say you met a guy a year ago and you had a fling that you both enjoyed," I grew redder with every word. "Would you be flattered or freaked out if he showed up a year later, and said he still thought of you and well, kind of still loved you?"

"A year?" The waitress asked, stunned by the vast amount of time on the table. "Must've been one helluva fling."

"Right." Sean agreed. "Let's say it was the best fling ever. Like a ten-point-oh on the Richter of flings. Would it freak you out if they showed up on your doorstep with a bottle of wine, spilling their guts out to you?"

"Objection!" I said. "Leading the waitress."

I took down half of my bloody to the face.

"So," the waitress cooed my way. "Is this the enamored little teddy bear, still in love after a year?"

"That wouldn't be completely inaccurate." I said.

"Still got a thing for this girl then?"

"Something like that."

"A thing!" Sean couldn't help himself, the bastard. "*Try obsession.*"

I nodded in defeat.

"Well. I don't know what to tell you." The waitress began, folding her arms and propping herself up, half-slouched on one leg. "Sounds crazy to me, but crazier shit has happened…and worked out. Two of my first cousins got married last year despite the entire family being against it." Jay and Sean's heads perked up, as they did to anything that whispered taboo. "And you know what, they're happier than any quote-unquote normal couple I've ever met. Love is strange. It comes and goes for some of us, hangs around for others. Just do what feels right," She paused a moment and leaned up against the wall in an attempt to make her opinion seem all the more casual. "Just don't let your head get in the way. That's all. *So what.* It's been a year. Man up and do something about it or get over it…and in the meanwhile, take the time to get over yourself. That's the first thing men have to do in my opinion."

Sean and Jay were thoroughly enjoying the unabashed waitress as she rained blows of wisdom down upon me. I felt no need to take cover, however, since I very much enjoyed the assault and battery…more than enjoyed it. Deserved it. Needed it.

"I mean. That's just how I see it." She continued on, "But hey. What do I know? I'm a lesbian."

"Perhaps that's why you see it so clearly," Jay offered.

"Hay. Ya can't bullshit a bullshitter. No one's got their shit down, least of all me."

"Here! Here!" Sang Jay.

"Praise be to thee, sister of the traveling hot pants!" Echoed Sean.

They raised their glasses, as did I.

We thanked her, she bowed, and we returned to our Sunday sacrament. When our food landed, my appetite was nowhere to be found. A festering had returned to my gut, the likes of which I had not felt since the sleepless nights spent in the d'if. It was something about what the waitress said in her spiel, something that was so close to home it felt right on the nose — an obviousness. One I had completely missed. Maybe my problem wasn't just the struggle of illusion, the problem of building up a fantasy that didn't exist, but that falling in love was, by my very makeup, second nature. It was the falling out of love that seemed at odds with everything I did, everything I was. Perhaps that is where getting over oneself comes into play. Maybe the real illusion wasn't the girl — but me — and the idea wasn't so much that I was deserving of her love, so much that I remained in love with her because I thought she would benefit from mine…it was the greatest lie I had been selling to myself this whole time. It was a selfish lie; the thought that June would be better off with me than without me — and finally, with the help of a stranger's wisdom, did it shed light on the easily missed questions everyone should ask themself from time to time:

"Just who the hell am I? 'The fuck makes me so special?"

And well, by confronting that lie and asking those quintessential questions of life, I guess I stumbled onto the art of letting go.

"You guys think you could love someone," I proposed, "and continue loving them, despite the fact that you will never be with them?"

"Of course." Jay answered, unflinching. "Love isn't something you can just turn on and off. It's beyond our control. You can't pick and choose how it comes out of you, and whom you put it on, it just does...it just is."

"Hm."

Now I was the one huffing on my sunglasses, wiping them down, looking at the reflection in the dual mirrored frames. I think, for the first time in a long time, I genuinely liked what I saw.

"What you thinkin', Frank?" Sean asked.

"I'm thinking I'm going to pass on the concert."

"Really?" They harmonized.

Both men leaned in and placed their elbows on the table.

"Yeah. I've been foolishly waiting for some external force to guide me away or whatever...but that doesn't seem to be in the cards. I think it's time I guide myself away and open up the door to greener, realer pastures."

"Well isn't this unexpected!" said Jay, unnerved.

"This calls for shots!" Sean belted, all too happily. "Shots I say!"

And shots we had. Whiskey at 2pm mid-autumn does something to the brain. Aside from killing cells and hazing memory, the warmth of the brown booze combined with the crisp air creates some sort of temporary paradise. The Paradise of Nothing Matters. We ate lunch and got another round. Standing up was going to be a chore; of that there was no doubt. And then Sean saw something that frightened him:

"Hoah. Gawd. Is that...?" His eyes were scared. Like he'd seen a ghost across the way. "No no. *Can't be.*" He regrouped and relaxed a bit. "Guys, check that lady across the street."

We looked. Our eyes matched his in disbelief for a moment. He hadn't seen a ghost; he'd seen a curmudgeon. A doppelganger of a curmudgeon.

"Fuck me. Could be Doris's twin." I said.

"She's in Russia, right?" Asked Sean, rather desperate for reassurance.

"Yeah...left when we moved out." Jay said. "Maybe a day or two after."

"Back to the Mother Country?" I asked.

"*Dah. In tha-cold-cold-vinter 'vere she bee-longs: Bel-ah-russ.*" Jay rolled his R's. His voice low and guttural, he had a knack for making it seem as if his vocal chords had been weathering vodka since the ripe age of two. "We were too gay for her apparently. She'd had enough. *Dasvidaniya Doris!*"

The statement made me laugh, "You guys are like, the least gay couple I know. As far as the spectrum of gay goes."

"Good lord," Jay glanced once more at the spitting image of our old landlady, taken by an unavoidable weariness as the frail old Dowager's hump passed us by. "That lady gives me chills just looking at her."

"All those good memories just come flooding back, eh?" I asked.

"That old witch!" Sean said. "To this day she still believes you died in a boating accident."

I laughed, "Unreal."

The waitress dropped off our tab. Jay motioned to pick it up but Sean stayed his hand.

"Which reminds us." He said. "That was about three hundred bucks we saved you…" Sean glanced down at the bill and then nodded my way, as if to say 'hey, want to settle up?'

I shrugged a little and made a gesture as to break out my card. Then Sean snatched the bill from the table and started laughing.

"As if, you-little-dwarf-boner." Sean's voice was cutesy. He pinched my cheek. "Maybe if that book-a-yours ever makes its way to paper."

I smiled, grateful for them – my older, better-looking brothers.

"Besides." Jay added. "We're proud of you. After handing you that flyer, I never in a million years would've thought you'd be rolling back up the river with us tonight."

"Me either." I said, still somewhat surprised that I was. We all rose, stammered each in our own way, dancing to the sauce-inspired music in our heads, and sauntered on down the red and orange and yellow leafed Havemeyer – the last charming street of Williamsburg.

The thought hit me again…*Goodbye June.*

'Me. Either.' I said the words once more, but this time to myself.

Internalized language, I now know, is always the safest and most effective form of communication with oneself. Particularly when two-sheets have become three.

Chapter 19

Ending Gently

"You ever look around and think, wow, everyone in here masturbates. Or poops. Or whatever." Sean asked.

"That would be a big fat resounding no." I said.

"Just asking. I mean, look around. There's four hundred people in here, at least. And they all do embarrassing shit. Ya know? Yet everyone walks around like their shit doesn't stink."

It certainly was a different way of thinking about the buzzing swarms of people in Grand Central.

"We walk around like that too, ya know." I said.

"Well I do it because my shit doesn't stink." Sean answered. "It is literally without smell."

Jay rolled his eyes. We were drunk and our convo had now fully devolved into the scatological. It was a good half hour before our 4:43 train would tear up the Hudson, and so, we did as we always had when wasted and waiting for the commuter rail, scared that social suffocation or ennui or the overall sadness of life might find us...we played with the shiny new toys in Grand Central's Apple Store.

"Oh yes." Jay said, flipping through apps. "Comes out with a poof of glitter, too. You should see it, Frank. It's magical. Unicorns are jealous of the man's dung."

"I'll take your word for it."

My phone buzzed in my pocket.

"Shit. It's the Mad Queen."

I thought about doing what most kids do who have a healthy relationship with their mothers and hit the ignore button and call back at a more conducive time for me. But, I had made recent promises to myself that I would be more open to her, whatever the circumstances. Whatever the madness, I'd focus on being a better son. Which is easier said than done, of course.

"How is old Victoria these days?" Jay asked.

"Oh ya know, same bat shit, different day — Oh Hey Mom, what's up?"

"Hey Bud, you wouldn't happen to be in the city, would you?"

The woman's got a sixth sense, I swear it.

"I am but I was literally just about to head back up the river. What's going on?"

"So you're in Grand Central?"

"Yeap."

"Oh goodness that's great. We really need your help. I'm near the Plaza with some other good spirited folks. Can you come up this way? We need extra hands dearly."

I didn't even need to ask. She was protesting something. That much was certain, but just what exactly she was protesting was always up in the air.

"Who is it now?" I asked. "The Surgeon General? Some Foreign Consulate? The horse carriages of Central Park?"

"Hilarious Bud. What a gift for comedy you have. When ever are you going to take to the stage with that act of yours? *We're all waiting.*" I bit my tongue, as her tone grew more serious. "You know they treat those horses like shit."

"I know. I know."

"Then why do you always have to joke about it?"

"The same reason anyone jokes about anything. To keep from crying."

"Good answer." She was curt and had no time for my drunken needling. "Now, will you come? *We need help.*"

"Well who is it?"

"Apple."

"*Mom.*"

"They're exploiting modern day slaves, Frank!"

"Tell me something I don't know."

"Then why won't you come?"

"Because."

"There is no excuse." She interrupted.

I raised my voice slightly, "You know almost every device I use is Mac-related, right? Me being there would be what some people might refer to as '*hypocritical.*'"

"Almost every Apple user is a hypocrite or in the dark! That's the whole point of this..." the Mad Queen was about to launch into another tirade but I was drunk and tired so giving in was a much easier way out.

"Alright! Alright! I'll come up!"

I made like I was going to throw the phone against the wall to Sean and Jay.

"El Madre hath spoken." Sean boomed in a deep low bass.

"Who is it now?" Asked Jay.

I pointed up to the glowing white icon hanging on the wall above our heads, "Our dearly beloved and unendurably evil, Apple Corporation...as if one was any worse than the next."

They smirked a familiar smirk — it was some sort of contentment lacquered with glossy smiles of adoration. I'm quite sure it had something to do with me sewing up old wounds with Vic but I could care less at the moment. I was on my way to go stand in a goddammed picket line. I wished then, that drinking in public were legal. Like in Vegas. I would picket all day long in Vegas. I'd picket the shit out of that place.

*

As I crossed fifty-eighth street, beyond the wandering tourists buzzing before me and the shopping gazelles clacking around in high-heels, past their blown out hair and the sunglasses that covered three-quarters of their faces (artfully camouflaging who was ugly and who was not, I might add), I could see an energetic woman clad in a denim jacket. The jacket was old, loud and proud, with union patches sewn on the shoulders. She was weaving in and out of a loitering group of people with the speed and pace of a sewing machine, pedal to the metal. It was happening all right, and once again Victoria Gently was at the helm of the movement. I made my way across the intersection to the park that sat picturesque in front of the Plaza Hotel and tried to track down the wide-eyed woman socializing and to my amazement, still bouncing in and out of the crowd like a pinball caught in a never-ending pattern. Then she saw my face and dropped everything mid-sentence. She embraced me and showed me around, introducing me as "her Frank" and "my Bud." It was somewhat embarrassing. I become the shyest creature that ever existed when we're together. Maybe that has something to do with her being the loudest creature that ever existed but I think it's more than that. I think kids fear their parents simply from the off chance that they might become them. Something like Newton's law in simian form. You know, actions and reactions and primates being primates. Add to that the horrors of being human and making mistakes and how those mistakes cause unwanted reactions...in your kids. *Well. That's effing science, man.*

I realized then I was still drunk and despite the leftover glaze of cheap bourbon, it was easy to discern there was high tension in the air. Everyone looked unsettled — ready and eager — but still, uneasy. Things were about to get under way. There was a wide variety of clever and searing signs already resting on the shoulders of protesters:

"PHONES MADE BY MODERN SLAVES."

"SOCIAL CORPORATE RESPONSIBILITY – AN OXYMORON."

"APPLE. A CREATIVE COMPANY UNTIL IT COMES TO THE QUESTION OF HUMANITY."

"TO USE A MAC IS TO USE A CHILD."

"THE FACES OF APPLE'S ROTTEN CORE."

And so on.

The last one was what really got me, and convinced me more than anything to stick around for the actual demonstration. It had a blown-up photo of an Apple sweatshop in China. A stark black and white image of a horrific looking room, overcrowded, dilapidated and dingy, full of innocent eyes slowly losing their light.

"What good do you think this will do?" I asked Vic just before everything started. There were only forty or so people standing around with a straggly white-bearded and gray-pony-tailed man holding a megaphone at the front. He had his eyes closed and appeared to be rehearsing the words for his upcoming denunciation. It seemed less like a protest and more like a bunch of people who got together to bang on some pots. I looked at the uber-rich filtering in and out of Bergdorf and couldn't help the feeling that we had somehow missed the real target.

"It will do more good than not being here." She said. "Even if we get a couple consumers to think twice. We've done our job. Who knows, the press is always lurking."

"Mom, even the president can't change the world." I said sternly, rather convinced my words were true. "What makes you think any of this will?"

I was sobering up and had gestured to the severe lack of numbers we had in attendance.

"It always starts with a few people." She said, her mind continually on forward march. She was stapling a sign to a two-by-four. "Anything good that has ever happened always started with a few people."

I wanted to believe her. She was after all, my mother and someone who genuinely cared about justice and treating people kindly. But. I don't know. I could only ever look at history as a horrible cycle that continually repeated itself. The only difference being it now existed on a globally informed scale. To me, the Internet changed everything and nothing. People are just desensitized now, that's all. What else explains all the horrible shit still taking place? Apathy? Laziness? Human Nature? And then Victoria Gently finally said something that cut to the bone of the world's problems, the marrow of the bone. She cut through me:

"To do nothing. To know and still do nothing, that is the greatest sin of life." She finished marking up the last two signs and gave them to two fellow volunteers standing by. She grabbed hers and threw the sign that was nailed to a wooden broom handle over her shoulder. "Today, people think a Like Button will cure the world of its problems." She shook her head and walked me to the front of the line. "Civil disobedience, Bud. That's it, the only weapon we've got. The only way to move forward is to stand in the street and make a bit of noise. And I know it's embarrassing to you 'cuz I'm your mother, but all I can say is…sometimes that noise gets heard in different ways. Annoyance on some occasions, insanity probably on others…but sometimes, sometimes it is heard not as noise, but as sound. And its message pings crystal with clarity and reverberates in the minds of everyone in earshot. It is there; only when we knock down the shields of apathy do we find that reservoir of goodness stored in each of us. And believe me, when it comes it comes with the force of a levee breaking, like a thunderbolt to the pacemaker of the human condition. You know what we call that, Bud? We call that a movement, and movements change the world."

She grabbed my hand and we walked across the street to the square, signs held high. I now know that this was what she meant when she told me she had become *awakened.* I couldn't tell you just yet if I was a true believer, but then again, I certainly couldn't tell you I was no longer proud to be her son.

✤

It was a light-footed walk back down Park Ave to Grand Central. Smoke from my Toscano flirted with the sun's reflection as it strewed fiery pinks on the face of the Metlife building. The temperature dropped along with the sun and loneliness crept in. I saw the makings of my breath. I liked watching the steam float against the waning spectral of the sun. The vibrant weather was redolent of the many nights I spent in Yosemite and memories, good and bad, peppered my brain. Inside the terminal, the glow of metropolis burned hot. The people were at it as usual, flying about and crisscrossing amongst each other at break-neck speeds like racers in a video game. I marveled at their Tron-like patterns for a good bit but soon, the marvelous gave way to the insidious. I figured then that the speed of things was what really kept us apart, kept us from seeing the most obvious fact in plain sight...

We're all on the same team.

I sat there on the steps, enveloped by a blanket of deep thought and wondered just how it all worked.

The Game.

The Racers and Their Teams.

I waited and waited but nothing came to me and I don't suppose anything ever will.

And then I looked up.

CPSIA information can be obtained at www.ICGtesting.com
Printed in the USA
LVOW10s0041130716

496088LV00027B/446/P